Four Tales *of* Intrigue

Four Tales
of Intrigue

PETER KERSHEY

Copyright © 2024 Peter Kershey

The moral right of the author has been asserted.

Apart from any fair dealing for the purposes of research or private study, or criticism or review, as permitted under the Copyright, Designs and Patents Act 1988, this publication may only be reproduced, stored or transmitted, in any form or by any means, with the prior permission in writing of the publishers, or in the case of reprographic reproduction in accordance with the terms of licences issued by the Copyright Licensing Agency. Enquiries concerning reproduction outside those terms should be sent to the publishers.

This is a work of fiction. Names, characters, businesses, places, events and incidents are either the products of the author's imagination or used in a fictitious manner. Any resemblance to actual persons, living or dead, or actual events is purely coincidental.

Troubador Publishing Ltd
Unit E2 Airfield Business Park,
Harrison Road, Market Harborough,
Leicestershire LE16 7UL
Tel: 0116 279 2299
Email: books@troubador.co.uk
Web: www.troubador.co.uk

ISBN 978 1 805145 27 1

British Library Cataloguing in Publication Data.
A catalogue record for this book is available from the British Library.

Printed and bound in Great Britain by 4edge Limited
Typeset in 11pt Minion Pro by Troubador Publishing Ltd, Leicester, UK

*To my brother Tom (1947-2021), who loved this world of intrigue as much as I do.
This is for you.*

Contents

Conversations with the Moon	1
The Castle Steps	157
Dream	271
Abrielle	295
Acknowledgements	318

Conversations with
the Moon

Prologue

The man sat on a stool at the bar at Louisa's Place in Market Harborough and drank from his glass with feelings of great sadness. He sighed as tears slid down his face.

"Anything wrong, sir? Bad news?" asked the barman quietly.

No answer.

"Sir, is anything wrong?" he repeated, concerned.

The man turned his tear-stained face to the barman. "Life. Life is just wrong," he lamented.

"Maybe it's not that bad. You may just need a little break, a rest. Another drink?" the barman consoled him and poured him another when he nodded his consent. "Just pack a few things into a case and get away for a week… maybe somewhere by the sea."

"I was by the sea not long ago." The man sighed and wiped the tears from his face with his palm. "And nothing."

"So go somewhere in the countryside."

"I was in the countryside two months ago… it didn't help."

"You're a tough case. But I can personally recommend a consultant psychologist based in Leicester who may be able to help you. I'm told that Doctor Rafferty isn't cheap, but he's got a very good reputation."

"He can't help."

"How can you say that? Go and see him. He'll help you."

"No, that's not possible," the man sobbed.

"Why not?"

"I'm Doctor Rafferty…"

Chapter 1

I go to a German language class at the University of Leicester, and I found this short story, which could just as well be about me, in one of the textbooks. My surname isn't Rafferty – it's Warburton. Paul Warburton. Of course, I'm not anywhere as well-known as Rafferty and I'm not even a doctor, but I am a psychologist, and at the moment, in the same mental state as Rafferty.

I don't usually hang about in bars. I usually get drunk at home, which is, of course, worse because there's no barman to console me. There's no one to console me. I guess that's why I don't let anyone get close to me. I'm all alone. Night after night I sit with a glass in my hand, drinking and muddling through life.

A year ago, my wife left me. I know that as a psychologist I should be able to address a situation like that, but I can't. We had been together for fifteen years! We had wanted children but couldn't have them. We really tried. We went through all the medical procedures – and nothing. All those horrible tests we went through said that we were both healthy. And still nothing. Nothing. Then my wife found someone else. A wealthy property developer. After some time she left me for him, said I was useless and that she couldn't wait anymore. It has been a year – and she doesn't have a child with him either. But at least she has money. Maybe.

I can't get used to it. I don't think it's something you can get used to. I'm alone. All alone. I am forty-two – as they taught us in German class: *ich bin zweiundvierzig.*

And time goes on.

The German course was an instinctual thing. I took it up, I suppose, in a subconscious attempt to grasp on to something, to save myself. Maybe it worked: at least one evening a week I'm not getting drunk, and I get to be amongst people. Otherwise, I'm alone and have no one to talk to.

Until one time.

Something strange happened to me. I was sitting in the lounge at home, in my wicker chair, staring into the dark through the patio doors and drinking. I was talking out loud to my absent wife, saying that she's a slut, that I hate her and that rich bastard, that I would kill her and him, too, that she shouldn't have done this to me. And then that I understood her, that maybe I could forgive her, that I still loved her… Kyley, please come back! I was speaking into the dark and no one was answering. Speaking, speaking. Silence. No answer. Drunk with loneliness and alcohol, I turned my head towards the dark sky, towards the bright moon.

"See that? Do you hear that?" I called to his face.

To my amazement, the moon answered.

"I see you, Paul, and hear you too."

Am I nuts? I thought. *Or did I just imagine it?*

"What do you see?" I whispered timidly.

"What do I see? An unhappy man who feels alone. So alone that he's calling to me in the heavens. So alone that in his desperate loneliness he looks into my eyes and hears my voice."

It scared me. Made me think I shouldn't drink anymore. Had I gone mad?

"Why do I hear you?" I asked stupidly.

"You have a gift, and ability, feeling and imagination that not everyone has. And with that, you have pain and despair. That's why you hear me."

"Isn't it possible without the pain and despair?"

"It is. But the pain is like an exponent. A number raised to the second power, and desperation is that number raised to the third," the moon explained to me. "The pain in your soul makes you more aware of everything around you. Even of me."

And that is how my conversations with the moon began. My wife gone, no children, and no close friends – just a few acquaintances that I wouldn't want to bother with my troubles. And so I hurry, if I can, to get home, sit in my wicker chair in the lounge, and philosophise into the dark night.

Yes, I'm in a bad place right now. I'm alone and I can't stand it. I can't see the light. All day I listen to my patients' stories, which doesn't help at all. But I like my work. Where would I be without it? When I'm working, I can switch off my own problems. For a while I forget. The problem is that all day I hear nothing positive. No one comes to my office and says that it's a beautiful, sunny day outside, that the air smells like spring and the streets are full of beautiful girls. Instead, the exhausted manager comes to see me, wanting to know how to live so that his life has a purpose. Or the young girl comes, sick with anorexia, all skin and bone, and says that she's fat. Or – and right now I have a really terrible case – the bloke who was let out of prison comes. He had a bad time in prison, was bullied by the other prisoners, and he just wants to forget it all so he can sleep. How can I come home in the evening to that empty house, my head full of the dirt, pain and suffering of this world, and not drink?

The moon apparently regarded this as a rhetorical question and didn't answer.

"I can't," I answered myself. "I would go mad. I really would go mad."

"Drinking night after night is no answer," the moon spoke. "You already are going mad. It's simply another path to the same place. Just a lot shorter."

"I know this! I'm a psychologist and I know how these things end. I knew what to say to the guy who came in with similar problems. I insisted to him, in a scientific and important way, that cases like his were quite common, that he certainly had nothing to fear, and that we would handle it together. Then we analysed everything, took it all apart and looked for answers. I'm sure he left with the feeling that someone (me) cared about him, and eventually realised that things weren't so bad – that things were better. And why had he even come anyway? Good work by the psychologist. But who will convince me?" I raised my voice at this last sentence so he would understand why I had brought this man up.

"All psychology is a bit of a fraud." I sighed resignedly before heating up again. "I was lying to that guy, letting him think that I was professionally diagnosing his mental state. The truth is that his feelings of loneliness stemmed from the fact that he really was alone. Like me – he didn't have a wife, didn't have children, didn't have friends. He was alone. But I managed to persuade him that he had been professionally led out of a crisis. The reality of it is, however, that the relief he experienced actually came after he had found another woman. His solitude was no longer so tortuous – he told me this and thanked me for returning him to his life. I really felt like a fraud. And the worst part was when he added, with tears in his eyes, that he had found that woman thanks to me. No, he was no fool. Just a normal bloke who put his trust in me. But who will lie to me? Who? Can you tell me? I'm a psychologist who desperately needs a psychologist."

I was almost screaming those last few sentences, until I finally took a deep breath, and a dog started barking in the neighbour's garden.

"You are silent. You can't tell me," I whispered.

"What should I tell you?" shouted the moon. "Just like I can't mercifully mislead a GP who is dying of prostate cancer, neither can I reassure you when your soul is in distress. You have to just pull yourself together and believe."

"Believe? In whom or in what should I believe?"

"In a miracle, in love. Simply believe in something."

"Love, love – nonsense," I countered drunkenly.

"You want advice, and when I give it to you, you refuse it. I can't help you."

"There is no help for me? That sounds horrible coming from you." I woke up a bit and drank some more wine.

In this dream, I climbed up to the moon and together we looked down...

"That light below us, those are dreams," he said, "and those clouds, that is love."

"I can't be helped," I repeated, anxiety spreading over me from the words. I quickly took it back. No, it's not all so bad.

* * *

Every Tuesday evening I go to my German class. One bright spot after all. I'm not trying to fool myself into thinking that, someday, I will learn to speak German fluently, but I always go to class. There are about ten of us, and most are women of various ages. It's refreshing when we talk about the difference between '*ich bin hungrig*' (I am hungry) and '*ich bin hungriger*' (I am hungrier). Or when we sing *Weht im Wind* (*Blowing in the Wind*) – then we feel like schoolchildren who still have everything in front of them.

I like to watch the women. For example, I realised that they move their lips particularly beautifully when they pronounce foreign words. Take the word *betören* (beguile) – the lips first touch each other, the upper teeth brush the lower lip and then the lips form an 'O' as the breath comes out. Thrilling, exciting.

And in the evening, when it gets dark, I sit in my lounge at home, pour myself a large glass of wine and start a conversation with the moon.

Then I ask: "You say that you're only a spectator – the one who sees all the threads that tie us humans together. What are you talking about? How am I to understand that?"

"I've been travelling the sky for millions of years," he answered, "and from these heavens above earth and with these millions of years of experience, I see each of you. I see into your hearts and into your souls and I see that you are all connected by one thin thread. You are all somehow connected. Some of you are firmly anchored in the web of those close to you. Some of you hang by one or two threads—"

"And me?" I interrupted impatiently. "What about my threads?"

"Your threads?" He thought about it. "I see one – it's hanging behind you, torn off."

"Kyley?" I asked.

"Kyley."

"And what else? Tell me what else you see," I urged him.

"I see one more thread. It's distinct and it leads... to the future. I can't tell you anything else about it."

"You can't?" I wondered. "Why? Who can tell you what you can and can't do? You're a heavenly body. You are the universe!"

"Yes, I am, and I could look into the future, but you human beings are forbidden to know your future."

"Why?"

"Because you couldn't handle it. You are mortal, and if you knew the end of your days, you wouldn't be able to live normally. It's for your own good that you are not to know your own future."

"I don't want to know *when* I'm going to die, but who this thread that you're talking about is connected to," I persisted.

The moon remained silent, maybe trying to see the end of the thread, and then, as if he were scrutinising it, he answered just to himself: *Sometimes it's all connected.*

Chapter 2

"Are you sleeping?" Emma whispered. "Look at that beautiful moon."

Kieran didn't answer. He was lying on his stomach with his head turned towards Emma and his eyes closed.

"Are you sleeping?"

He raised his hand in answer, touched her bent leg and edged his hand up slowly, from the knee, along her smooth thigh, slowly, very slowly, across her hips to her naked lap.

"Stop it," she whispered, but didn't move away.

She used those two words often. She knew that in a way they excited him, whispered while he was touching her, and also that they seemed placating and soothing when they were having one of their arguments. Even now they had their effect. He opened his eyes, lifted his head, looked into her eyes and then with an unwavering expression, and as if following the traces of his hands, he began to kiss her tenderly – on the knee, the thigh, the hips…

"Stop it. He's looking at us."

He stopped. "What? Who is looking at us?"

"The moon, the beautiful moon."

"Come on, what are you talking about?" He didn't get upset and continued kissing her tenderly. "Let him look," he said, without even turning his head.

She watched the shining disc. It peered into the room with all its magnitude. She stretched out her legs and toes as if she wanted to touch it; she reached for its centre. She didn't notice the touch of Kieran's lips, just the light of the moon which slid along her skin and arched along the curves of her legs and hips.

Then the scene broke when Kieran blocked the light of the moon with his body and pulled her bent legs almost up to her breasts. In this discomfort she no longer trusted his tender kisses, and primeval instincts took over. As always – it was now each for themselves…

Once she had written: our lovemaking – two bodies wrestling together for the spoils.

Through the half-open window, through which the moon had peered into Kieran's room, daylight now streamed. Even through the closed blinds, flashes of sunlight hinted at the sunny morning.

Emma awoke slowly. She lay on her back and resisted opening her eyes.

Thoughts rambled through her mind: *I'm awake, it's morning, Kieran…* She opened her eyes. The rays of sunlight through the blinds broke up the darkness of the room. She leant on her elbows. The space next to her was empty.

"Help," she moaned.

Through the open doors of the kitchen, a newspaper rustled.

"Get up, lazy. It's almost eight."

She fell back on the pillow. "Now, at night? No, I don't want to."

A chair scraped in the kitchen and Kieran appeared in the doorway, just as God had created him.

"You know that joke—"

"Don't tell me jokes in the morning. I can't stand it!" She buried her face in the pillow.

"A telephone rings in a hotel room..." Kieran would not be discouraged. "A sleepy man fumbles with the phone.

"'Hello?'

"'Good morning, this is reception.' He hears a pleasant female voice. 'Are you the guest who wanted to be woken up at seven o'clock?'

"'Yes, that's me.'

"'Well, come on! Get up! It's almost nine!'"

She laughed despite herself. "Jesus, that is so dumb you have to laugh."

He sat down on the bed by her with an ambiguous look on his face.

"Would you like to be woken up nicely?"

"You already woke me up nicely."

"Would you like to be woken up in a nicer way?" He nuzzled up to her.

"No... I've already laughed enough this morning." She wriggled out of his arms.

"Now, hold on, are you saying making love with me is something to laugh about?" He was shocked.

"Sometimes it's even a horror."

He thought about whether this was an insult, but Emma had already jumped out of bed and opened the blinds.

Right after breakfast, Kieran hurried to get to his office by nine, even though he ran his own company, which produced promotional items. Emma refused his offer of a lift and said she would take a morning walk through the town to catch the bus home.

Home was in Kibworth Beauchamp, fifteen minutes or so away by bus, and walking to the Market Harborough Square bus stop would make her feel good. It really was a beautiful morning. It was the middle of October and the warming sun made one forget that winter was coming; it seemed like the autumn would never end. The sun shone into the people's pale faces and brought life back to them. Like on every other sunny day, people were rushing in all directions, but in this light, it was somehow more joyful, as if this time they were going someplace different.

Slowly walking down the sunny side of the street, she stole glances at the faces, felt the ubiquitous energy and tried to soak it in. She often had a problem sharing the mood of the crowd, the general merriment or general sadness, but in this moment her joyful feeling prevailed.

The waves of scepticism and anxiety that occasionally flooded her mind were calmed by the rays of autumn sunlight, and like a well-built boat, she could bob along on those waves with her thoughts and the awareness of the success she had achieved. She wasn't even thirty yet and she was a good writer, at least good enough that she didn't have to rush off to an office for nine every morning. She made a living at it, sometimes. Sometimes just barely, but she could wander down the street in the morning, warm herself in the autumn sunlight, sit in the park, daydream... think about how her character's story would continue, write a note in her notebook, an idea – like the one now; she writes it into her memory: *the hero of my book is a coward... it doesn't really fit anywhere, but it seems funny.* Maybe she will use it sometime, but probably not. Maybe tomorrow it will seem stupid.

Sometimes there were feelings of gloom and doubt, maybe as the price for her comfort, but she was probably just overthinking things. But how else? After all, she went deep into the thoughts of her characters. She let herself down on a thin rope to the depths of their consciousness, and then like a miner, covered in sweat, she dug and extracted before clawing her way back up. She empathised with their fates, experienced their joy and pain – and wrote...

Yes, writing was beautifully intoxicating – to think up a story, and characters, give them names, an appearance and nature, look into their dreams and determine their life paths. When she wrote, she was like God: she created a world, her world, in which her rules applied.

She decided not to hurry home; the sun was so pleasantly warming.

Immersed in her thoughts, she walked through the town square, past Tesco Metro, through the Commons car park and over the bridge spanning the River Welland, and there she was, in Welland Park. She had her choice of empty benches. She sat on one that had been nicely warmed by the sunlight. She closed her eyes and put her head back towards the sun.

Yes, it was about going down into the consciousness of her characters and empathising with their fates. She had always been sensitive and overly aware. This often made her glad because it allowed her to do the work that she does – write. But sometimes she regretted it, because she saw earlier and deeper into things that were often better left unseen.

It also often happened, without her even intending it, that her literary characters reflected the characteristics, moods or behaviour of real people who existed around her. So, for example, she has been writing about a dying feeling, about love which is no longer like it once was – and then, with a start, she recognised herself and Kieran in those two young people.

Even she herself didn't know where the thought came from. After all, everything was fine. Or was it? She had been with Kieran for three years. She slept at his place a couple of nights a week, and then he slept at her place, because she had her own place too. They went together to the cinema, to the theatre, out with friends to a restaurant, took trips, two weeks by the sea in the summer, skiing in Austria in the winter. Everything was as it should be. But even so, lately she had been feeling... how to say it? Alienated? Cold? Disinterested? No, those words were too strong and couldn't express her feelings and the real state of their relationship precisely. Surely it wasn't so serious, and she shouldn't be so hypersensitive, she would tell herself.

Her little sensors, however, detected a slight vibration and just a glimpse of a shadow in his eyes. But this was enough – just the flash of a shadow and everything was shaken. Yes, some things were better left unseen.

Outside the window, the moon shines, colouring the night white – the colour of a small and silly love, which has died away.

She opened her eyes, and a stream of light banished the shadow from her mind. Why did her thoughts run in this direction? Even this morning she was thinking of life with Kieran, she now realised. Right after waking up, and then when Kieran was cracking his jokes, thoughts went through her head, somewhere in the back of her mind, thoughts about their relationship. It's not like it once was.

She shut her eyes again and returned to her memory. Kieran had already left when she had gone naked into the bathroom – she liked to walk around the house that way, as long as she was alone, but even Kieran's presence usually didn't stop her.

There was a feeling of freedom in her body and soul. In that moment, however, absorbed in thought, she hadn't even noticed it. They had made love in the evening, but it was as if there was no love in it. Only their bodies' thirsts were quenched. Their bodies drank, but their souls, at least hers, remained thirsty. She thought more about those moments in the morning. How she had turned on the shower to wash away the rest of the night and all its gloom. How the flow of the water had drowned out her thoughts of Kieran. How the warm water had fallen on her face when she put back her head. It had drummed on her skin and closed eyelids, flowed down her shoulders and between her breasts, slid down her stomach and caressed her thighs, the hot water hitting the bottom of the shower tray. She had stood there, her whole body absorbing the warmth, moving only her face slightly away, as it hurt from the lashings. Then she had closed her eyes, but with her head leant back, she had noticed the light from the lamp above the mirror as it penetrated her eyelids – *luminous darkness*, she had thought – and the water from the shower hummed monotonously.

She had listened. She had breathed the steam in through her nose, and the roar of the water had sounded strange, like a windstorm. The combination of these sounds had ripped through her mind and made her think of eternity and the time that had passed, and which will continue to pass. She had seen the Earth, the moon and the sun, which together run through the universe. In this moment of insight, she had seen herself floating upstream against the current of time. At first slowly, then faster, ever faster, and finally at an insane speed where everything had fused in a blur of colour. The windstorm had abated, the flight slowed, the contours returned to the picture, and she had seen herself: a child. Perhaps she was the daughter of prehistoric hunters who huddled in a cave trembling with the fear of the incomprehensible...

Could she confide in Kieran with some of these thoughts? She couldn't.

She saw the sun through her closed eyelids. *Luminous darkness*, she thought again. She listened. What did the sounds of the park awaken in her? Rustling tree branches.

Approaching steps which don't stop and immediately moved away. Distant voices. Birdsong. Noise from a nearby street full of cars. A few seconds of silence, when she heard her own breath, but then again, immediately voices, birds, cars.

The ubiquitous presence didn't allow her to enter the space, against or with the flow of time. One couldn't dream at ten in the morning. All her senses were fully awakened and her focus forward. They wanted to take it all in – to see, hear, feel… In the luminous darkness under her eyelids, she then saw… a penis. It reared, drenched in October sun, like a messenger from the universe, like the lord of the world.

She opened her eyes. No, you couldn't dream at ten in the morning, but the warm rays of autumn sun can thaw the images that lay in hibernation somewhere in the mind.

She laughed.

She walked briskly along the tarmac path and headed to the town square to catch a bus home.

Chapter 3

I awoke with difficulty. My heavy eyelids wouldn't open. I felt cold, terribly cold. *Wake up, open your eyes*, I prodded myself.

Finally, I looked out through the slits of my swollen eyelids. God… I was sitting in the wicker chair. I had slept here all night. I could only move my eyes, and I rolled them in all directions attempting to get my bearings. I was sitting – lying – in the chair. Cold, cold. I tried to lift my left arm, which was behind me. I couldn't.

The thought *I have to get myself on the ground* flashed through my mind. I leant over and, with great effort, edged out of the chair and onto my knees. My left arm was asleep and wouldn't cooperate. I tried to move my fingers. They moved only stiffly. It took a few minutes before I could manage to stand up. On the table I saw two empty wine bottles and a glass lying on its side on the chair. Only then did I remember the crisis of the night before and was disappointed in my failure. Where had my commitment to a new life gone? Ugh…

The light above the mirror in the bathroom ruthlessly exposed the state of my soul and punished me for yesterday's attempt to drink myself out of this world. I was forty-two years old; I looked like fifty right now and I felt one hundred. With both hands I leant over the sink and looked into the mirror. At thirty, my hair had already started thinning, revealing a bald spot. Maybe I had made the right decision in not trying to save it with a comb-over, instead going for a very short haircut. As long as my hair was cut short, I looked neat, kind of sporty, maybe even youthful... but not great. Now, with my hair at this length, it looked too long, sticking out comically.

Eyes? They're brown, big – and they were able to 'speak'. They were able to praise, reprimand, ask and answer, caress and laugh – they could even kill. Now, however, they were silent. They just looked at the reflection in the mirror and were perhaps a little frightened by the face decorated with the two red buttons. I don't know you, but I will wash you; I remembered the silly joke. Then it was time for shaving. And when I had a hot shower and then a cold one right after that, I felt much better. The cold water after the shaving tightened up my skin a bit. And my eyes? No, they weren't laughing, but they weren't killing.

I didn't even consider breakfast, so I just sat down in the kitchen with a mug of black coffee, and with the remote control, turned on the TV that I had on the shelf.

Kyley had wanted it there.

"If I'm cooking on Sunday and you're watching TV in the living room, then I need a little company in here," she had said.

Now it was keeping me company.

The news. Two dead on the road, a night-time break-in at a supermarket, stabbing... the world entered my flat… I always wondered what good it was to tell people that someone had died on the roads yesterday, a person was stabbed, something was stolen, someone cheated. For what? A lesson? A warning? Nonsense. The disasters on the screen were so far away they might as well be from another world. Almost no one learns anything, and today more people will die, there will be another stabbing and another robbery. Only the most sensitive people, those who didn't take risks in cars, who didn't stab others, and didn't steal, were really scared by the news. And their conviction that the world was a very dangerous place to live in only becomes stronger. And they close themselves off even more, feel even more anxious and more distrustful… until one day they end up in my office. That's the only thing the news was good for. Otherwise it's for nothing. Yes, of course it raises the ratings – that's what it's all about. Most people yearned to see the misery of others, and in the warmth of their living rooms were hypnotised by the crippled fates of those who were struck by misfortune yesterday.

The weather forecast. Finally. I turned the sound off with the remote. This was the game I prescribed for myself when the pain over losing Kyley became unbearable.

"Hi. How are you?" I greeted the weather girl and read her lips.

"Fine, but I feel like sleeping more. And you?"

"Yeah, it's the same for me. I'd like to sleep… and I have a headache."

"You shouldn't drink in the evening. That's what it's from."

"I promised myself that I wouldn't anymore, but…"

"So promise me. Say: yes, I promise here and now that I won't drink anymore."

"I promise here and now…" I felt like a mad person. "I am a mad person, who talks to the television."

"And to the moon."

"Are you poking fun at me?"

"No, heaven forbid. I also talk – with the moon, with the sun, with the clouds; look, I have pictures here of all of them."

"You're poking fun at me. You're twenty-five and you don't know what loneliness is. You're beautiful, so how could you know? Your world is full of nice words that try to capture your attention, and full of looks that silently try to do the same. Loneliness – you know it when you suddenly find yourself in it."

"I guess you're right. Yes, I'm young. Is that a sin? Is it a sin that I inspire love?"

"A sin? Of course it's a sin. Because, what is a sin? It irritates and frustrates those of us who are disappointed, resentful and ageing. A sin – it's your young body in the eyes of an old woman. Your bright smile when she only has teeth in a glass on the night table. Your nakedness, when she will only undress with the lights off. A sin is your love when I whisper to the moon in the night. A sin is the man who made you laugh… while I just babble on here."

The two hosts on *Good Morning Britain* smile on the silent screen.

* * *

My office was in Leicester, but more and more often I saw my patients in the office in my house in Great Bowden. I was seriously considering giving up my office in Leicester and working permanently from home.

Today I would stay here. The former prisoner would come in the afternoon, and I had to prepare. Suddenly I felt nauseated. Residual alcohol? I thought about it. What next? Well, it's not so hard to answer that question myself: I will drink myself to death if I don't pull myself together. I know better than anyone how it will turn out. There are a few men, and even women, who come to therapy having thought that they could wash away their pain, gloom and shadows with alcohol.

They didn't.

It just looks like that at first, I tell them; the world seems disgusting, people evil – you drink five pints of strong lager, and everything is fine and happy, the gloom has been washed away. In the morning, however, you realise that along with all those problems that you have flushed into the toilet, you have also flushed a piece of yourself. Just a little bit, maybe not even enough to notice, or maybe you just smooth over the missing piece. And so you keep drinking, and little by little you find yourself being flushed down into that toilet, stinking of booze, and full of worries, gloom, and shadows.

Yeah, that's what I tell my patients. Yes, ladies and gentlemen, that is how things are – and I'm here so that I can pull you, standing chest deep and desperately stretching out your hands, out of the gutter. Maybe a bit of a peculiar explanation, but it works – and some understand.

But who will pull me out?

Silence.

I stayed in the kitchen a while longer and then went to my office. It's a medium to large-sized room on the first floor of my Victorian house in Great Bowden. Two wardrobes by the wall, shelves with books, a sofa, a comfortable chair and a massive desk that dominates everything. It doesn't go with the wardrobes and the veneered shelves made of particle board. It's enormous, massive, honest. I remember how hard it was to get it up the stairs to the office. We'd even had to take the banister off so we could turn with it, but it had simply had to be in the office.

It had originally belonged to my father. He used to sit at it in the evenings and write fictional wartime stories which he would then tell my brother and me. When he died, we gradually changed almost all the furniture in the house, but I had kept the desk and guarded it as a precious relic.

Often when I sit at it, I remember my father and his fictional wartime escapades, which even now seemed as if they were rising from the rings on the massive desk. Unfortunately, in contrast with father's stories, at this desk I studied the records of my patients' statements, and it's usually not such fun to read or listen to. It's my job. What can I do? This desk forces one to be honest, so it's to the benefit of my patients that here I often find answers to their questions, and medicine for their misery.

I turned on the recorder and started the recording of the last session with the former prisoner.

'To lose your freedom, being locked up, is in itself a bad thing,' his confession started. 'I broke the law, yes – I had sex with an underage girl... it wasn't rape. We loved each other. She was fourteen and I was almost thirty... we really loved each other. I should have known better, but I lost my head. And then it all came crashing down. Angry parents, endless police interrogation, the cell I was kept in, and in the end a trial in the Crown Court.

'I got three years. I'm a sensitive person. I took it very badly, and I was terribly afraid... and what you fear most usually comes to pass, doesn't it?

'Losing your freedom is in itself a bad thing... I don't think I'm able to talk about all of it, but besides the loss of freedom, there was exposure to violence and humiliation from the other prisoners and even the guards. I was labelled a sex offender and put on a sex offenders register.

'I saw evil. I don't know what else to call it. It was absolute evil. Evil that, even after all these years, wakes me up at night. Evil which... stank like those mattresses that I laid on. Evil that suffocated... like the stale air in the cells. It was the moisture that gathered on the windows... and the drops ran down and drew more bars – there was no escape.

'Three years. Three years. Those thieves and rapists preached to me about morality... they called me Fucker... No, I can't talk about it.'

'*Try to,*' I had persuaded him gently. '*Talk it out.*'

After a while he had calmed down a bit and then spoken some more.

I hadn't scheduled anyone else today other than the ex-prisoner, and I didn't have group therapy until one, so I listened to the recording for the rest of the morning. I made notes, and it was only with difficulty that I could maintain some distance from the horrors coming out of the recorder.

When I went to Bowden Stores and Coffee House for a bite to eat shortly after twelve, I felt distress, hopelessness, and that feeling of resignation that comes with winter approaching all settle in my mind. And suddenly I had a thought. It swooped in from somewhere in the universe of my brain, shining like a comet – yes, a comet is what I would compare it to. It was not a new thought – I knew I'd had it before. It flew in and waved with its tail. Only at that time, the sky – my mind – was overcast with worries about children, family, work…

Today was much clearer.

Chapter 4

Emma stopped. She held her breath so as to not scare her thoughts away. Yes. Yes, that was it. She continued walking, slowly at first, then faster as the tempo of her thoughts picked up. She ran out of Welland Park and headed for the square to catch the X7 bus to take her home to Kibworth Beauchamp. The sunlight blinded her, but she was oblivious to it. Her mind was working on an idea…

Yes.

At home she stretched her aching back and comfortably leant back in the chair in front of the laptop with her hands clasped behind her head. She read over the few sentences she had written and was satisfied. She had succeeded in capturing the moment when her heroine, Michelle, came to the decision that would change her life.

Yes, writing was intoxicatingly beautiful.

It was only the beginning of the story, but she already knew that she would like this woman. Once she had taken her through the whole book, all the way to its happy ending, and she had written the last lines, she would be sad to say goodbye. The end was far away. They still had a lot to go through together. She would put all her fantasies into this story. Perhaps she would conquer unknown places in the human soul. She knew where to look for those places. They were deep, down at the bottom of every soul, where one could only descend on the end of a thin rope.

She would try.

She would descend to the bottom and uncover layers that had been forming for centuries...

* * *

Emma walked naked into the bathroom, the mirror again her companion for today. She turned the water on in the bath and today, unusually, looked repeatedly at her reflection. The light was flatteringly dim and suddenly it occurred to her that it wasn't so bad: *I'm still a beautiful woman!*

She stepped into the bath and the heat of the water rose to her body and even warmed her mind. She slowly sat down and stretched herself back until her hair dipped in the warm water. Then, leaning on her elbows, she raised her head... and suddenly felt the weight of her hair as it had been years before.

She closed her eyes and was certain that she was a fairy with long, heavy hair.

'Turn around for me!' She remembered Kieran's excited words – and she did as he said, her hair lifting as she turned, circling her body from the momentum so that her breasts glowed out of the black like... how did he say it? Like two volcanoes ready to erupt. The running water drummed on the surface and drowned out the world. She hesitated for a moment, and then shifted in the bath until the water was pouring in her lap. It fell between her thighs, pulsated, shattered, sprayed… and roughly stroked, patiently stroked. Oh, life!

The sound under the surface darkened, rumbling monotonously as if from the bowels of the Earth. Her breath quickened and her breasts, like two volcanoes above the water, were ready to explode. Then the harsh, unrelenting force broke through the thin crust and released a geyser of hot lava which flooded her body… Panting, surprised with herself. *When did I last experience such pleasure?* She thought back. *Has it only been months? Or is it already a year?* She couldn't remember.

When she lay down onto the bed, the curious mood of this evening remained with her. She finally knew what would happen next. She fought back the tears, but they rolled from her eyes. *Don't cry, just don't cry…* She didn't wipe away her tears, but sleep stopped them coming. They dried on her face and changed into invisible crystals of salt, an avalanche sprinkling small wrinkles, whose rumbling disturbed her dreams.

* * *

Emma had a taste for coffee, so she got up from her laptop and went into the kitchen to make it. When the din of the water in the kettle signalled that it was boiling, she laughed because it reminded her of the scene in the bath.

And what of it? Of course it's her own special experience. Why, it offers so much: the sweet, warming environment of the bathroom, the uninterrupted nakedness, the pleasant warm water, the roar that drowns out the moans and sighs, and the current – constant, warm, strong…

A woman who insists she has not tried it is lying.

Kieran called before noon to tell her he was going out of Market Harborough and had to cancel their lunch together.

"I'll be back in the evening. Will you come over?"

She let him wait for the answer. "Yeah, I'll come." She sniffed, annoyed at the change of plans. "What does that mean – 'out of Market Harborough'?"

"Sorry. I'm going to Luton. A company there accepted my quote – imagine that. I sent them a quote for a shipment of five thousand production labels. I told myself that I'd overdone it, and nothing would come of it. And they placed the order! Great! I'm going over to work out the details and sign the contract."

"What does that mean – 'I'll be back in the evening'?"

"You're kind of nasty today," he grumbled. "Between eight and nine."

She had another comment about 'a company in' on the tip of her tongue but she let it go. Why should she know the name anyway?

"So, okay, I'll be at your place before nine." She hung up. Was she the problem, or was he? Or both of them?

* * *

She wouldn't go to lunch alone. That was exactly the limit of emancipation she didn't want to cross. A woman alone in a restaurant sent too strong a message: I am single, childless, desperately looking for someone to marry and have kids with, because as everyone can see, it's high time. She was exaggerating, but still, she wouldn't consider going alone.

* * *

Beth was the owner of a Market Harborough bookshop. She was almost a generation older, but she was a friend who, if it was possible, would drop everything to help.

And she didn't let her down even today.

"They're all the same," she comforted her as she sat down at the table by the window of Pizza Express overlooking St Mary's Place. "They should get over themselves."

In contrast to her petite figure, sweet expression and occupation, which was actually more of a calling, she always spoke directly, almost harshly. Emma never had to go further for sharper words. Her words never held the ignorance or obtuseness of the football fan, and in order not to degrade or offend, she didn't use vulgar words unnecessarily. She used her words rather as a shortcut.

'They should get over themselves.' It was all in there: mockery of the self-centredness of men and outrage over their unreliability, but also the determination to get by even without them...

"Don't you have the feeling that they are..." She clicked her tongue, looking for the right word. "How should I say it? Unfinished, primitive? Don't give up yet. I'll help you out."

Emma sighed in agreement, but Beth went on.

"In my next life, I want to be a man. I ask Chris how he can lie around watching television all afternoon. He says he's tired from work. Ha-ha. Bullshit, I tell him, you're lazy. He goes into an explanation of the historical reasons for the 'rhythm of life', that for thousands of years they've hunted, and they have it in their genes to focus, hunt, rest, focus, hunt, rest… During the day at work, he 'focused and hunted'. Now he was resting. You've been making fools of us, I tell him, for thousands of years. The truth is, you've enslaved the world and especially us women, and now you can afford to live such a life."

Emma took advantage of the pause and slipped into the debate. "Calm down. It's not like I'm getting married."

"What's wrong? Is Kieran annoying you?"

"I don't know," Emma continued again, while the waiter served their food. "I just have a feeling lately that things aren't working. Or that our relationship has put us in another dimension – from 'I can't be without you' to 'I can be without you.'"

"And, for Christ's sake, the only thing left is 'I don't want to be with you.'"

"Exactly. With feelings like that, a woman can't be thinking about a wedding. Let's change the topic. Ask me what I'm writing."

"What are you writing?"

"Nothing. I'm searching. But no, I'm writing, writing… only, I don't know what will come of it. I don't have a framework. Just a foggy idea that it will be a story of a woman my age, a bit disillusioned with men, with the man she has at home. A woman who is thinking how to go on… A little love, a little sex – so far with a man."

They both laughed at this last sentence.

"I hope you'll spice it up… with something a bit stronger," said Beth, narrowing her eyes.

Both remained quiet and suddenly the space was filled with a special charge. Until Emma broke the silence.

"So far, they're just snippets which maybe I'll somehow put together. I'm learning to think with the head of a slightly older woman. I'm circling and waiting. I'm curious myself where it will lead."

"You're learning to think with the head of a slightly older woman? A woman almost twenty years older? I'm curious what you'll come up with."

"Perhaps nothing. It'll end up in the drawer and I'll have to start again. And so what?"

Beth was suddenly serious. "Will you have some wine? Rather not, hmm?" she answered with a sad smile. Suddenly it was not the brash and energetic woman sitting here.

"Is something wrong?" Emma asked, waving at the waiter.

"I envy you," said Beth.

"Envy? Me? What could you envy about me? My troubled relationship with Kieran, or my few poorly selling books?"

"No, no. Even though I could envy you both of those things. Especially the books. Seriously. They're good. But I envy your enthusiasm… your taste for a fight. Zest. Youth?"

"You envy me? You envy my enthusiasm and zest? Am I hearing you right?"

Emma reached her hand across the table and with her fingers, touched Beth's hand.

"You surprise me. As long as I've known you, I've wanted to be like you – strong, intelligent, beautiful. What happened?"

"I'm weak, stupid, and ugly." Beth sighed sadly.

"What are you talking about? What happened that suddenly you're sitting here like a pile of unhappiness?"

"I don't know. I'm getting old. Fatigue or something. For weeks and months, I've been thinking about myself. I don't enjoy work, I don't enjoy reading, I don't enjoy writing, men, women…" She smiled bitterly. "I'm at an impasse and I don't know how to get out."

Beth noticed the waiter, already back behind the bar, with a slight smile on his face and raised eyebrows, so she slowly pulled her hand from Emma's touch.

"What will your heroine do with her unhappy life?" She didn't wait for an answer and went on, "I found myself a shrink."

"Wait a second – like a psychiatrist?"

"Not exactly a psychiatrist, but a psychologist."

Neither said anything. Emma processed this surprising information and Beth enjoyed a sudden sense of relief. The waiter watched them with a sly smile and was certain that these two women, who were now gazing long into each other's eyes, had 'something' together.

"And?" Emma interrupted the silence.

"And what? I simply have a psychologist. I go to him, I talk, he records it – I allow him to: it's his method – and at the next session we discuss it and he erases the recording."

"Does it work? Is it helping you?"

"I've been there twice, and my next visit is tomorrow. I can't say. Maybe."

Emma looked at her incredulously. "Who is this man anyway? How did you find him?"

"Bullshit." Beth brushed away the hint of doubt. "He's fine. My GP recommended him. Paul is his name. Good-looking guy, by the way."

And that is how Emma first heard the name Paul Warburton. And what of it? She was surprised by the slight chill that she felt. Again those sensitive little sensors which registered a passing shadow. It occurred to her that everything seemed slightly flared... and she smiled despite herself.

Chapter 5

It was four in the afternoon and the ex-convict hadn't turned up. I sat behind the massive desk and waited. It was the first time that he hadn't turned up on time.

I read through my notes again. I turned on the recording.

'Evil which... stank like those mattresses that I laid on. Evil that suffocated... like the stale air in the cells. It was the moisture that gathered on the windows... and the drops ran down and drew more bars – there was no escape.'

I pushed the stop button. I'm ready.
He hadn't turned up.
Four-thirty. Where was he?
Time went by.
I looked at the tree rings on the desktop and unwittingly traced their shape with my finger. I ran my finger along them, and like the needle of a record player for vinyl records, I sensed with my finger a long ago sound.

Are you sleeping? You're not sleeping. Sleeping, sleeping, and in the dream, you are dreaming...

How did it go after that? Almost all the words ended with 'ing', making it sound like a song.

I'd forgotten how it went.

Music sounded. It was quiet and friendly, and sounded as if it came from a distance. Or from the depths of time. Even the sing song rhythm. And finally an old sound, which reminded me of my parents tuning the radio stations a few years back. A faraway sound that you don't hear anymore these days. Whistling, humming, rustling… and then voices, music and again whistling. What did it remind me of? The end of the song *I am the Walrus* by The Beatles. Yes, exactly.

I like The Beatles' music. I'll never get tired of listening to it, and I have listened to it since childhood. *Eleanor Rigby* occurred to me, and I don't know why.

He was not going to turn up. That was clear. He could have let me know.

I decided to use the time to prepare for the next day's session. Beth Brooke, forty-five years old, bookshop owner, I recalled. Her name suited her – small, slim, pretty brunette. I read in my notes: mid-life crisis. Children grown, independent, have left home. Routine job which she has been doing for almost twenty years. Married for twenty-five years.

I played the recording from her first visit.

'I don't want to stuff myself with antidepressants because I don't think my gloomy moods are the result of any mental problem,' she had stated quite sharply, differently than I had expected.

I had quietly agreed with her.

'It's probably just several unpleasant factors together. The children have left the nest. Nearly twenty years in a business that really takes nerves – I sell books. You wouldn't think so, hmm? One husband for twenty-five years… I'm not expecting a miracle, but I want some advice about what to do next. I can't do it myself.'

'From what I'm hearing from you, and my overall impression of you, I have to agree that you're not in need of therapy. And I even have doubts that you're a case for therapy. I apologise, I don't want to make light of your problems, but really, from what I've heard so far, I'm not able to discern any anomalies. I would say that everything is basically normal, and if you're tired from your monotonous job and from your husband, please don't expect that I will recommend that you change them both. You could be back here within a year saying that everything is a hundred times worse.'

'I know. I reckon I'm just not good at describing my problems clearly. You know, I've been in books for years, and during that time I've developed… how should I say it? A distaste for drawn-out babble. For those long sentences, which you are using right now, and which your presence is forcing me to use too.'

'I'm sorry, really. Okay. Again. Try it your way.'

'All right. I can't act like you're not here, but I'll try… Everything is really pissing me off.'

She had got me. You could even hear my laugh on the recording.

Then her tongue had come untied, and she had really let go. She'd talked and talked, and when she thought it was appropriate, she'd said: 'Ungrateful bastards, lazy asshole on the couch, or – fuck them all.'

When we had finished and she'd left, I'd realised with embarrassment that after that session, I somehow felt a sense of relief.

I turned off the recorder and walked to the window. Outside it was growing dark rapidly because the sky, clear during the day, had become overcast. It hadn't rained and didn't look like it was going to, but the clouds brought the evening nearer. It would be a long evening. Again that tightening somewhere in the chest. *Eleanor Rigby*, I remembered.

* * *

Outside was already dark when I poured myself a large glass of wine, turned off the light and sat down in the wicker chair by the window. From the perspective of my profession, the worse way to stave off anxiety.

The moon was only partially shining through the veil of clouds, but the brighter spot in the sky betrayed its position.

"Do you hear me?" I tried.

"I hear you. I even see you, Paul," boomed the moon from the deep within.

It took me by surprise. I took a sip of wine.

"Do you know what songs are? Does music reach you?"

"Of course. Not all music reaches my ears, but that which does – and not only to my ears, but what flies further into space – is beautiful. Seen from space, there is nothing better than what you, as human beings, have created."

"That wouldn't have occurred to me," I wondered aloud, "music is surely beautiful, but don't you think that we have achieved even more?"

"Hmm," he said doubtfully.

"You don't like our buildings, our cities, our... work?"

Silence.

"Have you perhaps seen something better somewhere else in our solar system?" I kept trying.

"Why do you think your cities are better than... ant cities, for example?" the moon said finally, really infuriating me.

"Ant cities? Did I hear you correctly? You're comparing ant cities with those built by humans?"

I drank the rest of the wine in my glass. It had really pissed me off.

"Your cities aren't better," the moon continued fiercely. "You build them in contrast to nature. You don't respect it. Pompously trying to humiliate it and... it's stupid. Ants wouldn't do that. Even I would never do that."

I took a breath to defend all of mankind, but then I gave up.

"Do we really look so stupid from the heavens?"

"Not only from the heavens." After it had been quiet for a while, he added apologetically, "But music... you make music beautifully."

I poured myself another drink and wondered if I should continue in this discussion. I took a drink before trying to change the subject, but the moon prevented me.

"Have you noticed that all your efforts, that struggle that you engage in daily with nature, always slowly, but inexorably, turns against you?"

"What do you mean?"

"Almost everything you do," the moon snapped. "Cities. You build them for your own comfort – big, concrete and asphalt. But so noisy and dirty that they're uncomfortable. I sometimes look into ant cities – anthills, as you say – and I've never, never seen ants fleeing in droves from their cities to the countryside. They respect the millions of years of proven ways – and they don't have to run from themselves."

"Maybe you're right. You're definitely right – but only if you judge human activity based on its influence on nature. Almost everything is bad here. But there is another point of view, and from that we are exceptional, unique in the world, and perhaps even in the universe – you would know best. We humans can create! We build tall buildings, houses, theatres, bridges... and we make them beautiful, and they often even speak to the soul. Our sculptures and pictures express emotions – sorrow, joy, love. Who else can do that?"

"What would your sculptures be without my light? Black shadows in a dark night. And nature also creates pictures and sculptures, but you have forgotten to look around you. You don't see them. The sun setting, the peaks of mountains that rise to the heavens... but those thousands of tiny beauties – except for a few individuals among you – you don't see. You create things that you think are soulful and beautiful. Perhaps they are – but only for you. They don't reach the universe. No, I repeat, the only thing that you are exceptional in is your ability to create music. You have created it and can rightly be proud of it. Nothing else. Nothing worth mentioning."

"What about our technology?" I fought on. "Isn't it wonderful what we have achieved? Look – a mobile phone; if I want, I can call to... Australia! I just punch in the number, and I can speak with a friend in Australia."

"Give me at least one reason why it's good to be able to call Australia. As far as I know, you don't have any friends there."

This is how absurd our conversation was. Time and wine flowed on. Where had my resolve gone? We could have gone on trumping each other's arguments all night, until the new day washed over us, but that didn't happen.

"Does God exist?" I asked, right as the mobile phone on the table started to ring. *A sign* – the first thing that occurred to me.

"Australia," the moon muttered tersely.

I squinted at the display; it blinded me, and so the wine had done its... I gave up.

"Hello? This is Paul."

"Good evening, Doctor Warburton. I'm calling... I don't even know why... perhaps, just to say goodbye."

I immediately sobered up. The prisoner. The prisoner was calling me!

"What are you saying? Why are you saying goodbye? Where are you going? Are you driving somewhere?" I poured questions out in apprehension.

"I'm not driving away... I'm flying away."

"Where are you flying to? Where are you calling from?"

"Where am I calling from?" He was quiet, and for a few long moments, we listened to each other breathe. "I'm ending it, Doctor... I can't go on. I'm sitting in the window of my flat and I know it's ending. Nothing will stop me. Before I do it, I just wanted to tell you... thank you for everything you did. But there is no help for me. Don't blame yourself. Without you, I would have done it long ago..."

I shivered with the way he spoke so calmly. I recalled the three-storey building and how he lived on the top floor.

In a flash, I had decided: "I'll be there in ten minutes. Give us both a chance. Go back into your flat and wait for me. Give us both a chance, I'm coming immediately," I spewed incoherently. "Hello? Do you hear me?"

He didn't answer. He'd hung up.

I hurriedly pulled my sweater over my head and ran down the stairs to my car parked in the garage. I set out on my way, not even wasting time to close the garage door.

Market Harborough had not yet gone to sleep. It danced as if decorated with lights. Yes, it was a dance. A wild dance. It was a whirl of lights that I found myself in the middle of. Surprised, I ignored the lights that flashed all around and just hurried. There, to where I could see and where several dozens of lights twinkled and looked like stars in the late October sky, there where he was waiting for me, perhaps even more desperate and more in despair than I was myself. Even in my mind, the lights danced. Had the world around pervaded me, or had my turbulent mind spilled out into the space around? A light storm. I noticed that it wasn't thundering. Flashes of light streaked across each other, but the thunder was missing. It was quiet. And in this quiet I was reminded of the question: does God exist? I sat there for a moment at the traffic lights. The silent storm arrested. Through the car windows I looked around and searched for the bright spot in the sky where the moon was hiding. I didn't find him in the flood of light around me.

"Do you hear me? Does God exist?" I screamed.

No answer. The lights began moving again. Faster, faster, faster. Quiet lightning intersected the space, crossing over itself and entering my mind…

Suddenly, it thundered menacingly.

Chapter 6

Slumped in the chair, he listened to the hum of the shower. He rubbed his head with the towel and left his hair to dry. Without combing it, he looked like a porcupine. Michelle walked out of the bathroom, a towel wrapped around her body, the knot at her breast, and with another towel she carefully dried her hair. He watched her with a mischievous smile on his lips. The towel around her body was narrow and could only cover her top or her bottom. She chose to compromise and knotted it so that her chest swelled above, and half her bottom peeked out.

"What are you smiling so slyly at?" She checked herself from the knot down.

"Oh, nothing. I just – it's so nice with you. Come here."

She stepped towards him, still drying her hair with the towel. He put his arms around her naked thighs.

"Let me go, my hair is wet," she begged, but didn't move from his embrace.

He stroked her thighs, then moved his hand upward, higher, past her hips, under the towel and up to her cool breasts… The knot didn't hold, and the towel slid down to the floor.

She leant towards him for a kiss. Her not quite dry hair fell over his face. With a smile, she pulled back.

"Hold on, let me finish, otherwise I'll look like you."

She closed the door of the bathroom behind her and, with the hairdryer, blew dry her mane of hair. Then she combed it. *Hair – it's still the best thing I have*, she complimented herself. Forty-nine sounds awful, but not even her figure was bad. She raised her arms and laced her fingers behind her head. Breasts like before, but only when I have my arms up. If I put them down, it's worse, worse, even worse… forty-nine. No, that's in the past. Now it was year zero.

She leant closer towards the mirror.

'Happy zero birthday.'

She was startled by her own words. He was twenty-two years younger. She could be his mother. The thought invaded her mind, but she pushed it out again. And so what? What of it? Why should she chase him away? Why shouldn't she live her dream?

Yes, she remembered, it all started with a dream.

In the dream she put the stethoscope to his chest.

'Are you afraid of me? Your heart is beating as if you've just run a marathon.'

She couldn't see his face; it was hidden in the mist. She squinted her eyes.

'What's your name? We know each other from somewhere, don't we?'

The young man didn't answer, just nodded his head in agreement, and with that movement, disturbed the misty veil surrounding him. Suddenly, a flash of his face.

'You're the young man from the park! We see each other every morning.'

He remained silent.

'Yes, I recognise you,' she said with a laugh and thought, *I recognise you. And I know from that expression that you like me. You always look at me that way, not moving your eyes. Even I don't move. It's sweet. Just your look pleases me, not to mention your smile, which always enchants. A discreet, almost imperceptible smile, but I notice it, I feel it. You smile with your eyes.*

The young man in the dream remained silent.

'What's your name?'

He didn't answer. He just nodded his head, dispelled the fog and smiled with his look.

She looked in those eyes, and somewhere deep inside, the magma within her shifted. Then she felt his lips on hers. He remained silent even between kisses.

She didn't have that dream by chance. She knew the young man, or she'd at least seen him on her way to work. She walked to the office every day. It was barely ten minutes, half of it through the park, so it was a nice morning walk. Even that one time, she recalled. She was hurrying with small steps – that is all the narrow skirt allowed – to get to the office by nine. She had been thinking about Michael – her husband. He had cheated on her, she had known it for a long time, but it still hurt, nonetheless. Maybe even more and more. What kind of life was this? What was he thinking anyway? That he would have fun with other women, catch up on what he had missed... and I would run from the stove to the window, cook, iron, and wonder when he would come home? In the morning, he had acted like nothing had happened... Michelle, Michael... I'd like to give him a kick.

Immersed in her thoughts, she crossed the street and continued through the park. In the shade of the beautiful greenery, she better remembered the young man she always ran into here – and the dream that she had had the night before. Would they meet today? Involuntarily, she squinted her eyes to examine even the silhouettes of distant figures. No, she didn't see him. She realised that it upset her mood more than it should. Today had not started well.

She slowed her pace, the sun flashing through the tops of the trees. *What can I say? My dreams are becoming mixed with reality. Anyway, that young man I see on my way to work smiles at every halfway good-looking woman... And even if he didn't, what about it? I'll stop him and say, 'Hi, I had a dream about you last night.' Why do I even want to run into him anyway? Why am I even looking forward to seeing him? He's handsome... but not that handsome. I'm longing for sex... Yeah, but I can hold out. Flirt... a little.*

She sauntered on. Her subconscious slowed her steps to increase the likelihood that she would run into him. She threw her head back and closed her eyes... *Yes, I know – I need, I really need someone to love me. Is there someone out there who would love me?* She returned her gaze to the passers-by. *Hello?* No one, nothing. No one noticed the desire written in her eyes. *There's no one in my world to care about me. My world is this park, the street I have crossed, the waiting room at the office, the office...*

She walked out of the park. She was dazzled by the sunlight, but she was oblivious.

"Ma'am... ma'am!"

Not until the second time did she realise it was directed towards her.

"I've been waiting here for you," he said. "I didn't want to startle you in the park," he continued, as if he had not just plunged from the flood of light like from the mist in her dream.

The young man from the dream!

She looked into his face, into his eyes, unable to react in any other way. Was it him?

It is... maybe the only one in her world that...

"We know each other a bit, we pass each other here in the park... I'm Adam. Maybe I'm mistaken... I hope not... but it seems that we have something we want to say to each other."

"Yes? And what?" It was the only thing she managed to say, and to cover her embarrassment, she added, "Yes, I remember, we've passed each other in the park... And what do you want to say to me?" She held his gaze.

He faltered. "I think... I have the feeling that there was a sort of suggestion in our looks at each other."

"I've got terrible eyes, young man," she exaggerated, "there was no suggestion in my look."

He acknowledged the advantage she had and – maybe just to carry out the fanciful scenario – he said, "Can I invite you somewhere this afternoon for a cup of coffee?"

"No offence, but I don't go for coffee with young men that I occasionally pass on the street." She smiled at him and turned to continue on her way.

"I'm sorry, forgive me," she heard his voice say.

She didn't answer. She bit her lip so as not to scream – *God, I'm so stupid!* With a victorious stride, she walked away but felt defeated in her soul.

Was he really giving me a chance? He surprised me. That was not me who answered him. Those were reflexes taking over my brain. Reflexes that every woman has developed against passes like that. If I'd seen him coming, if he had smiled like at other times, if…

She was angry with herself and at him.

That was several weeks ago. He waited for her every day, always greeted her with a smile, and they exchanged a few words. She ended up going for coffee with him after all… and then several more times…

Now they were here, in his flat. They would make love together… for the tenth time, or was it the twentieth?

* * *

Emma got up from her laptop and walked around her flat. She thought about Michelle. Her little big love had not been in the plan, but came as love does: unexpectedly, as a small first step and a harbinger of a new life. No, it wasn't an act of revenge for her husband's infidelity. Her Michelle was not like that.

'I wanted to experience what love is,' she had confessed to Emma, 'and through Michelle I did. I wanted to meet my knight. It is I who needs, really needs, someone to love me. I was Michelle and Michelle was me. Yes, without originally intending it, Michelle has become my reflection; I was writing the story of a woman and then I realised that it was actually my story, my ideas, and my dreams.'

Emma stopped at the window. It was already dark outside. What time was it? Gone seven. She would go. She had promised Kieran that she would be over well before nine. *Compulsory love*, she thought. Or what should she call their relationship? *Habit. That's life. That's how it goes. What do you want? I'm afraid of loneliness.*

She looked out the window at the buildings. Many lights, at least. *I'm afraid of loneliness.*

She quickly dressed and in a few minutes was rushing down the street. She waited a while at Kibworth Beauchamp square for the X7 single decker bus to Market Harborough.

Most of the seats on the bus were taken, but she found a seat near the back next to a nicely dressed woman. On the other side sat a young man on his own wearing in-ear headphones. An older lady and a young woman sat in the seats behind them.

Then a man sat down in the empty seat, dark-haired with nice eyes. Her eyes noticed that his were nice a few seconds before she had even realised it. She averted her gaze, as a longer look would be inappropriate. Too late. A signal had been sent, and for the remaining stops she felt the call of his eyes.

When she got off at Market Harborough square, she was extra careful that the expression on her face didn't give him even the slightest bit of hope. Oh, these men. She was no longer hurrying. There was time enough.

All those who had got off the bus passed ahead of her, and when they saw the green pedestrian pelican signal, the orderly crowd scurried across the crossing.

Emma, in a moment of indecisiveness, started to increase her pace, but had to slow it again when the signal turned red. She sauntered towards the crossing and closed her eyes, imagining in her mind hearing the sound of a clock. *Tick, tick, tick*; she imagined this being a signal for the blind ticking like a clock which fixed her in its tempo. She hesitated. It was as if her heart and breath aligned with the frequency of that imaginary clock. *Tick, tick, tick*; her eyes were still closed. *I'm blind.*

Just as a blind person, she concentrated on waiting for the imaginary change. *Tick, tick, tick...* She opened her eyes and walked towards the green signal for pedestrians. One step, a second, third... *Something isn't as it should be*, flashed through her head. Cones of light, emerging from the right, were curving towards her and moving too fast.

Oh my God, I've made a mistake! It's my mistake! Why did I close my eyes? she thought, in a moment of eternity, when the lights, with eerie slowness, chopped through her legs. And like a raging bull, horns picked up her body and tossed it into the air. *The windstorm*, she thought. *I'm flying again against the flow of time where everything is fused in a blur of colour.*

Then the storm without its rumbling was swept away and stopped. Silence. *Tick, tick. tick...*

She saw herself: a child, cowering down in a pool of the incomprehensible. No, it wasn't my mistake.

Chapter 7

Lightning, and for a split second I see a face. God's face? I appeal to him – it must have been God. Or an angel? An angel with a woman's face. Was it a woman's face? Definitely. A terrified woman's face. It was a woman! A terrified woman's face... and then lightning lit up the sky again. God.

My brain finally assembles the whole mosaic from those perceptions. *God, if you are there, tell me that I didn't hit her.* I raise my eyes to the rear-view mirror. Horror washes over me. There was no doubt, the shadow on the street could be nothing but a body lying there. I hit her! I hit her!

A film runs through my mind: I stop the car, the prisoner forgotten, run the short distance back and immediately bend down over the motionless body.

But my arms and legs keep driving.

In the film, I lift the head of the injured woman so I can see her face and I wipe the blood away. Is she dead?

In reality, my fingers are convulsively clutching the steering wheel. Seconds pass and I drive on. My body is a soulless machine. I am in autopilot, able to depress the clutch and shift gears, go in the direction of the programmed destination, slow down before the next traffic lights.

The car slows and his soul, which had just a moment ago been bent in horror over that woman, catches up to its body. Back, back, it orders itself.

I do a three-point turn, again gain control and manage to go back. I'm surprised at how far I have gone from the scene of the accident. It takes several minutes before I see the several stopped cars and a crowd of people ahead of me. Slowly, almost at a crawl, I get closer.

A man in the middle of the street gestures for me not to stop and to keep going. I roll down my window and want to say… Our eyes meet. I'm speaking. Or rather just moving my lips, but no voice comes from me. The man doesn't want to hear anything and furiously waves with his arm.

"Keep going. The lights are on green."

I pass by him and search for the woman with my eyes. In the flickering of the shadows and figures, I can't see her.

I turn round further up the road. I go a few dozen yards when an ambulance whizzes past me from the opposite direction. With screaming sirens and blue flashing lights, it turns into the place of the accident.

Minutes pass by and I stop on the edge of the road and get out of the car. My legs are giving out and I feel sick. I vomit. God, what have I done?

I hear the roar of a helicopter landing in nearby Symington's Recreation Ground. I see the blue flashing lights of the moving ambulance coming towards me with sirens screaming into the night, turning off St Mary's Road towards the helicopter.

An air ambulance. She is being transferred into an air ambulance.

She's alive, she's alive, she's alive…

The prisoner – I had forgotten about him.

Again I drive past the place. The crowd had disappeared, but the area remains cordoned off with police tape. Only four cars remain on the edge of the street, two of them police cars. I should stop, but autopilot is again controlling the steering wheel. The prisoner. I depress the accelerator pedal lightly and at the road junction, turn right towards Edwin Court, the prisoner's block of flats.

My soul has caught up to my body. The light storm has ceased. I injured that woman. *Maybe I killed her*, goes through my head. I have to go back and confess. I have to. But first I will talk to that nutcase. It's all his fault. I'm angry with him.

Road junctions, road junctions everywhere – in my mind and in the streets between the row of some Victorian houses. I become confused. But then I remember that he lives in a modern block. In Edwin Court, on the Kettering Road. Is it the next street? A few trees and bushes block my view. I'm not sure. I pass the bushes and want to turn.

The scene which greets me as I see the other side of the three-storey building takes my breath away. The blue flashing lights of more police cars stab my eyes and my heart, ominously portraying the now familiar scenes of these places of misfortune. The police, the ambulance, the police tape across the road. I understand. I'm in shock and I can't tear my eyes away from those lights.

You idiot, what have you done? Why didn't you wait for me? Not until now do I notice the policeman leaning towards my window. He says something, but I don't hear him. After a moment, I finally lower down the window.

"You can't go any farther, sir. There's been an accident. If you live here, turn round and park a bit farther down."

"What happened?" I whisper.

"Some bloke fell from the window," he said in a gruff voice.

He says something else, but I don't understand him. My soul again leaves my body and runs towards the lights while my hand puts the car into reverse.

Home, I want to go home. I drive slowly. The drivers who pass me make angry gestures. I don't have the energy to react. I can't go faster; I can't even wave my hand as an answer to their furious gestures.

I had to put the car out of the way. It took ages before I finally managed to park in the garage.

Back home I collapsed into the wicker chair. On the table an empty bottle of wine and a partially empty one. It made me feel nauseated. Was it a dream? I wish it was. God, if I could just wake up from this dream. How many times had I appealed to God today? In vain.

My mobile phone rang. I was terrified. Another sign? Maybe I had gone mad. I was holding the mobile, which didn't stop ringing with that tone that at other times seemed pleasant. I couldn't see the display.

"Hello?"

"Good evening. This is the police; I'm Sergeant Maynard. Can you tell me your name?"

My mouth went dry, and my thoughts swirled in my brain.

"Warburton. Paul Warburton," I rasped resignedly.

"Mr Warburton, we need a statement from you regarding an incident that took place this evening. Can you give me your address? We're unfortunately going to have to talk to you tonight. We'll send a police car over to you."

Like an obedient machine, I dictated my address. After I'd ended the call, I realised that the policeman must have known from my submissiveness that I knew what I had to explain.

But do I know? Is it the accident? Or the prisoner's suicide? Or both?

I couldn't even think about it.

After a moment: *They found a record of our conversation on his mobile. That's how they found out about me. That's why they are coming.*

Not even ten minutes had passed when the doorbell rang.

"Good evening, Mr Warburton. Can we come in?" began Sergeant Maynard, showing his warrant card as he spoke. He started out politely, but then immediately spoiled it. "Otherwise, you'll have to come with us to the station."

"Come on in."

There were two of them, and another one, if I noticed correctly, stayed in the car.

"My name is Sergeant Maynard; we spoke on the phone a short while ago. Are you familiar with the name

Alex Holler?" he began as soon as he had taken a seat in the living room.

I was sweating and my mouth was dry. I coughed to fill the awkward pause. Should I confess to everything? Not confess? There was no time to think it through.

"Yes, I know a Mr Holler, he comes to me as a patient. I'm his psychologist."

"Psychologist? Ahh. Now I get it why he had you saved in his mobile under the name Psycho." He laughed. Yes, he laughed like it was a joke, but the tension in those minutes wasn't broken. In fact, his laugh struck me as being sinister and dangerous.

"Psycho? Really?" I stammered. But then I couldn't take it any longer: "What happened? Why are you here, gentlemen?"

That decided it, I realised in the next second. Now I would have to deny everything.

As if someone had waved a magic wand, Sergeant Maynard suddenly became serious. He looked right into my eyes, and I had the feeling he was using an x-ray to scrutinise me with his stare.

That moment seemed to last for ages, and I managed to hold his gaze only thanks to the dullness of the alcohol and sudden fatigue which had fallen over me as a result of all this distress.

"What happened? That's what we came to ask you, Mr Warburton."

"I don't understand."

It went through my head that there was no way he could know that I had another reason to carry out this farce.

"You really don't know why we came to talk to you?"

"I understand that something has happened to Mr Holler, but I really don't know what."

I didn't even blink.

"All right… Everything – so far, at least – has indicated that Mr Holler committed suicide tonight. And we're here because shortly before he did it, he dialled your number. What did he say to you? What did you talk about together?"

Everything went dark before my eyes. Again the nausea.

"That's terrible." It was all I said, and perhaps it seemed convincing.

"What did he say to you? You spoke to each other for over two minutes before he jumped. We have several witnesses who have all independently verified the time of the act."

I took a deep breath and overcame the nausea.

"Yes, he did call me… we only spoke for a moment. He apologised for not coming to our session this afternoon."

"And? What else did he say? You spoke to each other for over two minutes."

"He said… that he wanted to say goodbye, that he wouldn't be coming to therapy anymore… that he was flying away."

"You didn't understand from those words that he was speaking about suicide? He didn't say directly that he wanted to end his own life?"

"Excuse me," I stammered, "at the moment I'm in a rather difficult life situation… I've got some personal problems… I've had a drink this evening, and when Mr Holler called, I may not have exactly been in the best position to read the indications he was presenting. I just listened to him – that he didn't intend to continue our sessions and that, as he said, he was going to fly away."

The policeman was looking at both the empty and the other unfinished bottle of wine and accepted my explanation reluctantly.

"I repeat: he didn't express directly that he wanted to end his own life?"

"No, he didn't express that directly," I concluded.

"He didn't leave a note, but you, of course, would know the reasons that could have driven him to suicide."

"Mr Holler had recently been released from prison and was still experiencing trauma from the hardships he'd experienced there."

"Do you have any records of his sessions?"

"Yes, I do. Written and… an audio recording."

"We're going to need both of those," he stated firmly. "You have the right to refuse us this, but then we'll come back with a warrant."

The other officer had his notebook open and was writing something into it. He then took the file with the reports from the sessions, and the recorder. Then they said goodbye.

I remained sitting in the living room and didn't see them to the door. I heard the car drive away and then it was quiet.

Silence.

Even my thoughts were quiet and calm. Yes, I was waking up. I felt cold on my chest, but also soothing waves of being conscious that I was waking up.

It was only a dream, I thought, on the threshold of sleep.

I fell asleep – in the grace of awakening.

God knocks on the door.

May I?

No. Not yet, Paul.

Chapter 8

No, it wasn't my fault, goes through Emma's head in the air ambulance, where she's unable to discern that this isn't the most important thing at this moment. Now her mind betrays her completely: I flew to the stars…

Beth! What is that loud whirring noise?
Is that shining spot above me the sun?
Am I flying to the sun?
No, it's just a lamp above my bed… Beth! Beth, do you remember? The lamp… do you remember?

It has been almost a year since we were together in Enigma Cafe Bar in Market Harborough and got drunk. I see it as if it was today: we were laughing, acting like two deranged people and complaining about men. We don't need them! What good are they?

You are looking into my eyes. You are a beautiful woman, and you are smiling with your eyes. You are older than I am, but the wrinkles around your eyes only seem to decorate your face.

We are laughing and we don't know at what.

Tears of laughter are running down our faces, and the smeared make up only makes us laugh even harder. Enough. We try to compose ourselves.

We look around to see if anyone is watching our antics. Hopefully no one. You wipe the tears with a tissue and say, 'I'm going to pee in my knickers.' Another explosion of laughter.

The tables are separated by wicker screens, but the next table has apparently noticed our merriment. We hear a few comments and hear them laughing at our infectious laughter. That is really enough. We wipe our noses again. We compose ourselves. It seems the hysterical laughter has passed.

'We only live once,' you say out of nowhere.

I look into your eyes and attempt to trace the reason for your sigh.

Suddenly you are serious, and you say, 'Life is getting away. You have dreams, ideas, desires and you say, today I can't, but tomorrow I'll fulfil them. Tomorrow comes and you say again, I can't today, but tomorrow... tomorrow, tomorrow, tomorrow...' You run your hand through your hair and go on. 'Let's stop, dammit, and say, not tomorrow, but we'll do it today. Because tomorrow – there might not be a tomorrow.'

Your eyes tear up and make you look sad. We look at each other and we are different than we were a few minutes ago. Completely different. And suddenly in those eyes of yours I see a challenge, curiosity, desire... and I feel your bare leg against mine. Nothing more, just the warm, friendly touch of your bare foot which sends a wave of excitement through me.

'I've been thinking about it all evening,' you reveal, and we don't say any more, transfixed by that touch of your foot. The long look we give each other perhaps betrays to the waiter our secret, otherwise hidden beneath the tablecloth, but it doesn't matter.

Outside the window it's already dark. We finish our wine. Already the second bottle. I feel your leg against mine. It's burning. I look away and say something, move a bit in the seat and offer myself to your touch. The warmth inches up towards my knees... I hold my breath and so do you. Yes, I want it. Do it, do it. Fingers are between knees, which are still pressed together as if they had decided on their own – no. Another look into each other's eyes – why not? Tomorrow? And my knees relax. They don't move apart all the way, just enough to let your bare foot in. I shift in my seat and move as much as I can towards that touch, all touches.

I have your foot under my skirt and the world splits in two – the world under and the world above the table. Above the table are our burning faces and ears, a bit of shame and looks around, because in our eyes, which give everything away, there is wild desire; and under the table is the wet between my legs (and there a storm is spinning the world into one maelstrom), covered with a small, warm female foot.

I return the pleasure. My bare foot touches your knees. You are sitting upright, as always, your chin resting in one hand as if nothing, while the other hand takes my foot and moves it into your lap. I lean my chin on my hand too and say something. I push my foot into your pubic area and feel the moist warmth. I understand men.

We practically run back to your place, where you were going to be alone tonight, but then when we are standing across from each other, each on one side of the bed, we no longer hurry, and we savour the seconds and minutes of the impending rapture: like my reflection in a mirror you unhook your blouse and then your skirt and we lie next to each other clothed only in our underwear.

I want to turn off the lamp above the bed, but you beg me not to. We are lying face to face, speaking only with our eyes. I stretch out my hand and touch your face with my fingers, across your chin and neck my fingers move down, stopping at the edge of your bra and then sliding in to touch your naked breast. I have never touched the naked breast of another woman. It's soft, softer than mine. Or am I just imagining it? You close your eyes and toss the unhooked bra to the side. I toss mine aside too, and you lean over me until our breasts touch. Now we are both finally naked. I feel your lips on mine, they just gently brush, and then they are kissing my throat. They don't hurry to my breasts, and only after a while do I feel them on my nipples, and here too they stay for a long time, until I unwittingly, but eagerly, gently nudge them down to my stomach...

Through half-open eyes I look at the lamp overhead, while the light loses itself in the dark and then returns with the rhythm of a pulsating vortex that pulls the moist and wet down to between my legs...

The loud whirring noise continues, but the light disappears and comes back, disappears and comes back.

"Beth! Beth."

"Don't speak. Stay calm. We're almost at the hospital."

The light above her head is momentarily blocked by the head of a man. In a brief moment of lucidity, she understands the situation and remembers the horror she's experienced.

What do I wish? To wake up in the dream I was dreaming while I slept.

I want to fall asleep and wake up in that dream. I want to fall asleep and wake up in that dream. I want to fall asleep...

Chapter 9

"*Live from the Harborough FM News Centre in Market Harborough on 102.3 FM – first for news across South Leicestershire and North Northamptonshire:*

"It is 10pm and I'm Carrie Mee.

"News just in: a woman was seriously injured in a hit-and-run incident in Market Harborough this evening.

"The incident happened at the junction of Northampton Road and St Mary's Road at around 8:30pm, with a car travelling at speed hitting the pedestrian on a pelican crossing.

"The pedestrian was a woman in her late twenties who was attended at the scene by paramedics, and then taken by air ambulance to University Hospital Coventry to be treated for life-threatening injuries.

"Leicestershire Police are appealing for witnesses to the incident to come forward and would also like to hear from anyone who may have dash cam footage of the car prior and during the collision.

"Next item..."

* * *

The world entered my house.

Most people bask in the misery of others, and in the warmth of their living rooms are hypnotised by the crippled fates of those who were struck by misfortune yesterday.

I recall my own words. This news, however, isn't just meant to frighten, or 'entertain'. This news is a challenge and a request at the same time, addressed to all the decent people in their warm living rooms. There is a villain and a coward somewhere among us... help us catch him! Don't let this criminal escape punishment! Get him!

Get... me.

The world has entered my house and is talking about me.

The voice of the young reporter says, "The driver responsible didn't stop and sped from the scene of the accident."

The young woman speaking about the cowardly driver is looking at me from the TV screen tuned into BBC East Midlands, and I am scared that she will suddenly thrust her finger out at my face and shout, "That's him! Get him! That's him!"

It's daytime outside the window. It has washed over the night of terrifying dreams – and next comes terrifying reality.

Yes, it's me who hit that young woman on the pelican crossing yesterday evening and fled the scene. Those are the facts. I am a villain and a coward. I failed. No, that's not really how it was. I... didn't want to... I wanted to...

After a few sips of coffee, my mind wakes up and the agonising thoughts begin to run through it. I was drunk, that's why I didn't react right away. Drunk? Drunk behind the wheel...? I realise it would be impossible to lie. I wanted to help the prisoner! I wanted to help that poor lost man... I am looking at the TV screen, but not taking in anything that is coming out of it.

All the cells of my brain are engaged in creating a picture of last night's events and trying to gather together the whirlwind of thoughts. Not even one is processing the picture and the other news, the other adversities that were surely coming from the TV screen.

After a while, my eyes offer my mind a picture of the young woman presenting the weather, then small sparks, somewhere in the folds of my brain, in subconscious recognition of the face, and, like a drowning man who lunges for the floating piece of timber he spies in the seconds above the surface, my hand flies to the remote control like to a lifesaver.

"What have you done... friend?" I lip-read.

"Friend, you say? After all this... we are remaining friends?"

"Why wouldn't we? I know how it happened. You caused a serious accident. Its mishap was a terrible thing, but you did return to the accident... you were just desperate and upset... that is why it wasn't until later, when the woman was already in the care of others."

"I wanted to help the former prisoner. It was a shortcut. I knew that it was a matter of minutes – I felt it... that's why I got behind the wheel drunk."

"I know, but... you promised me that you wouldn't drink anymore. Remember? You didn't keep your promise."

"Wait here a minute, don't go away," I beg.

I turn off the television. The silence becomes deeper. I lean back in the kitchen chair, put my hands behind my head and close my eyes. I don't want to see anything, and I don't want to hear anything. It's futile; under my eyelids I see the film of the storm of last evening and flashes of the young woman's face, and I see the lightning. But I hear no thunder... I open my eyes. I tell myself that I have to keep my eyes open – so I don't see.

After a moment, I realise that I have no idea what state my car is in. I go down and partially lift up the garage door. I have an old Land Rover Defender, solidly built, that I bought on the spur-of-the-moment when Kyley left in our almost new BMW. In the poor light of the garage I see that the headlights are intact, but the passenger-side windscreen is cracked, and one sidelight and one indicator light dome is broken. I lift the garage door up fully and drive the car out so I can see it in the light of day. I see that the bonnet is dented, otherwise nothing else. The battle of woman versus the three-ton machine goes decidedly to the machine. I drive the car back into the garage, thinking to myself that I have to get this damage fixed sooner rather than later.

When I go back up the stairs to my office, I feel the nausea again. I hold onto the handrail, and when I finally get back into my office, I have barely enough strength to pull the chair out from the desk and slump down into it. No, I couldn't work today, not in this state.

Beth Brooke is scheduled to come at ten this morning – I will call her first. Group therapy is scheduled for two in the afternoon, and I will cancel that too. I open my laptop and find my clients' contact information, which I keep a record of for just these reasons – when it is necessary to inform my patients about a change of programme. I punch Beth's number into my mobile. She answers almost immediately.

"Hello? Beth Brooke."

"Hi, this is Paul Warburton. I apologise for calling at the last minute, but unfortunately, I'm going to have to cancel our session today." I pause with disgust at the lie that I will have to use to explain further. She doesn't insist on one.

"You don't have to apologise. Really. I was just about to call you too – that I wouldn't be coming today… but I will need you all the more later."

The last words stop me.

"Has something happened to you?"

She is quiet for a moment, though there is no doubt there are tears, and then she answers.

"Not to me, no. Nothing happened to me, but… excuse me…" Again she is quiet for a moment. "Last night my friend was in a hit-and-run accident… she was hit by a car on a pelican crossing. Did you hear about it on the local news? I'm on my way to the hospital. I don't know how she is… Her boyfriend called me – it seems bad."

The world swirls around me. I don't know how or even whether I said goodbye to her.

God, you are there! But why are you persecuting me? Why? Why?

I don't know how long I sat there and just stared at the tree rings on the desktop. The initial shock turns into an apathy from which I very slowly emerge. It's simply not possible. My client tells me that he wants to kill himself. I hurry to him to talk him out of it and on my way, I hit a young woman. It takes me a while before I can pull myself together, and in the meantime, she is helped by others. I want to at least stop the prisoner, but it's too late – he has already done it. The police. Questions. And in the end, I find out that the injured woman is the friend of another one of my patients. That absolutely cannot be a coincidence! God…

I pull myself together a bit and call the alcoholics anonymous that I try to help once a week with group therapy. I cancel the session for today. What next? What should I do? Should I go to the police and confess everything? Should I confess that I hit a woman on a pelican crossing while drunk and then fled the scene? They will lock me up! I will end up going to prison!

'I saw evil. I don't know what else to call it. It was absolute evil. Evil that, even after all these years, wakes me up at night. Evil which… stank like those mattresses that I laid on. Evil that suffocated… like the stale air in the cells. It was the moisture that gathered on the windows… and the drops ran down and drew more bars,' I recall the words of the prisoner.

I'm going to prison. I'm afraid, but I don't deserve anything else. I have decided. I will end it. I will go to the police; I can't do otherwise.

I don't know how long it took me before I turned my determination into action. Half an hour? An hour? I have to do it; I will not be able to live with it.

I got dressed and phoned for a taxi. I rejected the idea of taking the car – I wouldn't be able to drive and besides, the damage needs to be repaired before bringing attention to myself. It occurred to me that I could call Sergeant Maynard – I stored his number in my mobile from yesterday evening – but I decided not to. I would give myself up at the local police station, which is a short journey away from Great Bowden, where I live.

I got the taxi driver to drop me off on the Union Wharf off Leicester Road. Not directly at the police station. I decided to walk the short distance back. Not until now did I realise how nice the weather was. The sun was shining and although it was only the end of October, it was pleasantly warming. It couldn't, however, dispel the gloom in my mind.

I passed people without noticing their faces. I probably didn't want to notice; in that morning sun, they were happy and carefree. I envied them, just as I envied the man about my age who was laughing loudly with a group of his friends outside the newsagents on the opposite side of the road. Short laughs, lasting only a second, but they said it all: I am all right, healthy, carefree… An attractive woman swaying her hips just ahead of me. But I didn't enjoy the sight of her; instead, there was pain in the anticipation of soon losing all this beauty.

I have had the feeling lately that I have lost everything. Kyley left me and I was at rock bottom. I thought that it couldn't get worse. I drank. How petty were my problems of yesterday compared with those of today? And what of tomorrow's? Happiness is a trait – I recalled my own theory. If you don't have that trait, then it will be you who is robbed, who becomes ill, whose wife leaves him, whom misfortune happens to.

Leicestershire Police was the sign next to the entrance to the building. *Police, police, police* shone the words on the cars parked in the car park at the rear of the building. *Protecting the Community*. Protect from people like me; it stabbed me in the chest.

I stood just outside the entrance and took a deep breath for that last step. Will I be locked up in a police cell before being interviewed? Will I be able to tell my parents living in Northampton my side of the story? Will I be able to inform my patients…? These sorts of practical questions kept occurring to me. I was convinced that I would be going to prison for the first time – at least one lighter thought flashed through my mind.

I walked. One step, the second, the third… My mobile began ringing in my pocket. *God. No, I don't want any more! Everything bad has already happened, has it not?*

"Paul Warburton."

"Doctor, this is Beth Brooke…"

"Hello, Mrs Brooke. How can I help you?" I said awkwardly, fearing the worst.

"I'm sorry to call – I know we cancelled our session for today… but I really need you right now… you know…" she sobbed into the phone.

"I can't right now, Mrs Brooke."

She ignored my words.

"I went to the University Hospital in Coventry. They didn't let me see Emma, but I know a doctor there and he brought me up to speed."

"What did he tell you? How is she?"

"She's going to be paralysed from the waist down. Her spinal cord is severed. He said that she'll never be able to walk again."

No, I understood that everything bad was far from being over. There was still lots of misfortune to be had.

"I'm in town, Mrs Brooke, not that far from my office," I lied. "Can you make your way there?" said someone totally alien in a voice I didn't recognise, from deep inside me.

"Thank you. I'll come. Can you wait an hour?"

"I'll be waiting for you."

I stood for a while in front of the entrance to the police station. *Should I not just end everything and go through those doors?* I thought feverishly. Instinctively, I looked up at the sky and found the moon. White-masked between a few clouds and looking down.

"Was that you? Or the boss?"

Quiet.

I turned and phoned for a taxi to take me back to home. *Fine, I will just do this one thing.*

* * *

I didn't have to wait long. She rang the doorbell and as I opened the door, she walked in, pushing right past me.

"Sorry," she apologised. "I'm totally out of it. I'm really sorry. Hello."

"Hello, Mrs Brooke," I greeted her for the second time in a short period. "Don't worry about it. Let's go to my office."

In the office, she took a seat. There she dug in her handbag and pulled out a pack of tissues.

"Such a mess." She wiped her nose and went on. "I've known Emma – she's my friend, you know… Emma Lineker – for many years. We met through books – she writes them, and I sell them. A young, beautiful, talented woman… I can't believe what's happened."

She paused. Perhaps she was waiting for me to ask how it actually happened. She couldn't have any idea that I knew better than anyone.

"I'm not here for myself, Doctor, even if it's a shock and I'm very upset…"

I stiffened. "Hold on, I don't understand you. I thought it was you who needed help. What's going on?"

"Emma's spinal cord is severed. The doctor I know said that the injury is so serious that he can confirm… that she won't be able to walk. She'll end up in a wheelchair." She paused for a moment so that, without even knowing it, those words could stab me even deeper in the heart.

"If this is true… I would like… I wish you would help her. I've only known you a short time, but I would really like it if it were you the one who helped her… to survive this somehow."

I got up from the desk, went to the window and looked out. *Is that you again?* I looked for the white moon in the sky.

"How exactly did this happen to her, Mrs Brooke?" I whispered into the silence.

"Last night, around eight-thirty, as she was on her way to her boyfriend's, a car hit her on a pelican crossing here in

Market Harborough. They say that the driver left the scene without stopping, but I don't know anything else about it."

"Where did it happen?" I grasped at the last shred of hope.

"On St Mary's Road, at the junction with Northampton Road."

I stood at the window with my back to Beth Brooke, lest my face betray my despair.

It was her, there was no doubt.

"What's your opinion, Doctor?" she interrupted the long silence.

"I… don't know. I really don't know how to answer you. The hospital will surely provide everything needed for your friend. Of course, they will try to help her from all angles – they'll treat her injuries and even provide her with psychological help. I… I cooperate occasionally with the hospital on similar cases, but it depends on the wishes of the patient. You simply can't know at this point whether Mrs… Miss Lineker… will want my services at all."

"Yes, of course. I guess I'm getting ahead of things, but still, if things do develop like it seems they will, can I ask you for this help?"

Panic seized me and it took great effort to hide it. I had been caught in some insane film or in a vortex that was spinning and gaining speed.

"Please," she whispered.

"I repeat… it depends on your friend's wishes. From the sound of things, she's now going to undergo some essential operations, then later if she wants my help…" I took a deep breath. "I'll try."

When Mrs Brooke left, conveying her gratitude, I collapsed again into the chair behind the desk. I was resigned. In the past few hours, I had been sucked into a vortex in which I was writhing around, and which it wasn't in my power to get out of.

Chapter 10

"What do I admire most about you?" Michael thought about Michelle's question.

She sat across from him, wearing just the robe that she had exchanged the short towel for in the bathroom. She threw back her head and shook her hair as a prompt.

"Yeah. What do you like most about me?"

He was smiling with his eyes and didn't hurry to answer.

"Is there anything you like about me?" she asked, faltering.

He crouched down silently and took her bare foot, put it to his mouth and kissed her toes tenderly.

"Legs," he said only.

"Legs?" Michelle was surprised. "I think I would have guessed my legs last."

"Why? They're beautiful; smooth, with nicely shaped calves and thighs, which are soft and warm. When you put your knees together, your legs and your hips make a curve that drives men crazy."

"And when I move my knees apart?" She laughed.

"If you move your knees apart when you're lying down," mused Michael, "then they're like arms inviting me for an embrace."

"That's nice. Legs create arms that invite you in for an embrace. You said that rather beautifully."

"Will you embrace me?" he whispered.

She became grave. "Turn out the light."

"No." He smiled.

"At least dim it… please." She leant forwards for a kiss.

Then she got up, and softly staring into his eyes, sat down on the bed. Slowly she lay down on her back and, with her knees pressed together, lifted her bent legs until the robe slid down those legs and, in the dim light, revealed the warm curve of her hip and thigh. Closing her eyes, she undid the knot in the robe, which slid from her breasts, and in that position, she moved her knees apart.

Michael got up from the chair and walked over to her. He let the towel slide down from his waist and, with tremulous anticipation, lay down in Michelle's 'embrace'.

* * *

Emma licked her dry lips. "Water… can I have some water, please."

The nurse moistened Emma's lips. "Open your eyes. Try."

Her eyelids fluttered, and for a split second, opened.

No, I won't open them… I'll never open them again.

Emma gave up, and under her closed eyelids the film ran on: the story of Michelle, who is Emma (or of Emma, who became Michelle).

Chapter 11

"So you see, Paul, could I have told you, or even hinted, at where that thread which is bound to you leads? I couldn't have. I am merely a spectator who sees you, human beings, and whose fates are intertwined."

In the night illuminated by the light of the moon, Paul stalled on his answer for a moment.

After a while, he said, "You can move oceans... you couldn't have stopped her in her steps, or swerved my car out of the way? You should have killed me! Why did you let it happen? Why?"

"I can't interfere in your fate. I can neither bind nor tear the threads that connect you – I would become entwined in them like a fly in a spider's web and violate the law. I can do nothing but watch."

"The law? The law, you say?" I jumped on his words. "What do you think? That me hitting that woman occurred according to some rules of the universe?"

"You could say that," the moon mused. "There is a fundamental universal rule that determines the unimpeded course of things. Everything is given, the rules are set – the same for you on Earth, and in the whole universe – and any interference in this order always turns out to be a mistake."

"Wasn't that you who stopped me when I was going to the police?"

"No. I repeat, I can't interfere with your fate. It was just another coincidence. Chance caused your accident, even though you helped a lot, and it was by chance that you didn't go through with your intention to give yourself up. But it's also chance when two objects, or even whole galaxies, collide in space. Sometimes chance simply causes ripples on the surface of an otherwise undisturbed course of events."

"If an undisturbed course of events is the basic norm of this world, why were we blessed with the ability to create?" I wondered. "Why are we given the power to change things?"

"You're not. You were blessed with the ability to learn, and it's usually with insufficient knowledge that you 'create' the chance – or rather, the accident – whose effects will eventually be eliminated so that things can again go on undisturbed."

"That sounds ominous," I said. "Does that mean that one day we, as people, will be…" I looked for the right word. "Stopped?"

"And we're back to square one; I can't reveal anything about your future."

"But you're hinting."

"No, I'm not even doing that. Everything depends on you, on your knowledge, and whether someday you will understand that you can't straighten rivers, cause lakes, seas and oceans to dry up, build concrete cities, kill beasts, cut down rainforests, cause climate change to change the course of things. Do you understand?"

"Are we to perhaps give up on progress? Should we get rid of our mobiles, our cars, and return to the trees?"

"Progress? I don't understand. Have you come to understand something, made progress somewhere? Have you progressed in your understanding of life, and its meaning? You've never been further from it. Cars drove you from the shores of this knowledge and, together with mobile phones, paradoxically, moved you all further apart."

The moon's last words seemed to thunder from the heavens, and they echoed in my ears so they hurt. Then it went quiet, hidden behind the clouds, but the words still sounded and created the impression of an ongoing debate.

I was still looking for the words with which to continue. Yes, when I look around, I see all around me that he's right. We have lost the path. But is it even possible to stop and say, enough, no more, let us go back and start again? No, I can't imagine it. It's difficult for people to learn from the past, let alone from an inkling of the future.

Then I noticed the silence and the fact that my 'worldly' reasoning had led me from my own big problem. What next? I know the name of the woman I hit: Emma Lineker. Her friend has taken it into her head that I should be the one to help her – and somehow live.

"You know my story. Tell me, what am I to do? Can I stand before that woman and act as if nothing happened… and just do my job?" I called to the heavens.

The moon didn't answer. Its silence reminded me of his inability, or rather unwillingness, to interfere, even with advice, in human fate.

What now? I asked myself. *What next?*

I sat for a long time in the chair across from the window, repeating my question, looking for, and not finding, an answer in the silent sky. In the middle of the night, I got up, deathly tired. I took the untouched bottle of wine and poured its contents into the sink. Fine, I would wait for things to come. I had no idea how long I would wait.

Chapter 12

The wet roofs of the houses opposite and the harsh greyness outside made the little flat seem warmer and cosier, but at the same time magnified the grim tones of the women's conversation.

"You know what was strange? The whole time I was in the hospital, not counting those awful states I was in after my operations, I had erotic dreams. And most of them were scenes full of images of women's legs; I felt their touches…" Emma paused and closed her eyes to hold back the tears.

Beth put her hand on Emma's and was quiet too. What could she say? What words could ease that pain? Should she impart courage with her voice, or regret with her whisper? Neither one; whatever Beth could say now would be wrong. She knew it and that's why she remained quiet.

Until Emma broke the silence.

"I even had a dream in the air ambulance which was taking me to the hospital, or maybe I was delirious, I remembered our fling long ago. The touches of our legs against each other." She took a breath to suppress her crying. "When I thought about it later, I thought maybe the memories were induced by the blinking lights of the air ambulance – maybe. But perhaps I subconsciously realised that there was something wrong with my legs. Yes, even at that moment I somehow knew."

The room was silent again. It was a long silence and it made Beth feel uncomfortable. She had to say something too. It had been almost two months since they had last seen each other. When Emma was in hospital she came to visit often, but later, when she was rehabilitating, she only went to see her once. They had spoken to each other often by phone, but in those conversations, they didn't touch on such things, and stayed more or less on practical issues.

Beth had found a flat for Emma that was wheelchair friendly, and she arranged for the sale of the old flat in Kibworth Beauchamp to buy the new one in Market Harborough.

"How do you like it here. It's nice, isn't it?"

Emma raised her eyes. "I like it, and it's nice and warm too. You know I like it." She sighed unconvincingly, but then immediately added, "I don't know how to thank you for helping me so much." She turned the wheels of her wheelchair and glided to the window. "You know, I couldn't go and live with my parents. Mainly because of how they are, but also because of me. I would die from those looks of sympathy." She straightened up in the wheelchair to look out the window. "You know I like it here, but I'm looking at a different world now – I'm only at the height of a person's waist. I see things on the table from a different angle, the view from the window is different… I'm like a child. A small child dependent on the help of others." She slumped in the wheelchair. "A child," she whispered again.

For a moment she shut her eyes and a windstorm sounded in her ears. Yes, I am that small child cowering down in a pool of the incomprehensible. Scenes from her previous excursions into the depths of her own thoughts flashed through her mind.

Beth didn't realise that Emma's thoughts had slipped away somewhere else.

"You're not going to be dependent on anyone. It won't take long, you'll soon be able to deal with everything yourself, and if there's a problem, you have me and Kieran."

Emma smiled bitterly. "Kieran? There's no Kieran anymore."

"How come? What happened?" Beth didn't seem to understand.

"I would be wronging him if I claimed that he'd dumped me…"

"Hold on. Tell me about it. He left you?"

"No, I took off," Emma joked bitingly. "I hit the pedal on this thing and sped away from him."

Beth was in shock. "I don't get it. What happened? He came to see you often and he was supportive, wasn't he? I'm sorry. I don't want to meddle."

"Look, don't you think I know that?" Emma pulled herself together after a long pause. "I repeat, I would be wronging him to say he dumped me. He handled everything fine. He was with me from the beginning of my stay in hospital and he even came to see me when I was in rehabilitation, but… it was sympathy. And I can't take that. I think, after all, that he was relieved when I was the one who proposed that we end it."

Beth gasped on hearing this, but when she looked into Emma's eyes, she reluctantly surrendered.

"Fine. You just have me... at least until you find someone more solid than Kieran was."

"I'm grateful for everything you're doing for me... even for these illusions."

"What illusions?"

"Find someone when I am wheelchair-bound? That's really an illusion."

"Emma, I don't want to hear talk like that. Life goes on. Why couldn't you find someone eventually?"

"I can tell you exactly why: because I won't be looking for him."

"Never say never. Maybe he will find you."

It seemed that the debate had lost its former grimness, but now Emma recalled, "Beth... I've been in this wheelchair now for over two months, but I can already tell you, no one is looking at me down here."

It was rapidly becoming dark outside and was a typical January day. The few trees and bushes growing in the shaded spaces between the houses had long lost their leaves, and the playground, full of children in the summertime, was now abandoned and glistening with the cold dampness of the winter.

"You can't just give up," said Beth, to break the silence, "and close yourself off from the world in this little flat... and then feel sorry for yourself." She spoke louder as she went on. "How can you say something like that – no one is looking at you down here? You're not the first, and you're not the last person whom something like this has happened to. You can't just give up."

"You can't give up; you can't give up and feel sorry for yourself," mocked Emma sharply. "And what do you suggest I should do? Should I go out onto the streets, bumping along the pavement, looking for a man I could harness like a mule to this wheelchair… and giddy up?"

"For a start, it would be enough if you began to write again."

"Write? Excuse me, how can I write?"

"As far as I know, you didn't write with your legs."

"No, I didn't write with my legs. I wrote with my head, a head that was fine, that could dream and didn't have to think, 'How will I turn on that light when that bloody switch is so high?' Fuck. Fuck!"

Emma screamed to get the pain out and Beth let her scream. She understood her. She felt with her. She could only vaguely imagine herself in her place. Could she handle it? She let Emma sob into the gloom and the silence of the room. Then she got up and turned on the light.

"Stop thinking about nonsense and write. I'll deal with what's necessary. The bathroom has been modified, and so was the toilet, everything is now within your reach. And we'll fix the light switches. You start to write and live."

"Write and live." Emma clasped her hands on her motionless knees; a heart could burst from that image.

"Yes, write and live."

Then it went quiet. They were silent for a long time, until Beth couldn't take it anymore.

"From time to time, I go to the psychologist I told you about."

Emma closed her eyes, knowing what was next. "And?"

"I'll get you an appointment. You can talk to him. It can't hurt."

"Out of the question," said Emma, without even considering it.

"Why?"

"Because I don't want to. How can he help me? Can he cure me? No! Will I walk again? I won't," she answered herself and went on. "He's going to teach me to live with it, but I don't care about that. I don't want to know how. With crippled legs you can only vegetate... to death. I can manage that without a psychologist."

Beth got up from her chair and walked over to the window. It was dark outside.

"I wish you would write again. Start for me. Write the story of that interesting woman... Michelle? I want to read the book."

Emma didn't answer right away. She listened to the silence and suddenly realised that she was hearing the ticking of the clock hanging on the wall of the room. *Tick, tick, tick.* It reminded her of the instant her life was turned upside down. She closed her eyes – *tick, tick, tick* – until she got scared.

"I can't write. The only thing I'm able to do is dream that story and watch it like a film on my closed eyelids... but write it, I can't."

"Why can't you?"

"I simply can't. I can't formulate the sentences. I have it in my head, I see the scene, but I'm not able to describe it."

"That's exactly why I think you should talk to Paul. He knows something about these heads of ours. I've convinced myself of that."

Emma looked at Beth with eyes full of sadness.

"I'm so very grateful to you, Beth, for everything you're doing for me. Thanks… But don't ask this of me. I'm in a different situation than you. My battered psyche has everything to do with these legs. No one can help me. Let alone a man. Understand. Try to understand. I didn't just lose my ability to walk, but also my ability to express myself as a woman. I'm not attractive. I'll never again hear: 'you've got nice legs'. Never. Do you understand that?"

Beth couldn't immediately find the words that might convince Emma, but after a moment she tried again.

"You're not completely right. You're a beautiful woman," she said quietly. "With beautiful hair – I always envied that about you. It isn't—"

"Stop it," Emma interrupted crossly, "I don't want to hear any more about it."

Beth looked away. "Whatever. I'm not going to be able to persuade you." She glanced at her watch. "I've got to go. The home help will come at seven."

"Thank you, Beth, for everything. And please don't be angry with me."

"How could I?" said Beth, walking to the door, trying to smile encouragingly.

Chapter 13

Often at night I am frightened by the idea that one day I will have to stand face-to-face with Emma Lineker. I wonder why I let myself do something so ridiculous.

Why didn't I tell the police what I'd done? Why? I ask myself.

But the answer is more agonising than the question. Like a coward, I hid behind the tempting opportunity that presented itself. I grasped at the rope that had been unexpectedly thrown my way, and foolishly and stupidly toyed with the idea that it had been some higher power that stopped me in my tracks in front of the police station. There was no higher power. It was only a coincidence that I took advantage of. I lied my way out of my obligation to report the accident with a noble promise to help. That is how I agonisingly judge my offence. As if I were seeing myself, I testify to my own cowardice.

Disgusted, I make a promise in the dark night to go to the police first thing in the morning. Yes, that is how this story should end: I pull myself together, knock on the door of the police station and say, 'Do you recollect that accident in October when a young woman was hit and crippled in that hit-and-run on the pelican crossing at the junction of St Mary's Road and Northampton Road? Do you recollect the case of the reckless driver that you finally gave up on because you couldn't find any clues that would lead you to him? I am that reckless driver. It was me.'

As the day gets brighter outside, my thoughts get darker. I recall the prisoner and his words: *I saw evil... absolute evil... I'm afraid.* I admit to myself that I'm afraid. Maybe it's just the tragic fate of the prisoner, to which I stood witness, that fills me with this insurmountable fear. I can't do it... and immediately I say to myself, *I must help her.* I promised. It's a crutch that I lean on the whole day. Who would I be helping by being in jail? No one. Out here I am benefitting all those drunks, anorexics, exhausted businessmen... and also Emma Lineker, who will one day call, write, send a message... and she'll come.

The day ends, night comes, and I reverse my thoughts.

Where do I get the right to enter her life in any way? I have entered once, with tragic consequences, and that's enough. Anything else that I do for her, however beneficial it is to her, is inappropriate. It's not right. These things simply are not done. My feelings alternate with the regularity of day turning into night: manly determination with cowardly reversal. Around and around.

The only relief is my work. Since the accident in October, I've worked like a dog, not giving myself even one day of rest except for Christmas Day. Perhaps another reflex to ease my conscience. A survival instinct that tells me, *don't stop or you'll go mad.* I work and work. I listen to the problems of all those people caught unaware by their lives. I would swap with them if I could. God, what I would not give to only have a problem with eating.

"Dear girl," I want to say, "are you concerned about being fat? I'm listening to you. Yes, I hear you." But in my head, I think, *girl, if you only knew I injured a young woman just a bit older than you. She's crippled now and she'll never walk again. I am to blame! It's my fault that she'll never walk again. Do you understand?*

I don't get an answer to the question I don't ask. I quickly make an appointment with another patient.

"Of course, come. Any time is fine."

"Mrs Brooke? Yes, of course tomorrow is fine. If you have time even this afternoon, you can come. Does that suit you? All right, I will expect you at five."

The sessions with Beth Brooke, of course, veer from the usual. They are full of tension. It's difficult for me to concentrate. When she's talking about her problems, I don't read between the lines, as I do at other times, but I'm always waiting for any mention of Emma. I'm waiting because I don't want to ask her myself. It's a difficult topic even for her, and it can't be avoided – and it always comes up.

"What are my problems with Emma?" she usually begins.

I try as much as possible not to let her see how hungrily I wait for this turn in the conversation.

"How is your friend doing?" I ask understandingly.

"How's she doing? How's she doing…? About as well as she can, but I wouldn't change places with her. I found her a flat because she wants to be alone. I found a carer, someone reliable to take care of her, someone who comes to the flat... and who she can stand. That's all. But I can't get her to go out and I can't convince her to begin writing like she wrote before. And..."

I want to ask the thing that interests me the most. I reckon it's written in my face because she doesn't let me finish and answers immediately.

"I'm trying to persuade her to come... to ask for a session with you, but she doesn't want to hear anything about it. She doesn't believe. She's given up. She's shut herself up in her flat, she doesn't want to see anyone or anything and, as she says herself, she just vegetates."

Her words hurt me. Beth Brooke, without knowing it, is rubbing salt into my wounds.

"So no one is taking care of her in the hospital or at the rehabilitation?" I ask wearily.

"As far as I know, in the hospital they are, but at the rehabilitation... it doesn't matter, the result is miserable. This is the exact moment when someone like you should talk to her. She's returning to her life, and she needs someone to trust, someone who will be able to help her."

"Yes, you're right, but she has to want it herself. That is necessary for the therapy to be successful. I can't force her."

"I know. I tried, but it didn't work. Maybe it just needs time."

"Time," I reply thoughtfully, "yes, time will solve it. Maybe in time she'll find the way herself. If not, then she may bring me only a feeling of despair bigger than what she's already experiencing – and that should be avoided.

Do you understand? Her mood will not stay the same; it will get either better or worse. And when I listen to what you're saying, I'd say... I'm almost sure that her depression will only get deeper."

We fell silent, and in the quiet of my office only the humming of the recorder could be heard.

"I'm sorry. I forgot to turn it off. We don't need to record this part of our conversation."

For a moment there was total silence.

"I like Emma, you know... We've known each other for quite a long time, and she's always been a good friend. I like her, and she's talented – she writes very well. Her stories are as if... how can I say it? Without blood, but about blood... about sex, but without sex... about love. She pulls you into her dreams. You read her book and suddenly you're not sure: did I dream that story? Am I sleeping and dreaming?" She hesitated for a moment but then went on again. "I admire her even as a woman. She's... she's beautiful."

I didn't interrupt her. I just sat, just watching and listening.

"She's convinced that with what she's suffered, she's lost her charm. No. Not at all. Nonsense. Her biggest advantage is not just her physical appearance, but rather..." She searched for the right words. "The waves of harmony that exude from her. You look at her and you don't see the ideal of feminine beauty. But you're enchanted, nonetheless. Hair, eyes, lips... beautiful, but separately, not in an obvious way. Together, however, underscored by the way she moves, she creates a fluidity that just radiates from her." She wavered a bit under my gaze. "I'm babbling, aren't I?"

"No, no. You speak very nicely about her," I hasten to answer so as not to interrupt her sincere declarations.

"I want you to know how much she means to me. I'm not stupid, I know that no one can teach her to walk, but to live and to write – the ability to live and the ability to write – only someone like you can remind her of that."

I was quiet for a while, ashamed by the compliment. *Tribute to a coward*, I thought for a second.

"I have a small favour to ask you." I banished the gloom. "Next time, bring me one of her books. I'll leave it up to you which one. I need to know Emma more, and I think her book may tell me a lot."

"I'll bring one." Beth said goodbye in the doorway of my office. "And I know which one."

Chapter 14

The next day, Beth brought me a book and cautioned that there was no time to lose. This unnerved me. In a situation where I still didn't know how to approach Emma or even whether I should attempt to, those words distressed and agitated me. Despite that, I hurried to my office, sat down at my massive desk and began flipping through the pages.

She writes about blood without blood, about sex without sex; I remembered Beth's words. If I understood well, that is only with allusions, provoking the reader by awakening in him his own fantasies, conjuring up rough or erotic scenes. *This could be interesting*, I thought. *For God's sake, as long as it's not that depressing humorous style that most female writers use today.*

I leafed through the book and skimmed over the text until a passage caught my eye:

The door shut quietly behind him. He didn't slam it as I did, though not sure why. After all, it wasn't really an argument. Just a sudden flaring up of something that had been smouldering between us for so long.

I stayed sitting on the cold bed. I pulled my legs up to my body and let my hair fall on my bare knees. A small spark had been enough. A small spark ignited by a sharp sigh, and in an instant, everything had flared and burned.

"Me or your wife," was that sigh. So the wife. Fine. How else... It was difficult, however, to fight back the advancing sorrow.

The darkness from the street outside entered my room through the window and merged with the shadows that had only a moment before crept along the walls and the floor of the house and somewhere into my soul. In order not to banish them, I left the light off.

Tears ran silently down my face and fell into my hair, while some slid, unrestrained, along my thigh as if along a slide into my lap. I sat there like that for a long time. There were no more tears to cry and the pain in my back brought me back to the world.

I lay down on the unnecessarily large bed and the pain returned, without relief, to my soul. Outside the night had taken over, with stars, and a moon which peeked in through the window. His light mercifully lit the corners and over time moved through the room until it rested on the bed at my feet.

I stretched out my leg, and like a swimmer poised on the beach, poked my toes into the beam of light and felt heat. I felt the pleasant warmth not only in my submerged toes, but throughout my whole body. It pervaded me... I put my other foot in too, closed my eyes and felt the energy that entered me, and was transformed, in my mind, into hope. When something ends, something also begins, I thought, heartened. The sun doesn't shine for just one flower.

I opened my eyes, reconciled, and watched the bright disk outside the window. It peered into the room with all its magnitude. The light slid higher and higher along the curves of my legs, at the knees and up to the thighs. It shone through the curtains and the pattern was projected on the smooth skin of my legs, so that they were suddenly dressed in luxurious stockings.

When I slowly bent my legs, they were undressed, when I stretched them out, they were dressed again…

I wouldn't run away from this scene, I thought, amused.

With the night, the light progressed further – across my thighs to my naked lap, across my stomach to my breasts. Then I lay curled up, covered only by the luminous veil.

In my mind I composed the verse that crept up on me. After a while I got up, throwing off my celestial dress and at the table I wrote:

Tonight I can't sleep, so I write to my loves that will be. On blank paper I catch the words flying through the Universe.

With my eyes I scanned the lines and paused over their content. With astonishment I read them again, and then again. They surprised me.

"Is it possible? Could it mean that…?"

I was afraid to even say it out loud. I leant back in the chair and thought.

"Yes." With embarrassment, I smiled. "It would be crazy, but everything suggests that this is how it really is."

Chapter 15

The city of Paris paused for a split second when the setting sun slipped beneath the horizon, but then started running again, at perhaps an even greater pace, in a necessary effort to catch up before the rest of the sunlight, still reflected in the sky above the horizon, was engulfed in darkness.

Michelle sat back comfortably in the chair and nodded in agreement at the waiter's offer of another glass of champagne. The small terrace is part of the restaurant on the top floor of the hotel and overlooks the labyrinth of the city with its mosaic of buildings and their roofs, and the network of streets interlaced in road junctions and roundabouts through which humming caravans of cars wander.

While Michelle sipped from her glass and looked out over the city from up on the terrace, Michael, her husband, three hundred miles away in their Leicester home, dialled her number with the suspicion that something wasn't right. Imagine his surprise when he heard the ringing of a mobile phone somewhere close in the house. The ringtone led him to the dressing table in the bedroom. He opened the drawer and found, along with the mobile, a short, hand-written letter.

I'm flying away – in answer to all your flights. Tonight I'm dining in Paris. And tomorrow? Who knows...

Yes, it was her answer to years of humiliation. She had always wanted to travel. Although she and Michael had gone here and there together – in winter they skied in the Alps, or went on a cruise to somewhere warm, and in the summer they visited cities of Europe – now it was about something else. This was her mutiny. No longer would she refuse to see what was so blatant, and on the threshold of fifty she would indulge herself in what she had long dreamt of: exploring Paris, seeing Dublin, Amsterdam, crossing the Atlantic to visit New York... but most of all, enjoying that wonderful feeling of freedom. She had been denying herself for a long time and for a long time she had been suffering. Now was her time. Michael? Poor Michael, she had written him a letter; it had to end sometime, better sooner than later.

My dear Michael, you came into my life at a time when I was no longer expecting you and when I was on the edge of leaving – where to is not important – but you caused me to stay, to pause... and so for a little while I selfishly warmed myself in your arms. It's time to say goodbye...

Perhaps he would understand and forgive her.

She sipped her wine and stared into the distance. The horizon darkened as the city lit up. *Life is so extremely beautiful*, she thought, thrilled by her renewed ability to perceive its beauty. She crossed her legs comfortably and casually let her elegant shoe slip from her heel and playfully swing from the tip of her toes.

She saw the two men sitting at the table opposite register the innocent movement, pause for a moment and then ask each other with their eyes, 'What were we talking about?'

She smiled to herself. She put her head back and gently shook her hair. *Life is beautiful.*

* * *

Emma opened her eyes and stopped the film. *I'd like to run away like Michelle, too*, went through her mind. *Be healthy and run far away. See the sea again, the mountains… travel and explore.*

Never before had her desire to travel been stronger than it was right now – when it seemed impossible. The setting sun was not visible from the window of her flat. Just the wet roofs of the buildings opposite and a few crooked trees. *Those trees are like me. Excluded from the company of others, imprisoned between the concrete houses, unable to move. Deprived of their forests, the touch of other trees, the sweet smell, silence, safety… life.*

She leant on the wheels of the wheelchair and moved closer to the window. The sky was overcast. Without stars. Not even the moon broke through the cloud cover to reveal its position.

"You know what I wish?" she said at random.

To her, the silence over the rooftops was a sympathetic answer.

"I wish life was beautiful again," she said in tears.

"Yes, I know," the moon said sadly from somewhere.

"I wish I could cross my legs and swing my shoe from the tip of my toes." She finished with the impossible.

Chapter 16

I read the book into the night. Though I hadn't originally intended to, I read it all. Very interesting reading. I had to admit Beth was right when she said it draws you into the dream. I would express it differently: like an impressionist painter with his brush, Emma creates sentences with her words that capture not sharp contours, but just the mood or impression of a scene. The girl who dresses her legs in stockings made of celestial light really is like something from a dream. There is so much eroticism in that – the darkened room with just the light from the moon covering (or uncovering) those feminine legs. *That must have been written by a man.* I smiled to myself.

I put the book down on the table and gazed out the window. The light of the office kept me from seeing into the dark night outside. I got up and switched it off. When I had sat back down at the chair behind the desk, I regretted it for a moment because the darkness surrounded me, pervading even my mind. How had Emma written it?

The darkness from the street outside entered my room through the window and drove away the shadows that had only a moment before crept along the walls and the floor of the flat and somewhere into my soul.

After a while, I got used to the darkness and said to the moon, "I'll recite you a poem. Would you like that?"

"I love poetry," answered the moon almost immediately.

"It's from the book that Emma wrote… and it's strange. As if…" I looked for the words, but the moon didn't let me finish.

"Get on with it!"

I leant back comfortably in the chair, closed my eyes and arranged the words in my memory.

Then I recited quietly:

"Tonight I can't sleep,

"So I write to my loves that will be.

"On blank paper I catch the words flying through the univers—

"and nothing more.

"And when the night progressed, my friend, the moon, came to my aid.

"What else could I wish for?

"I write to my future loves that will be,

"You were and are my everything."

I finished and there was silence.

"What do you think?" I couldn't stand it any longer.

"What do I think? Nice verse. I like that she writes to her future loves, those that were and are everything. Funny."

"And what do you think about '*my friend, the moon, came to my aid*'?"

"Of course. I inspire every budding poet. It doesn't mean anything."

"Really?" I didn't believe him. "Doesn't it by chance mean that Emma is a bit like me? That she can hear your voice too?"

The moon didn't hurry to answer. Hidden somewhere behind the clouds, he didn't temper the expansive night.

After a pause, he admitted, "Emma… yes. Emma is a bit like you." He continued in a sombre manner, "It was only a few years ago that she first looked up at the sky, amazed that she heard my words, and since then we speak together often. You discovered me through your pain, and she through her feelings. Understand? By the way, she's a beautiful woman."

"You've known Emma for years." I reconcile myself with this thought. "And you couldn't have…?" I didn't finish the question that I knew the answer to anyway. "Beautiful woman, beautiful woman," I repeat, irritated. "Isn't it enough that I crippled a young, talented woman? She has to also be beautiful – perhaps so my feelings of guilt are stronger and more painful?!"

"What is your pain compared to hers?" the moon snapped at me.

I felt ashamed. "Yes, I know. I don't have the right to feel sorry for myself. What is my misery compared to Emma's? I just sometimes have the feeling that this unfortunate story is being built on my shoulders like a house. Not all at once, but brick by brick it grows, burdening my back and breaking my knees. When will it end? How many more bricks will be laid? And the house that is being built, is it perhaps my next prison? Or grave?"

The moon ignored my metaphors. "She is a beautiful woman... and interesting," he said, more to himself. "Once we even competed with each other:

"I calmed the oceans and mirrored their shine,
"She tossed her hair, and with it... stopped time."

The words tore me from my gloomy thoughts. "Tossed her hair... and stopped time?" I had never before heard a more beautiful declaration. "She impressed you that much? She's that beautiful?"

"Beth has already told you about her; you look at her and you don't see the ideal of feminine beauty. Hair, eyes, lips... nice, but not in an obvious way when taken separately. Together, however, underscored by the way she moves, she creates a fluidity that simply radiates from her."

We were quiet. With my eyes closed, I tried to imagine a woman's face that would conform to that strange description. As if from a fog, it revealed itself to me. I couldn't focus onto the picture, and when I began to, the face began to turn away. As if in slow motion, her hair lifted with her movement and, in its momentum, wrapped around and covered her face. I was seized by a sense of despair. She tossed her hair... and stopped time. Instinctively, I reached out my hand to touch that hair.

"Emma!" I shouted into the night.

Chapter 17

The moon looked down from the heavens above. He saw the Earth and its oceans, and he saw Beth and Emma. *Strange world*, he thought for at least the hundred thousandth time.

> *The foam on the crests of the waves*
> *is the happiness of the world…*
> *and the dark depth of the ocean –*
> *is an ocean of pain.*

The moon spotted Emma behind the dark window of her flat. The clouds parted and she was sitting in her wheelchair with her face exposed to his shine. In the tear that broke through from her closed eyes, darkened the darkest abyss.

"Just this once." The moon sighed and let Paul's shout fade away in an echo.

Emma opened her eyes. She looked around the room.

"Did you hear that voice?" she asked quietly.

The moon calmly illuminated the corners of the room. "Cross your legs and swing your shoe from the tip of your toes? That's what you wish for?" He ignored her amazement. "That can come true… and if not, you can always toss your hair and stop time."

* * *

"Emma!" called Beth from the gap of the partially opened door.

She had a key to the flat. Emma had given it to her, but she didn't dare enter immediately, and instead waited to be invited in.

"Come on in," came a voice from the small living room.

"Why on earth are you sitting here in the dark?"

"I just felt like it," scoffed Emma.

"You felt like it. Winter is here, clouds are racing across the sky, and on top of that you want to sit in the dark. It's going to make you feel depressed."

"I do anyway, light or dark."

Beth turned the light on in the room, took off her coat and hung it on the coat rack by the door in the small hall.

"I'd like a nice cup of coffee. Can you make me one?"

"Wouldn't you rather make it yourself? Seeing as how I'm a cripple."

"I don't like that kind of joke," Beth bristled immediately.

"It wasn't a joke."

Beth sat down in the chair and looked at Emma sitting by the window in her wheelchair. The light reflected off the window and obscured her view. They sat quietly until Beth broke the silence.

"What do you see out of the window?"

"I was trying to remember an old proverb, and another one, a similar one, came to me."

"A saying. Let's hear it."

"The well-fed doesn't understand the hungry."

"Hmm…"

They were quiet again.

"Do you want to say that I don't understand… your condition?"

"I wouldn't say that you don't understand. It would be more precise to say you can't understand."

"That's the same, isn't it?"

"No, it's not. You can't understand, it's fairer to say. You're trying, but you can't understand. You don't have an experience that you could measure up against mine. To not understand means that you're not even trying."

Beth got up and went into the kitchen. She filled the kettle with some water and switched it on.

"How would you like your coffee, Emma, black or white? Remind me, do you take sugar?"

"Black, and no sugar, please."

"I'd say Paul has more than a standard interest in you," Beth said as she put a teaspoon of coffee into each of the two mugs.

"Who?"

"Who? Well, our shrink, of course. Paul."

Beth poured the hot water into both mugs. Emma manoeuvred herself over to the entrance to the kitchen.

"Who?" she repeated, not comprehending Beth's answer.

"The shrink. Paul."

"The shrink." Emma laughed. "What kind of interest?"

Beth was encouraged that Emma had not immediately dismissed the discussion about Paul Warburton.

"Whenever I'm there to talk, you come up. I'm always the one to begin talking, but you can see he's waiting for it and always eagerly asks questions—"

"Why do you talk to him about me?" Emma interrupted.

Beth ignored her. "Can you believe that he even asked me to bring him one of your books? So I lent him the most recent one."

"Why do you talk to him about me?" Emma repeated, but not sounding angry.

"Because, just like me, you're a case for a shrink… and, excuse me, an even more urgent case."

Emma leant back in her wheelchair with her hands clasped in her lap, in that unfortunate position that inspired sympathy.

"Why do I speak to him about you?" Beth regretted her rising tone. "We talk about everything together; about my life, to which you belong, so it isn't possible for you not to come up. He's a man who can be trusted. He comes across that way, and I do trust him. I believe that his interest in what is going on in my head… is sincere. I always thought that I knew myself, that there was nothing I couldn't handle on my own. And you see, I've worked myself into a state where the only thing left to do would be to drink… or to find a psychologist. I don't regret it. I don't know how he did it, but suddenly I see everything differently somehow – as if from above."

They went back into the living room. Beth put the mugs down onto the coffee table and moved one of the chairs so Emma could come closer in her wheelchair.

"Actually, I do know how he did it. He's a case, an example, of how to manage life and everything miserable it brings with it. He lives alone. His wife left him for someone else. I don't know that directly from him, but from the women who come into my shop. He seems so at peace, so balanced. You wouldn't say that he had problems too."

"Are you trying to persuade me again?" Emma asked quietly.

Beth picked up her mug, carefully took a sip and put it down on the table again.

"If you want to call this persuasion, so be it. I just want to talk."

"But I explained to you that no shrink can help me. He can convince me a hundred times over about the meaning of life and how to be happy but these dead legs of mine will always remind me where I belong, and where I'll always belong."

"All right then. Where do you belong and will always belong? Tell me. I'm interested."

"At best, among the pitied, and at worst, among the annoying, among the sick and repulsive."

Beth's eyes flashed. "That is, pardon me, bullshit what you're saying!" she exploded. "For God's sake, look at it from the other angle. You're not able to imagine yourself falling in love with a man in a wheelchair? I can imagine that. Why not?"

"It's different with women, don't you think?" Emma argued back, irritated.

"Yeah? How is it different?"

"I'm sure I don't have to explain to you what legs mean for a woman. I… now I could only attract some pervert who could get excited that before him… that he could take me like an inflatable doll, lay me down, spread my legs like he wants, and afterwards… pack me up again and put me away somewhere. It can never again be… normal."

"Normal, you say? What's normal?" Beth snorted and continued, "We can argue about this for a long time. I can tell you that our little lesbian tryst seemed more normal than sex with my husband. Yeah, don't look at me like that. After all these years of marriage, sex with my husband seems like incest to me – he's like a relative, a brother… or a friend. Whatever. You know? When I've lived with someone for twenty-five years and slept only with him… don't talk to me about what's normal in a long-term relationship, love, or sex. I'm telling you: nothing. Nothing. There are no norms or barriers."

Emma wheeled herself over to the window. Outside twilight had set in, and the late January chill of the winter crept in through the spaces in the window frames. Evening was approaching. Another evening, when loneliness hurts, the silence is the most excruciating, and her legs so cold.

"Are you trying to convince me that nothing's happened, that I'm normal? I'm not. I have a severed spinal cord and a broken spirit. I've been eliminated… I'm a cripple."

Beth tightened her lips, and it was clear which word she wanted to say.

"Bullshit! I'm simply trying to explain that no one is eliminated from this game in advance unless, of course, they eliminate themselves."

Emma couldn't hold back any longer and began to shout too. "I didn't eliminate myself! I was eliminated. Get it?"

"No, you took yourself out. You're not fighting," Beth answered, suddenly icily calm as if someone had waved a magic wand.

The room was silent. Emma looked out of the window, and it seemed that she didn't even notice the world. Beth watched her silently and forbade herself from feeling sorry for herself.

"I'm not fighting, I'm not fighting, you say. Well, what should I do?" Emma sighed finally. "A man simply can't help me."

"On the contrary. Only a man can help you. We'll invite Paul, and we'll do it as soon as possible." Beth said what had been hanging in the air anyway.

Emma didn't answer immediately. She stared at the window, perhaps trying to further elude her nagging fate, but like a mirror, the windowpane just returned her to the world of the living room.

"He'll come here, and you'll come with him?" She was resigned.

Beth happily blinked her eyes.

"Yeah, of course. I'll come with him. It'll be our ménage à trois. Just a normal ménage à trois, though."

Chapter 18

In the crowd of other passengers, Michelle slowly made her way down the aisle of the huge wide-bodied airplane, checking the numbers on the seats with her eyes. Patient and smiling, she waited until the man in front of her put his bag into the overhead locker and was rewarded with his smile and thanks. All of the passengers were unusually gracious and considerate, perhaps influenced by the smiling flight attendants, or masking their anxiety before the long flight, or perhaps it was caused by the fact that they were all in this together. Even the older woman already sitting in the seat next to Michelle's seat by the window willingly got up to let Michelle get by.

"It'll be a long night," she said politely when Michelle had sat down.

"It most certainly will," Michelle answered with her mildly accented English, "but sunny Mauritius will be our reward."

Yes, her next goal was the island of Mauritius. She had originally wanted to fly from Paris to Amsterdam, but the chilly autumn weather had led her to the idea of sunning herself not only in that splendid feeling of freedom, but also in real sunshine. She was setting out after it now. How easy it was when she could make decisions alone. She warmed herself now in the rediscovered realisation that life was beautiful.

The plane filled up with passengers. The speakers sounded with the encouraging voice of the captain, and the flight attendants, smiling indulgently, demonstrated how to use the oxygen masks and life vests – it was such an unnecessary ritual, but what could be done? Even a meticulous rule was a rule.

Through all this, the engines hummed darkly as the colossus slowly moved along the runway. A few long minutes of hushed expectation in the darkened plane as everyone suddenly ceased to be sure of the victory of human genius over the laws of nature. Only the young people in the back of the plane laughed loudly, constantly shouting something. Michelle, with her few semesters of psychology, understood these outbursts by the young males. The boys were just masking the fear they surely felt. She was certain that at the first signs of turbulence, it would be them who would be fearfully looking around, while the one who was loudest now would be shrieking hysterically.

Start. The huge several-ton leviathan hurtled along the runway, all the time gaining speed. No one, not even the young men in the back, attempted to shout above the noise of the raging machine. Take-off. The massive engines pulled the aircraft into the sky.

How brazen. Even above the clouds – which after only a few minutes of ascent were deep down below, creating the soothing impression of soft down pillows – the plane didn't straighten out, and boldly continued to conquer tens, hundreds and thousands of feet of height.

Flight level.

"Is it now okay to use the toilet?" The brave boy laughed.

The flight panel on the back of the seat in front of her was showing parts of Europe with almost all of Africa, and the two curved lines from Paris to Djibouti and Djibouti to Mauritius showed their flight path. The small red dot, which was the airplane, moved from Paris and set out along the arc on its long pilgrimage. Michelle watched the panel. *Just hopping over to Mauritius*, she thought when she saw these two arcs. *A hop and a jump.* The tension eased and the plane sounded with the clicks of seatbelts being undone.

Even Michelle made herself comfortable. She looked out the window and saw the fluffy down clouds far below. If to dream, then in the skies. If to live, then in paradise. She patted herself on the back again for the idea of flying to the island. What to dream about? God, there was so much. And then, *I'm in that wonderful age when I can't only dream, but also remember.* She smiled to herself. There's so much of that, too.

Over an hour into the peaceful flight, female flight attendants pushing a trolley were offering dinner, which interrupted her pleasant contemplation. Choice of salads and cold meats, fried chicken or vegetarian. Wonderful. Things just kept getting better. The red dot was now somewhere above the Mediterranean, barely moving along a fraction of an inch at a time. A delicious rosé wine eased the oppression of that endless stretch in front of the dot.

After dinner, the noise in the plane died down. Only the small spotlights above the heads of the passengers shined. The boys occasionally made themselves known through the humming silence. How old could they be? Twenty? Twenty-three? Definitely not more. God…

Michelle nestled down in her seat as best as she could. She was still watching the dot on the panel, and in her mind the plane took the opposite direction. It retreated into the past. It flew over her office, past her family – Michael, children, and then university buildings – until it circled above the student house where it landed…

"I can't believe we've graduated." The young, twenty-one year old student laughed while her equally young friend exuberantly jumped on the bed as if on a trampoline. Her oversized shirt flapped around her hips, at every landing revealing her thong and bare thighs.

"Yippee! I'm delirious! God, this is absolutely awesome!"

"Come and have some bubbly, Kyra."

Clink, clink. The Prosecco multiplied the insane feelings of the two happy graduates.

"We're going to get smashed. We'll go to a nightclub. We're going to dance all night."

"Yeah. We're going to party."

Both spluttered a bit when the bubbles went up into their noses.

"Hello, I've come for my shirt, so I've let myself in," said a voice from the bedroom door, but because of their laughing, they hadn't heard it open.

In the doorway stood Ben, fellow university student and friend; a tall, stocky lad nicknamed Tank, always ready to have fun. A week ago, the girls had been up in the lads' student house, and he had lent his shirt to Michelle, who had felt the cold, being in only a T-shirt. With tears still running down their faces, they looked at him and then at each other conspiratorially. They jumped onto the bed, sat down and hid their bare legs under the duvet.

"I can't give it to you now, Tank, because I don't have anything on underneath," said Michelle playfully.

Tank joyfully joined the game. "But I really need it. What are we going to do about that?"

"We have no idea." Kyra laughed. "I can't even lend you my shirt, although I have a T-shirt on under it, because it wouldn't be big enough for you, as you are a big lad."

Tank's eyes twinkled. He sat down on the bed next to the girls. They pulled the duvet up to their chins and laughed at him with their big eyes.

"Tell you what, Tank," Michelle said, feeling in a devilish mood, "you take off my shirt... and as a bonus, I'll let you have a feel of my naked breasts."

The girls winked at each other.

"What are you waiting for, Tank? Go on, take it off," they said while pulling the duvet down to their *midriff. But then Tank's hands quickly disappeared beneath the duvet and were now fondling the top of their legs.*

"Not there, Tank. You can have a feel of the breasts, but not the top of the legs."

They giggled.

"Tell you what, Tank, I'll undo the buttons myself," Michelle said and thrust out her chest as Tank took his hands out from under the duvet. "Tank, would you like to watch?"

He didn't answer. He just swallowed, as the eroticism of the moment trumped merriment, and his eyes betrayed his desire. She slowly undid the buttons, one after another. Suddenly all three were silent, just smiling stiffly. Finally the last button was undone, but the shirt still veiled everything.

"So now you can take it off," prompted Michelle.

Tank took a deep breath and pushed back the shirt. Michelle didn't move her body or even cover her nipples with her hands. She continued to push out her chest and show off her firm white breasts.

"Those are some wonderful tits," mumbled Tank, touching her naked breasts with the tips of his fingers. "Those are some tits…"

Michelle shrugged the shirt off her shoulders.

"Your hands are sweating, Tank," she said, letting him fondle her breasts.

"Want to see how my breasts bounce when I pull my T-shirt up over them?" Kyra entered the game.

She didn't wait for an answer. She crossed her arms, gripping the hem of the T-shirt, and slowly pulled it up over her naked body.

"Fucking hell," Tank panted, staring at her breasts, which plunged from under the T-shirt. And when the taut hem sprung loose, they swung in such a sexy way that Tank just groaned.

Sitting, the girls leant back on their hands. They tilted their heads back until their hair was touching the pillow and let Tank touch their breasts with his trembling hands.

"Does that make you feel good?" Michelle chuckled.

"Yeah."

Tank's face was flushed, and he panted with excitement as his hands slipped again under the duvet.

"Ha-ha. Not there, Tank. Keep your hands out of the thongs."

"Oh, girls, you can't do this to me. You can't leave me like this," Tank whined.

"Like what?" *They cruelly pretended not to understand.*

"Like... I'm really all horny because of you."

"No way, dear Tank... The only thing, perhaps, maybe – since we're having such a great day today – we could give you a little massage. What do you say, Michelle?"

"Have you ever had your dick stroked with four hands at a time?"

They had to throw the duvet over his head because he bellowed like an ox...

* * *

Ménage à trois? Emma thought in the silence of the room. *Well, we could say that...* And she smiled sadly.

Chapter 19

When you wait in suspense for something that you fear will happen, it usually happens when your fear has abated and you're not expecting it anymore. I call it Paul's paradox. There is truth in it. It was Friday afternoon. I was sitting in my office finishing up writing my case notes, and suddenly, after a long time, I longed for some music. That's just how it is with me. I don't notice music when I have troubles. Some people are the opposite: music can distract, soothe or help them break away from their problems. Not me.

When something is bothering me, I don't notice music at all. Inside my soul the strings, normally thrilled by the tones I hear, harden. Music then just goes right over them. It doesn't enter me, and is therefore pointless, because it would just act as a backdrop to my gloomy thoughts. My home is usually completely silent.

Today is different. My worries have disappeared. I put on The Beatles, which is particularly interesting because for them I have to be in a good mood, otherwise, trying to dispel the gloom, I become even more depressed even by their funniest songs. I listen to *Sexy Sadie*, and Paul's genius bass guitar at the end of the track thrills my inner strings. The melody is so simple and obvious. The whole song is playful.

Real music connoisseurs would probably cringe at such a comparison, but Beatles music seems to me almost Mozartian. Just as Mozart did in his time, The Beatles moved away from writing songs for the masses and bravely experimented with sounds, melodies and tones. Like him, they set out on an uncharted path of musical composition. They had fun when they played, and you could hear it expressed in their music. Connecting joy with the unrestrained. I am no expert, and maybe I am wrong, but in no other composer do I see that extent of playfulness and enthusiasm for new discoveries.

I was listening to *A Day in the Life*, one of their strangest songs, when my mobile phone rang. I had forgotten to silence it at the end of the work week. I looked at the display: *Beth Brooke*. The sound waves suddenly lost their ability to penetrate the space, as it became thick, and the music faded away. My stomach tightened. A premonition?

"Hello, Mrs Brooke."

"...Hello," she answered after a short pause.

"I was a little surprised that you have me saved in your mobile. Not so long ago I wasn't there. Or have you memorised my number?"

"I have you saved. Why not? We speak quite often."

"I'm sorry for calling now. You would have finished working and must be looking forward to the weekend. But I couldn't help it. Guess what – she agreed. She agreed!"

I understood everything immediately. What I had hoped wouldn't happen, had just happened. In an instinct of self-preservation, I still grasped at straws.

"Who and with what, Mrs Brooke?"

"Emma, of course. She wants to meet with you. To be more precise, she'd like you to come over to her place. Not a good idea?"

Brick by brick, I was reminded of the house being built on my shoulders.

"And she would like me to come with you."

"I'm afraid, Mrs Brooke, that won't work. It's simply not standard practice."

"I know, Doctor. I understand that, for you, she's not so important that you would want to commute for her sessions, but I really must intercede for her. Help her. Let's help her together."

"It can't work." I sighed resignedly.

"It will work. Believe me. Just our presence, our interest, will give her the kick she needs."

I couldn't resist Mrs Brooke any longer, and I especially couldn't resist my conscience, which had already long struggled with the flimsy fact that I would even stay free to fulfil the promise for Beth and myself; I would help as much as I could.

"When?"

"You're wonderful. How about early evening on Tuesday?"

"At six?"

"That would be fine. If anything changes, I'll give you a call."

"Where shall I go?"

"I'll pick you up at five-thirty so you don't have to look for it. And thank you. Thank you once again."

We said goodbye. So Tuesday at six. D-day and H-hour. A story a person couldn't make up.

* * *

Are you sleeping, Paul? You're not sleeping. Sleeping, sleeping, and in the dream, you're dreaming... I traced the tree rings on the desktop with my finger. *Eleanor Rigby* pulled me from my thoughts... I turned off the forgotten player. Silence passed in silence. Just as tributaries merge into streams, and streams into rivers, so the mistakes I have committed merge into a relentless torrent. Drunken evenings and a night-time drive through Market Harborough, an accident with cruel consequences for a young woman, running away from my responsibilities, and then the worst: I am going to lie to that woman, cheat her, laugh at her...

I was tormented with pangs of guilt the entire weekend. What should I do? God, what should I do? Can I still stop it? Should I go to the police? Should I refuse the therapy I promised? Therapy that cannot succeed anyway. No, I had let things go too far. I had left Emma with her inner struggles and let her suffer, and I let myself become a beacon that Beth was drawn to. I can't turn away now. I can't. Her spirit, as well as her spine, would be broken. She would be scared by the fact that even I don't believe. That spark of determination that Beth and I had ignited would be extinguished once and for all. No, no, no. I can't. I will let myself be carried further on the relentless torrent, but even in the short moments when I will lift my head above the ferocious waves, I still won't see the calm surface.

Beth picked me up at exactly five-thirty. In the car we greeted each other with smiles and set out on our way. I was quite calm, and I would dare to say that Beth had no idea how deep my despair was in those days. Perhaps the only problem was focusing on the geyser of speech directed at me. Helter skelter; it reminded me of the song by The Beatles. She talked and talked. I answered politely, but briefly, when she asked something. The lyrics of the song go through my head.

"This is where it happened," says Beth, pointing to the road junction opposite the PDSA outlet in front of us.

We pass the pelican crossing. I look out the window and am silent.

"This is where that so-and-so hit her and drove off. The police have not been able to find anything. That scumbag is still free. Doesn't it frighten you that maybe every day you run into such a person?"

It does. Every morning when I see him in the shaving mirror, I feel sick, I think without answering. *Look out, helter skelter.*

We are in a residential area making our way between the buildings. We find a parking place and Beth carefully reverses in between two cars.

"It's that building over there, but I'll leave the car here. There's only a small parking area over there, and it's usually full."

We walk the short distance on foot. I can feel my stomach tightening, but I forbid myself any sort of emotion. *You're at work, you're at work*, I repeat to myself.

Beth waves at a window on the ground floor.

"I'm sure she's watching from behind the curtain."

But the curtain doesn't move.

"See, I told you there wouldn't be any available parking place here."

She unlocks the door to the building. Right past the door are the wide doors to the lift, but we go up the five steps to the raised ground floor. Beth rattles a bunch of keys and unlocks the door to a flat on that floor.

"Hello, hello," she calls through the half-open door. "You have visitors. Can we come in?"

"Yes, of course. Come in…" I hear the voice of Emma Lineker for the first time.

Instinctively, I take a deep breath and follow Beth. Just no emotion, no emotion. What does her voice say about her? Young, thoughtful, sensitive, nice… pain, nervousness, expectation…

Beth goes in before me and announces, "Set the table! The guests are here."

I am grateful to her for slightly breaking the tension in this moment. She slips into the living room. She obscures my view. She bends and I hear the smack of a kiss.

"Hi." Beth stands back and points out towards me. "Doctor Warburton, Emma."

Eyes, a smile, and dark, straight hair that dances around her head with the slightest movement.

"Emma Lineker, Doctor."

I move closer, and when I am two steps away, she offers me her hand in greeting. I bend down slightly and put my hand out too. The film slows. We move towards each other with infinite slowness. There is total silence. Everything is blurred; only our hands move closer to each other. Just a few more inches. Eyes. Dark eyes. Eighth of an inch. A smile and hair that falls around her face when her eyes look at you. Touch. A cool, small hand in mine.

"Emma Lineker."

"Paul Warburton."

Beth smiles, and we smile with her.

"Have a seat," Emma says to us.

I let Beth sit in the chair she has chosen, and I sit in the other one.

"Can I get you a cup of coffee?"

"That would be nice. Black and one sugar, please," I answer.

Beth nods too and then immediately offers, "I'll make it."

"No, no. I can manage. I'll call you when it's ready."

From the kitchen comes the rattle of the mugs. We are quiet at the table.

I look around the flat. It seems, I would say, unlived-in. It doesn't seem to fit Emma. It's not the flat of a young, talented writer; it's a prisoner's flat. The furniture is nice, that is true, but otherwise there is no decoration, no character. A temporary place to live with no relationship to anyone, anything.

"It's ready," Emma calls from the kitchen.

Beth stands up and, after a short while, brings back a tray with three steaming mugs. Emma manoeuvres over to the table in her wheelchair. We stir our coffee and are grateful for the short opportunity to do something with our hands. We smile with our eyes.

"I feel I should say something first," says Beth, breaking the awkward silence. "I was the one who thought this all up… but I'll start broadly. Everyone who knows me, knows that I'm a woman who speaks her mind. I'll tell you what I think, whatever it is, and not everyone likes that. I never really worry about my problems. I always just solved them – bang, bang, and that was that.

"People around me always took me for a strong and well-balanced woman. I thought of myself that way, too, for a long time. Then forty came and at once I noticed some changes. Suddenly I was tired and annoyed, nothing was any fun, and I just crumbled from it all. It lasted a year or two. I fought it, but eventually I gave up. I closed myself off.

"Finally, I confided in my doctor, and she advised me to talk to a psychologist about my mental state. I refused at first – I'm not some nut – but in the end I gave it a try. I discovered Doctor Warburton here. He knows best all that we've discussed and dissected, and finally we found that weak spot in my personality and my way of life… I'm better now. I'm living a better life. I feel it that way."

She paused for a moment, sipped her coffee and went on. "What happened to Emma, happened. Of course it's a mess, and I understand her state of mind and her scepticism… but I also think that it's time to start living."

Emma drew a breath in protest.

"No, let me finish," Beth went on. "I said this to you not long ago and I'll say it again: it's time to start living and writing. You're a writer, you're not some top athlete. You can't run, you can't jump, but you can write. The only thing stopping you is in your head, or, let's say, your state of mind, and something can certainly be done about that." Beth grabbed her cup and took a sip from it. "I'm finished. So there. Whoo."

I had to smile, and inside I felt grateful again to Beth for that hoot.

My turn had come. I glanced in the eyes of the two women to check that it was in fact my turn to say something. For a moment I lost myself in Emma's gaze (God!), and then I began.

"If you'll allow me, I'll also begin a bit broadly. I met Mrs Brooke a few months ago when she came to me with her problems. She came regularly to our sessions. She talked about herself, about her life. We worked together. I recognised in her a truly strong woman who had only been led to me by a concurrence of all sorts of circumstances. She was always very straightforward and completely different to most of my other patients. I confess that after her visits, I always felt I had been lifted above my own problems. Yes, it's a paradox, but a psychologist feels relief after consultations with his patients."

Both laughed, and I now felt encouraged.

"Later on, Mrs Brooke mentioned you."

I hesitated for a bit. From this point on, everything I wanted to say was no longer improvisation, but part of my plan. In those sleepless nights, when I was struggling with remorse over what I had done and how much I had hurt Emma, I also considered my role in the situation I now found myself in. I thought about what to say and what strategy to choose if one day I stood face-to-face with Emma.

From all that I knew about her from Beth, and what I had picked up from her book – in her way of thinking and expression – one thing came to me: if I wanted to help Emma, if I wanted to give her back her zest for life, if I wanted to, as Beth says, give her a kick, then we would have to – I'm afraid to even say it – we would have to be friends! Yes, we would have to – Beth, Emma and I – become friends. Otherwise I wouldn't be able to get close to Emma. She is too intelligent and perceptive, and with her ingrained scepticism she would see right through any standard strategy I might choose. I would never be able to convince her if I spoke in the language of my profession. This is what I had come up with. I was convinced, and I bet on it.

"Later on, Mrs Brooke mentioned you," I repeated to emphasise precisely this fact. "She spoke very nicely of you, and it was nice to listen to. There aren't many friendships like yours in this world. Very often our topics of discussion veered towards you, and one day your friend Beth sort of asked me to help… help you adapt to your new life situation. I admit that I was, and actually still am, in a bit of a quandary with her request, because a proactive approach from you, Ms Lineker, was missing from the beginning. And without that, I dare say, this cannot work.

I interpret the fact that you finally invited me to this meeting as succumbing to the pressure that Beth, with all good intentions, put on you."

Looking into the eyes of both women, I checked the effect of my words. Beth was disappointed. Emma commended me.

"Besides, I'm convinced that with a friend like Beth, you don't need the help of a psychologist. Let's be honest, a man, even if he is a psychologist, can barely even get close to the kind of detailed analysis two good girlfriends can produce."

Now I saw praise in both of their eyes. I sipped my coffee and finished up my plan.

"Now, you're probably saying, 'So what are you doing here if you're not offering any help?' My answer is that, despite what I've said, my help is still a possibility. It depends on Ms Lineker. She just needs to agree, and we are ready to go."

I looked in Emma's eyes, searching for an answer. She held my gaze but didn't answer.

"What is the reason I'm here? Maybe it's presumptuous of me, but from the moment we began speaking about you, I couldn't help feeling that my relationship with Mrs Brooke, and hence with you, had moved from the plane of psychologist to patient to the plane of… the personal. I confess that the discussions with Beth were so refreshing, your reputation and book so interesting, that I couldn't resist the temptation to accept your invitation and get to know you better."

I wanted to say 'whoo', but I didn't.

"Well, that's great!" Beth rejoiced. "Why didn't you tell me that earlier? I was always so afraid of you. The three of us should have gone for a drink a long time ago. What do you say, Emma?"

"What do I say? That I'm relieved? I wasn't really all that excited about the thought that the three of us would all sit around here trying to get into my head. And to be honest, it wasn't just because of Beth that I invited you here, but also my curiosity about the man I had heard about so often… and only good things."

"Well, that went beautifully wrong." Beth laughed. "That calls for a drink. Will you have one? I won't, I'm driving."

"No, thank you. I won't have one either. I don't drink much, and besides, I'm still not totally sure that I'm not at work," I joked.

Emma immediately reassured me. "You're not at work, really. You're here on a visit."

Beth ceremoniously lifted her mug with the rest of her coffee.

"When I was in your office, I noticed that you like The Beatles. You have quite a collection of their CDs."

A little surprised, Emma and I waited for the punch line.

"We'll drink to the newly established Lonely Hearts Club."

This made us all laugh.

"So, to *Lonely Hearts Club!*"

The three of us toasted by clinking our cups together.

"I assume that you know something about my grim private life," I said, reacting to my membership in the club.

"Of course we know." Beth laughed, adding, "Damn, this is so… let's address each other informally."

Alarmed, I looked into Emma's eyes. She didn't notice, or she ignored it.

"Why not?" She lifted her mug again to toast. "Emma."

"Paul," I muttered flatly and repeated it with Beth. I realised that I was no longer driving this train I had set in motion.

"We should maybe have a small peck on the cheek, shouldn't we?" Beth announced, and immediately leant towards me.

There was nothing left to do but finish the ceremony. I got up and walked over to Emma. She was smiling. She tilted her head and turned her cheek towards me. Her hair fell around her face, and I could smell her scent. My head spun a little when my lips softly touched her cheek. I sat back down and looked at her. So this was the face I had been trying to imagine. She stepped out of the mist that had veiled her until now. I calmed the oceans and mirrored their shine. She tossed her hair… and with it, stopped time. Now I understood. God, how I understood.

It was after nine when we said goodbye. We chatted the whole time under Beth's direction. I talked a lot about myself and revealed things that maybe I didn't even want to, but I also learnt a lot. It was an interesting excursion into the world of women.

"That was the first time since it happened that I've seen her smile. And it's because of you," Beth complimented me on the way back.

"Because of us," I corrected her modestly and without enthusiasm.

"I promised that I would go back tonight and help her. This evening's carer cancelled. Will you give me your email address? I'll write to tell you what she thought of it all."

"I'll send you a text message." I sent it straight away.

"I had no idea how things would turn out tonight. It was really a desperate attempt, but it turned out as well as it could have. I have good vibes from it. Hopefully we'll be able to meet more often and get her to go out."

"Well, we promised that we'd all meet, but I'm afraid that getting her to go out in the near future might be a problem."

We stopped in front of my house. "Thank you again… Paul."

"You're welcome… and actually, friends call me Warbey."

She laughed. "Good night, Warbey."

"Good night, Beth."

At home I hung up my jacket, put on my slippers and ran up the steps to my office. I turned on the computer. I would wait until Beth wrote. I didn't turn on the light, and only the pale light from the computer monitor illuminated the room. Moments of silence punctuated by the sound of the computer fan. I sat – or rather, lay – in the chair behind the desk.

I thought about if this was what I wanted, and with difficulty I searched for the answer. I wanted to help Emma and I also wanted to resolve the situation that had arisen. It was the only possible solution. Friendship. Meetings, like today's, emails, text messages... the only possible way to revive her, give her a motivational kick. But could I have imagined that behind the term 'friendship' would lie touches, kisses? I could have, but it didn't occur to me, and it caught me by surprise. How had I imagined it? *Hello, Ms Lineker, hello, Mrs Brooke, I am writing to you again after a long pause. Imagine what an interesting case I have now... What do you think about it? I am looking towards your reply.* Something like that? Yes. And in the meantime, Emma! Beth! Warbey! The Lonely Hearts Club. God, if they only knew...

'The police have come up with nothing'; I was reminded of Beth's indignant remark. Were they still looking? Had they put the case on hold? My forehead began to sweat. What if they were still looking? What if that policeman – Maynard was his name – puts the two cases together? What if he realises that I was on my way to the former prisoner's? He was aware that I had had a drink. It would be enough to look at a map of the town, compare the time of the two events... and he would have me! I felt sicker than I had in a long time. God, what if it all comes crashing down? It can't happen. I'm mad. I'm just making things up. It will not ever happen! It can't. If it did... I would have to kill myself.

I shook my head to get rid of the thoughts. I couldn't think about it anymore. I would go mad. Beth still hadn't written. What could they be talking about?

I got up and went over to the window. The chilly January evening had changed into night. The sky was overcast.

"You know how this ends," I whispered to the universe,

and in my imagination, I saw celestial bodies inching through the black space.

"I'm just a spectator," the moon's incantation boomed from somewhere. "I can't tell you more."

"Why won't you give me advice? With your help, I could surely do so much more. I tried to help her. I really tried… to do something that would interest her, that would encourage her."

"That would relieve your conscience," said the moon harshly.

"Yes, that too. In that fateful moment, I ruined Emma's life, but also my own. I made a mistake. First one, then immediately a second, a third, and then another and another… I know that if I had stopped and rushed to help Emma, things would be much different. I would have been punished and sitting in prison. Things should have order. But in those few seconds that I had to make that decision, I missed my chance… and then I was afraid. I was afraid. Yes, afraid. Am I a coward?"

The moon didn't answer, so I answered myself.

"Yes, I likely am, but… but I'm not a bad person. I would like to make amends, which is why I endured that insanity and in this roundabout way again entered Emma's life. Is it another mistake?"

I didn't get an answer to this question either, but perhaps only because of the beep of the incoming email.

I hurried to the computer. Beth.

Hello Paul, at this late hour I'm finally sending you the promised email.

After leaving you, I went back to Emma's and was there up until now. Imagine that when I went back into her flat, she was crying. She was inconsolable, and for a long time I tried, but didn't succeed, in finding out what was happening.

Maybe we were too optimistic. Have we made a mistake? But it looked so promising. It makes me feel sad, and I'm sorry to make you feel sad too. All three of us will fall asleep tonight with sorrow in our souls... how fitting for Lonely Hearts Club.

Kind Regards,
Beth.
P.S. I promised not to mention the tears. Let me be forgiven.

Tears. I didn't expect that. After all, there was so much laughter. How can I even pretend that I understand the human soul? I couldn't bear to sit behind the desk anymore and went back to the window.

"Is that perhaps your answer? Have I only made another mistake?"

The whole universe was silent. The celestial bodies soundlessly inched their way through space.

Silence. Painful silence.

The cosmic mechanism purred on, untouched by my fate.

I stood at the window and let the thoughts flow lazily through my tired mind. Time also flowed lazily and sliced up the night.

Tears. Not always an expression of hopelessness. They always bring relief (if only I were able to do so), and sometimes they are a new beginning, coming between what was and what will be; I worked to comfort myself.

I wished.

Chapter 20

"I hate Beth for putting me in such a situation, and myself… Did Paul come to look at me like some kind of new species? I hate him for looking at me that way, and I hate myself for looking at him the same way. I was powerless. If I wanted to escape, I would have had to crawl on my hands… like a seal. It's humiliating. I hate—"

"Enough!" shouted the moon. "That's enough. Beth loves you and wanted to help you, and Paul… what did he do that was out of the ordinary? He visited you? He also wanted to help – especially you, but maybe even himself."

"He wanted the solace of seeing someone worse off than himself? That's why he came?"

"No, certainly not. He feels alone. He's alone. Maybe he wanted to repay a debt."

"Repay a debt? Who does he owe one to, and what? I don't understand you at all. What do you know about him?"

"Perhaps he's made mistakes in his life, and he wants to make amends. Who knows?" The moon refused to confess. "He has a broken heart and a broken soul. Just like your broken spine keeps you from moving, so his broken soul keeps him from living his life freely. Nothing hurts more than an injured soul. Trust me."

Emma softened. "I saw the pain in his eyes. I glimpsed it. Yes, that's what seemed so strange about him – he joked, but with flashes of sorrow in his eyes. Why? What's bothering him? You must know."

"I am only a spectator."

"Yeah, I know, you see all from the heavens. You see into hearts and into souls. You don't give advice. You don't answer."

Silence. Painful silence.

Emma was sitting straight up in her wheelchair so she could peer over the window frame to see the night above the roofs of the houses. The lights of the town and the black clouds in the sky made the stars invisible. One could only guess at what was behind that invisible wall. She closed her eyes. Luminous darkness, she realised, just like long ago… and in that luminous darkness she saw herself floating in space. She flew over the town. She climbed higher and the light below became the starry sky.

Am I flying upwards or downwards? I want to go up, above that wall of clouds that's suffocating me. I want to fly to the stars.

She flew through the fog, never-ending fog.

She heard the moon cry, "Warbey!"

Finally. Nothing but stars above her head. She let out a deep breath. Above her head, stars, and below, clouds made of down. She floated through space, relieved.

"I want to write!" she screamed into the infinity.

She opened her eyes.

"I want to write again," she whispered in the silence of the room. She tilted her head back and watched the clouds above the roofs of the houses.

Her mind changed in the calm of the night sky, a dark sky blinking with the light of the stars. Flames flickered in the darkness and suddenly a thought flew in like a comet. She caught it and carefully formed it into sentences. Then slowly, unless she frightened away the idea that had just been born, she reached for a pen and pad of paper and wrote:

'The star seemed so close,
So I set out towards it on a journey.
The closer I came, the further away it was.
Space. Heartened by the thought that though we were back to back,
We might be moving towards each other.'

Emma read over the short text. Then again one more time, and then again and again... Did it make any sense? Did it have a head or a tail? Yes, perhaps. She had put the idea on paper. She had written it.

She wheeled over to the laptop on the desk and typed out the sentences. God... Who did she have in mind? Who was she writing about? About Kieran? No. Emma looked around the room. *This is my world.* Could she travel to the stars from here? Bare walls, a desk and a computer, a television, a coffee table and a couple of chairs. Nothing else. She wouldn't think it possible that a man could ever enter this world. But he did. He was here. He sat in that chair and talked. He made jokes with a sad expression on his face. Such a contrast. *It intrigued me. Yes, I was thinking of Paul. I had written those few sentences about him. Without even knowing it. The two of us, though back to back, might be moving towards each other.*

Such nonsense! We are not back to back, and we are not moving towards each other. Neither of us. How are we alike? We're not. He's going his own way. Perhaps Beth diverted him a bit when she spoke at length about me. He came. He looked around. We chatted a bit. And off he goes.

Me? I'm going my own way too. From the window to the desk, from the desk to the window... today into space. I'm nuts. Will I ever manage to get out of this world? Will I lean into the wheels, push myself over the threshold of this flat and go? Where? Into the streets?

From the window, Emma saw where the broken slabs had lifted up in the snicket. She'll not be able to get over that spot. She would have to go into the street. She was terrified of cars and can't go there. She would die of fright if they were passing by her only a few inches away.

How long will Beth enjoy helping me? She has done so much for me. She handles everything, makes arrangements, comes to see me... What if one day she doesn't come? Tomorrow. What if tomorrow, or even today, she doesn't come?

Emma was horrible to Beth. She was acting hysterically and couldn't explain to her why she was crying. What could she have done? She didn't know herself. She should have died under the wheels of that car. It would have been better. She would not be suffering, and she wouldn't be troubling everyone around her.

Around her? Who was around her? Her family, whom she tormented by not wanting to torment them with her presence. The carer, who she guessed likes her as much as a seamstress likes her sewing machine, or a saleswoman likes her shop. She's just doing a job.

Beth… She clicked on her email page and typed Beth's address into the new message box and wrote:

Dear Beth,

Tonight, actually yesterday, was so strange. Several times I surprised even myself. First of all, how I stared at Paul like a halfwit (I had no idea what the first man to cross my path after the accident would do to me). Then there was my hysterical scene – I'm truly sorry. And then there is the fact that after such a long time, I finally pulled myself together and wrote a few sentences…

So I'm writing to you.

He almost knocked me off my wheels. Who? Paul, of course. Interesting man. You said once that he was a looker. I wouldn't say so. He's not very handsome. But what fascinates me about him are his eyes. Those big eyes that seem to speak. Did you notice? They look a little sad, but he can ask and even answer with them. An interesting ability. He's funny. And that contrast between his sad expression and his funny comments… that really got to me.

When you had left together, I felt such terrible sadness and also anger at the fact that I couldn't go with you. I envied you going down the stairs and out to the car with him. I watched you as you pulled out of the parking lot and couldn't handle the flood of emotions at the loss of these ordinary things.

I'm sorry. I'm sorry that I couldn't control myself even when you came back and I raged on about my inability to go with a man down the stairs, to the car, sit next to him...

I still haven't got used to this. I'm still not able to just sit passively and watch. I would like to, I wish... and I forget that I can't. I forget that I am, and always will be, only a spectator to ordinary things like walking, standing around, moving from one seat to another.

I'm writing and writing. I can't even count the sentences I've written. Are they making sense? Hopefully so. Hopefully at least I've got that ability back.

What definitely doesn't make sense is my crying over spilt milk. I know. I will learn to suppress it somehow. Take these lines as a small writing exercise, as proof that I can again put my thoughts (even silly ones) on paper. I will have a look to where I ended up with Michelle. In my imagination, I'm surely much further.

Lonely Hearts Club? Yesterday I felt like the loneliest member. I'm writing – and it's better. Not that I'm not lonely anymore. I reckon I still am, and will be, but I'm reconciled.

Sincerely,
Emma.

Chapter 21

I went by bus, and the rest of the way I continued on foot. It was only a short distance from the last stop, not even a five-minute walk. Where was I going? To see Emma!

Beth wrote to tell me that she'd got a letter from her.

A letter, she wrote, actually, a short email. But it's a huge success, Paul. She's writing! That's what we wanted, hoped for. I confess that after that last scene I had lost some hope. She was in such despair when I left. Only a few hours passed, and she sends an email! I couldn't believe my eyes. She only wrote a few lines, but what she wrote – simply wonderful. A breakthrough, a turn... I don't know what to call it.

I'll start from the end: she wants to continue writing her book about Michelle – who is a woman about my age, and also pretty apt for membership of the Lonely Hearts Club. I had really hoped she would finish writing this book one day. It will happen. Now I believe that.

And what else did she write? Are you sitting down? So sit down. She has a crush on you! Yes, a crush. She likes you! Your eyes, smile, jokes – you simply scored...

I really had to sit down when I read those lines. Another brick had been placed on the ruins that were being built on my shoulders. Like an idiot, I had gazed into her eyes. I had provoked her. What else could she have read into that look other than interest, admiration. And she returned it. But I couldn't help myself. There was no other way. She's – I didn't even want to think it, I didn't want to say it aloud – she's beautiful. Her eyes, lips, smile, hair... God. I barely slept that night. I stared up at the ceiling and tortured myself with my imagination. We will meet, our Lonely Hearts Club. We will exchange looks that will betray everything. I won't hide my admiration; I won't hide what I have felt from the first moment I saw her. I won't hide my love. What I will have to hide is the past. I will always have to cover up that fateful moment that was our first 'meeting'. Will I be able to? I must. I must.

Sergeant Maynard. Was he still searching? Was he still picking at the case? Would he appear one day at my door and say, "You lied to me, Mr Warburton." What if he does? What will I do then?

There would be an explosion, a huge explosion. A nuclear explosion above mine, Emma's and Beth's heads. I would have to kill myself...

Those were the thoughts that had gone through my mind.

* * *

Beth called a few days later.

"We're meeting at Emma's. You may want to go by bus; we're going to celebrate a bit. What, you ask? Well, we have to toast the book about Michelle that she's working on again."

Shortly after that, Emma called me too!

"I would be glad if you came. Beth is going a bit overboard, but apparently the fact that I want to continue writing other books too is reason to celebrate. Well, so be it: a small celebration. I'll be very glad to see you."

I stupidly asked who the book would be about.

"The hero of my book is a coward," she said mischievously, unaware of how the sharp arrow struck my heart.

* * *

I'm standing at the pelican crossing, my back to the PDSA outlet on the town square. I close my eyes. My mind spinning with a whirlwind of thoughts, fears, remorse, anxiety, attraction, desire… How long can I keep this up?

Tick, tick, tick, ticks the signal for the blind. I recognise the feeling when a film is running through my head.

"I will end it!" I resolve in the film. I can't do otherwise.

It's the only solution, I think, and with great relief step in front of the wheels of a huge pick-up truck. I felt no pain when the massive machine broke my bones and tore through my body. Light alternated with darkness.

Light, dark, light, dark. Noise alternated with silence. Darkness and silence.

Only the light of the moon shone and from afar sounded his voice: "Will your paths ever cross?"

They are two parallel lines – she on one, you on the other. Then you embrace her… in eternity.

I opened my eyes and stopped the film.

The pedestrian signal turned to green. I looked to the right, then to the left – just in case some nut… and then I stepped out onto the pelican crossing.

The Castle Steps

Chapter 1

Aisling is a beautiful name. Aisling.

It's in the semi-darkness of the casino gambling room that she's absolutely drop-dead gorgeous. The flickering lights of all colours frolic across her skin and along the deep neckline of her blouse, and then follow the path between her breasts. There is a mysterious way she's shielding her bare legs right now, decorously crossed at the knees, and after a moment, seriously spread. When she's not even breathing in the tension of the outcome of the bet, she remains very beautiful. Like a pianist, with her back straight, now with one leg bent under the stool and the other extended and propped up on a high heel, she taps the keys with her long fingers. Then with her palm to affirm the chord, and it reverberates in its luminous expression again; it accentuates that tantalising beauty of hers.

There's not a trace of disappointment on her face when the game is over. She puts another token into the machine and spins the roulette wheel again. But she's not alone here. Her extremely attractive appearance is making the eyes of the men sitting at the machines next to her wander over her curves. They don't see the other women hunched over their keys here. They are not even trying to fight for a sliver of those looks, in humble acknowledgement of the unattainable level Aisling sets here.

Who is this woman? they all ask with their stares, even though they actually know her. They know her by sight, for whenever they come here at this time of day, they almost always catch a glimpse of her. She sits upright behind a slot machine, her fingers on the keys, her skirt short. Her dark hair is cut short, and she has a deep fringe falling over her forehead as if to cover her dark eyes. They don't know her name, though. They don't know it's Aisling, because Aisling rarely speaks to anyone here. She comes in, sits down at her gambling machine, puts her hands on the keys, and plays. The game's background light music emphasises the mysterious appearance of the silent beauty as Janis Joplin's song *Piece of my Heart* plays on.

This, at first, somehow doesn't fit the picture, as Janis's singing is full of passion and pain, at times like the roar of a wounded animal, contrasting with Aisling's coolness. But when she tosses her hair and for a split second you look into her dark eyes, there's the same music and pain and passion in that look. When she looks away, there's the cry of a wounded animal.

Aisling. She won't let anyone know her name here. Perhaps she's ashamed of how Irish it sounds; perhaps she's too critical of the name and doesn't really know how beautiful it is. But perhaps she doesn't see anyone here who is worthy of knowing her name. Who knows?

Like a pianist, she sits upright and plays that futile game. The coins jingle and the notes rustle and one by one disappear into the bowels of a machine programmed to go straight into the thieving coffers. Only the bright and flashing sequence of colours is her reward.

She believes that all she has to do is hang on, not give up. One day there will be a victory fanfare, it could even be now with this coin… But not yet? Never mind. She must keep playing, she mustn't give up. Mustn't? She mustn't, she thinks. She can't, because it's her only hope of getting out of the debt she's run up.

Janis Joplin is singing *Cry Baby*. How fitting.

Chapter 2

There are three of us who share my garden: me, Russell Steel; old dog Rusty; and the mole. When the summer day draws near and the shadows of bushes stretch across the tended lawn, then my garden is at its most beautiful. Not that it's not beautiful at other times; it is, but it's at its very best in the early evening. It's when the sun sinks over the horizon that the lush green lawn darkens softly and looks then like a carpet inviting thickly coiffed hair to lie down. Or at least to take a few steps, bare feet leaving a trail in that thick manicured lawn as slow as the sand on the beach. The rockery assembled from large white limestones radiates accumulated heat. This appears to light up the flowers that grow through it in all colours in flats, or just clusters, between the stones.

At the same time, I came to realise that I don't actually like the expensive pool anymore, which I invested in this splendour years ago. Although indoors, I now mask it in vain from the rest of the house with trees and shrubs and bushes, as it bothers me, and disturbs me.

I have changed. It wasn't so long ago that an indoor swimming pool, a big fancy car, a big house and money in general were synonymous with happiness for me. Now that I've achieved all that, I've come to understand that this isn't the way to happiness. At least not for me. I don't get any satisfaction from the kitschy blue surface of that pool, or the ridiculously expensive customised Maybach I have in the garage. Good, but not great. No excitement.

What pleases me most is nature in its natural beauty. I just love the flowers in the rockery. I love watching the wings of butterflies fluttering from one bloom to the next, the birds in the branches of the trees, and the silence. But coming to think about it, this isn't really silence, but just a composition of the most natural sounds. Sounds like the rustle of leaves in a gust of wind, the squabbling of sparrows in a thicket of thieves, the buzzing of insects… Previously unthinkable, but the molehills that break the sterility of the grassy area leave me at peace. I don't lay traps for the mole that caused the horror. Well, what the heck, it's just that a mole has taken up residence in the roots of the tall spruce tree that looms in the corner of the garden. Where else would he go? He lives under my spruce tree. At least I don't feel so alone in this big house with a huge garden.

I bought the house over twenty years ago. It's a pre-war six-bedroomed house, well-constructed, in very good condition and, importantly, it's to my liking. When I bought it, it needed only very minor attention, apart from redecorating. It stands alone on a slight slope in The Woodlands area of Market Harborough. The Grand Union canal, frequented by narrowboats, is at the bottom of the garden, and is shielded from the house by a number of established trees. These don't obstruct the view of the large garden, but only pleasantly shade the terrace, which is glued to the south wall of the house.

The patio is my own work. I designed and largely built it myself, and it's accessible from the living room. It's not that large, just big enough for a medium-sized wooden table with six matching chairs and a couple of clay pots with flowers. Narrow stone stairs lead down from the patio into the garden, and then onto a romantically undulating, stone path. The path isn't very long. It skirts the garden and at the end it stops behind the rockery – the greatest jewel of my garden. Behind the rockery there is a large grassy area, several trees and shrubs to hide the patio, then a lawn and, finally, trees that seem to be part of the small number of trees beyond the garden fence.

On these summer days, my greatest pleasure is to walk down those few steps from the terrace and then, squatting or on my knees, crawl through the rockery, transplanting flowers, loosening the soil and pulling weeds amongst the large sandstone stones. I love the smell of limed soil and I don't mind getting my hands dirty and dirt caked behind my fingernails. I don't mind getting yellow and green palms from working amongst all the flowers and grasses. If I wasn't a successful businessman, I'd certainly be a gardener.

But fate had had it otherwise. I was twenty-five and had the drive, enthusiasm and desire to get rich, be independent and buy an expensive house and car. In a small rented workshop in Corby, I'd started making cardboard packaging of all kinds: boxes for fruit and vegetables, then for shoes, for foodstuffs, for TVs and all sorts of electrical appliances… boxes for everything. It was a good venture to get into, almost every manufacturer of anything needs cardboard packaging. Thirty years went by and the company in Corby grew to a size of a large factory, employing a sixty-plus strong workforce. I got rich.

Proud of my success, I bought this expensive big house with a garden, and like anyone who's made a fortune, I sunk a big pond in the nicest part of the garden. I made my dream come true, but as my grandmother would ask, "Did you make your dream come true, Russell? Good on you!"

Good for me. Looking back, I realise that I don't really have anything. I made it to the top, yes, but it's windy up there. A rather cold wind blew my friends away. They've stayed down and they're tired of walking with their heads tilted up. I'm alone. Women? I haven't had time for them. I've been working from morning till night, and meanwhile, out there, the world has slipped away from me. The world of learning, of wooing, of love… I missed it.

At fifty-five, I slowed down, lowered down the window of the Maybach and looked around. Too late. I feel it's too late to look. The women walking along pavements are intrigued by this luxury car and search the driver's seat. We meet gazes, freeze for a second and then pass each other with a look in their eyes that might even be forgiving… but I see my face in the rear-view mirror. I shouldn't be, but in reality, I'm a middle-aged man, a bit overweight with greying stubble of beard and hair. A successful businessman. But I don't want to live with the feeling that I bought a woman.

So I crawl on my knees through my rock garden, tending to the flowers and thinking. Thinking.

If only I could make time go back... Would I have gone the other way? At twenty-five, I'd be running after girls and marrying one and having three children with her. Would I be happy? Happier? I would be. I guess I would be.

If only I could turn the clock back. Time. How strange that word sounds and how accurately it describes something. It's short, and it's more of an adverb, like a *thump, thump*. Like when something flies past at high speed, whizzes by and goes... *time-s* with an ominous 's' at the end.

I'm fifty-five years old, but I feel like my life has whizzed by. It really has whizzed by. Have I wasted it? What's the best I've achieved in my life? Founded the Cardboard Fabrications Company in Corby, producing carton packaging? No, it's not. Because that's lying dumped on most rubbish tips in the world. Except for developed countries, where it's recycled.

So, what?

Rusty. Yes, it may be funny, but it makes me think of my dog, Rusty. His story might seem insignificant, unworthy as proof of the fulfilment of my life. It was really just a story, and yet I'm glad to look back on it, to find a little something of which I can be truly proud.

I'd taken up exercise at the time; I bought myself a racing bike. Perhaps I got fed up with my current way of life and being a bit overweight. Finally, the difficulty of breathing on the way up the stairs made me decide to do something about it. A couple of times a week, I would cycle out of Market Harborough along quiet country roads, over slightly undulating terrain, to torture my body.

It was a beautiful summer day, quite hot for my age and condition. But I pedalled hard. Suddenly, wherever it came from, a German Shepherd appeared not far from me. A big, hairy dog. I was terribly frightened, because I hadn't expected such a thing in this remote place. I pushed hard on the pedals in an attempt to save myself. My heart was pounding with fear and fatigue. Only after a moment did I turn apprehensively. He wasn't running after me in a frantic attempt to tear me apart. Rather, he was staggering, limping and pawing his front leg, perhaps injured.

I stopped. The dog took a few more tired steps… and then he also stopped and, panting heavily, fell.

I looked at him and he looked at me. He was lying down, not begging, just saying with that look: *I'm not well*. I turned round and approached him. He lowered his head and waited. He had a bad gash on his left front leg. It wasn't bleeding, but flesh and bone was showing through the hair. I laid the bike down and leant over him. What's about to happen is what's about to happen.

But nothing happened. I stroked him. He just looked up at me and sighed. I had a water bottle in the holder on the bike frame, poured some water into my palm and held my hand to his mouth. He gulped greedily. I did it again, twice, three times.

"Enough, buddy," I told him.

He was still panting and looking away.

"What about you? Who do you belong to?" I looked around. No one anywhere in the vast fields around. "Where's your owner?" I whispered to him.

I picked up the bike. He tried to stand up. He succeeded, but he was tottering on three legs. Helplessly I walked on, and he, poor fellow, staggered painfully after me. I felt sorry for him. I laid the bike down again and stroked his back.

"Wait here, my friend. I'll come back for you. Will you wait?"

I headed for the main road. When I turned around after a few yards, he was tottering in my direction. I raced home as fast as I could. I reversed out of the garage in my fancy Maybach and hurried back out of town. I stopped on the country road and looked around for the dog.

"Rusty!" I called him by the name of the dog my parents gave me when I was a child.

He ran, or rather staggered out of the field of barley, wagging his tail happily. *You haven't left me*, he said with that tail.

I bent down to him and said, "Rusty, you rascal, what have you been up to?"

I picked him up carefully. He probably wouldn't have made it to the car on his own. He didn't protest, just moaned weakly in pain as his sore leg swung out of my arms. I realised that in my haste I had forgotten to grab a blanket to put him on. What the hell; I put the dog on the back seat and drove him to the vets. The expensive, light-coloured leather back seat was immediately full of sand, and the bloody gash on his leg left an indelible imprint on the leather upholstery.

Rusty. So Rusty came to me. He'd been convalescing for a long time, but I didn't regret the time or the money. When he was fully fit, I put an advert with a photo into the *Harborough Mail*, the *Leicester Mercury* and *the Northampton Chronicle and Echo*, hoping the real owner wouldn't get in touch. No one did. So he stayed with me.

He sleeps twenty-three hours a day and dreams his doggy dreams. Only when I come back home does he clumsily get up and run to meet me. We're really happy when we greet each other.

When I die one day and confess my deeds to God, I will say, "I made a hundred million cartons while I was alive – and saved one dog."

And God will say, "That's not a small thing at all, Russell… that one dog you saved. That's a lot."

Yes, so that's how my life values have evolved; the desire for money and expensive things has turned into an admiration for the most ordinary bits of nature, and I consider my greatest life achievement to date to be saving one dog.

With such a philosophy of life, I can't help but feel alone in this world. I feel alone. I am alone. To most, I'm a greedy businessman driving around in an expensive, fuel-guzzling Maybach. To fellow businessmen, I'm the weird guy who wears shorts, T-shirt, a baseball cap, and rarely shaves. I'm not taken in by either. I don't really want their approval.

I'm on my own!

What more could I ask for? I think to myself as I sit on my patio. It's a late summer evening, Rusty is lying at my feet, a mole is gobbling somewhere in the back garden, and I'm dreaming. What am I dreaming about? Not about riches, not about things, I'm dreaming… about a woman. But it's not a desire for sex, not really… With a sense for beauty, I dream of beauty. I dream dreams that don't come true, and they stay dreams, they stay the soft tingle of thoughts, they stay the lovely smells, they stay the sweetly pretty sadness. I sit on a cushion on my up-market wooden patio chair, my elbows resting on the armrests, my fingers, with dirt behind my nails, intertwined in my lap. I look out into the darkened garden and, as if on a theatrical stage, I act out an act of my reverie in it. The trees and bushes, and the water shimmering in their branches, and the dark sky with the moon and a thousand stars all co-create a magical backdrop for me. Even the music sounds. It comes from somewhere, perhaps from the treetops.

And then, in the moonlit, dense no-mow soft lawn, I see footprints… Nothing more, just one footprint after another forming. First a slow step out of the thicket of bushes, pausing for a moment, and then that ethereal invisible being swathing the lawn's soft density, tiny steps and a long leap. Bare feet imprint themselves in an arc – first the whole feet, and then just the toes of those feet. Perhaps dancing… Who? Who is the dancer who hides from me, drawing only footprints in the thick, soft density of the manicured lawn? I don't know. I've never managed to reach her, and perhaps I don't want to. I don't see her face, only the footprints she draws and the smell I smell when I walk barefoot in those footprints at night… and I smell her hair.

The Castle Steps

"Wait a minute," I whisper to her.

The footprints stop. They wait, and I walk closer... towards the fragrance. I'm within reach when they take a step back, then stagger. I can smell a wisp of hair. I hold out my hands, but only reach into the void. I see the imprints of bare feet crumbling in the steps. They stop and wait again. They beckon. I sit down on the soft lawn, tired, and watch the footprints.

They are silent.

It's a still summer night without a cloud in the sky – perhaps only the music echoes in the branches of the trees. The sky is full of stars when I tilt my head. I close my eyes. The music has stopped. Silence... and into that silence rustle approaching footsteps. I hold my breath so as not to startle them. They're getting closer and closer... I don't open my eyes as she curls up next to me and lays her head in my lap. A dancer – my dream. We've never been closer before.

Do I want to see her face? Do I want to touch that hair? Yes, I do. Yes, I do! The time has come...

Oh my God. I had to laugh. When I opened my eyes, I saw... Rusty. He was snuggling with his head resting in my lap. I had to laugh. I laughed the laugh of a fool into the night. Then I buried my face in Rusty's coat to stifle that crazy laugh until I was in tears. Crying. I lay down on the soft meadow lawn without a trace, tears streaming down my cheeks. Rusty laid his head on my chest, because that's all a dog can do... but maybe, only the dog knows, he did the most he could do.

I calmed down. I looked up at the night sky full of stars.

I'd give a lot of money... so I wouldn't have to buy love, I thought absurdly.

Chapter 3

Company business matters often take me to Prague, where I have business associates. I'm so glad of it. I love Prague – they don't call it the 'Golden City of a Hundred Spires' for nothing.

I particularly love the Old Town. I love wandering the ancient streets, breathing in the atmosphere. Peace then enters my soul as I walk the stone pavements through the centuries, leaving behind our hectic times and immersing myself in the melody of the ages. Yes, a strange, soothing melody pervades those narrow streets. Charles Bridge, the sculpture of the Madonna and Saint Bernard, Ludmila and Little Wenceslas, and all the other statues that watch our steps, and watch over us as we lean over the sandstone blocks and watch the Vltava river.

Unchanging and yet different every second, is the river. The masses of water roll in silent amazement because they are in these places for the first time. Few of the waters have been here before; they have evaporated here and fallen again in a rain of drops in an endless cycle.

Sometimes I feel that I, too, was here once upon a time. Not a month ago, or last year (which is true), but centuries ago; a few cells of my brain, like those drops in the river stream, carry this ancient information. As I climb the castle steps, my favourite, the view is familiar... I have no doubt I have been here before.

But my visit to Prague today begins unromantically in the lounge of the Michelangelo Grand Hotel. I have a meeting with new business associates from the Czech Republic. We have been corresponding for some time and have more or less agreed on the quantity of goods to be purchased, the delivery date, the price and the payment terms. Now it's just a matter of signing contracts and also, because of the sizeable amount of goods and money we are putting into play, we want to get to know each other personally. It's a huge contract and perhaps that's why I don't want to lie to them: I didn't opt for a tie and dark suit. Instead, I arrived dressed in an old, faded, worn-out T-shirt and a worn pair of jeans. That's just the way I am. Anything else would be a sham.

We're sitting in the lounge, and I feel like I've gone a little overboard with the sincerity. The two young, very smartly dressed gentlemen in business suits are leafing through the contract and they're embarrassed.

"Yes, Mr Steel, you know," they explain, "we have tentatively agreed to pay you a thirty per cent advance, but after all... we don't know each other that well. We would welcome a small change to the contract, namely that the agreed price will be paid in full after the goods are delivered."

"Which is a sign of greater unprofessionalism, gentlemen: my unshaven face and poor choice of dress or your demands for a change in the terms of contract we have been negotiating for so long?"

The Castle Steps

I circle my empty glass on the tablecloth, waiting for an answer. I'm not backing down, I know it. They suspect it, but they're still trying.

"We are a reputable Czech company, sir. If we sign a contract with you with the stipulation that we pay the agreed price within thirty days of delivery of the goods, then you can rest assured that the money will be in your account within thirty days of delivery."

"I am a serious businessman, gentlemen. If we stick to the pre-arranged deposit, you can be sure that the goods will be delivered to you on the exact agreed delivery date."

"Your last word, sir?"

"Take it or leave it."

We've signed for a thirty per cent deposit here.

I know I've frayed their nerves a bit, but in about two months, on the agreed delivery date, they will receive the ordered goods of the highest quality. They'll be more than satisfied.

For today, however, I have excused myself from the next programme – lunch together followed by a social over wine. Only my head of sales will attend. I'm in a hurry to get to my favourite places – when will I have time to wander around Prague again?

I rush to the Vltava river, Charles Bridge, the castle steps. It's a beautiful sunny afternoon and thousands of sightseers have set out for the same destination as me. I don't mind. We're all in the same mood and we don't get in each other's way. On Charles Bridge, the crowd is packed like sardines and it's quite difficult to make your way through to the other side. I push my way through the crowd and between the souvenir stalls. When I can't go any farther, I lean against the sandstone blocks that form a protective railing, alternately watching the river below and the stream of sightseers rolling across the bridge.

The river murmurs and the bridge hums. I like it here. I love it. Strange: I, who have abandoned things and gazed at the inherent beauty of nature, feel comfortable in this setting. Perhaps it's true that, over the centuries, man's work turns to nature. It merges with it. It's as if for a million years this bridge has been growing into both riverbanks.

But it's when you look upwards, towards the horizon, that you're rewarded by a truly unforgettable panoramic sight. Over a thousand years, the gables of the magnificent Prague Hradčany Castle, the largest ancient castle complex in the world, has adorned a place on the hill in front your very eyes. Today, Prague Castle, besides being the seat of the head of state, is also an important cultural and historical monument, with St Vitus's Cathedral the most visited site in the complex.

But, seemingly unlike everyone else, I don't stop to view; I move on. I want to get to the castle steps – they are a particularly magical place for me. I don't know why; perhaps it's the romantic backdrop of steps lined with high walls, the image of which I have remembered for centuries. I walk down Mostecká Street, across Malostranské Square and continue along the narrow Zámecká Street; a little farther and I'm already climbing the first of the castle steps. There are a lot fewer sightseers here, only thinned-out groups pass me by and the occasional single person.

The Castle Steps

A group of teenage girls descends towards me, laughing and giggling.

I haven't quite made it to the top into the castle grounds. I don't want to go any farther. That's enough. I toss my cap and sit down on the step. It was worth the effort. I savour the sight of the red roofs of houses that those high walls allow me to see. I squint my eyes in the harsh sunlight but enjoy its warm rays.

Yes, I am in one of my dream places.

Time passes slowly here. Time, which determines everything, dictates everything, is afraid of these steps. It slows down, it doesn't rush down like great water; like honey, it flows down. It creeps through the streets through which I came and is swept away by the Vltava river. It rolls lazily in its waters, leaving the Old Town with them, and at the first rapids, goes wild and continues on its way.

I lean my back against a high brick wall and watch another small group of teenage girls coming down. Their legs glow out of their billowing skirts; *like roe deers going to the river to drink*, I thought. *Dancers.*

A silk scarf flutters over the girls' heads and waves a greeting to me. Was it a greeting? And did it belong to me? I suppose not. Just a mischievous gesture by one of them. But the scarf slipped from her hand and, carried by the air current, rose and fell, twirled and writhed, to then spread out on a cushion of air, stand still for a moment and then frolic again. No one chases it, no one misses it... so in the hands of my invisible dancer, it continues to dance above the castle steps.

My dreams are coming true. The dancer waves the scarf at me. It is a greeting, I'm certain now. After all, the young lady notices the loss and comes back those few steps. She runs briskly and bends down to retrieve the scarf, which the dancer has already fearfully put away. We look at each other; she frowns into my unshaven face and fidgets with her catch until her pale thighs are revealed for a split second by the fluttering skirt. I look past her, glad when she turns away quickly. Then she disappears from my view into the crowd.

I remain seated, leaning against the high brick wall. Time passes by, not hindering my dreams. I'm dreaming... projecting an image of those legs exposed for a second.

With a sense of beauty, I dream of beauty.

The number of sightseers has dwindled, only the occasional group or individual stomping down or huffing up. Now, at this moment, there is even complete silence. I close my eyes. No sound. Or is there? Yes, that familiar composition of the most natural sounds: the rustling in the branches of the trees that overhang the high wall on the other side, the chirping of birds, and the city humming darkly and monotonously below.

And suddenly, in the murmuring silence, there is the sound of footsteps. I'm listening. They're coming from below. They are breathless footsteps, and they certainly belong to a woman.

Clack, clack, clack – a young woman in expensive leather shoes.

That's how fate occurs, I think...

Footsteps rustle on the steps and then clack on the straight stretch. They're quite close when I can't stand it and open my eyes...

Dancer, is my first impression. A slender young woman. A lithe stride and her hair dancing into her eyes with each step. Short dark hair, a deep fringe, pale face and perhaps freckles on her cheeks. Eyes? I can't see their colour, though our gazes meet. I momentarily forget that I'm actually afraid of beautiful women, and stare – until eyes frown dismissively.

I lower my gaze apologetically. Footsteps whisper past, receding... one step, two, three... She pauses. I don't turn my head, worried that I'd have her calves at my eye level. I freeze. What's going to happen?

The unbelievable thing happens... Maybe I was expecting a rebuke for the long look, or that she would ask what time it was, or, 'Do you speak English?' Instead, her shoes clack two steps down... and coins clink in the cap I had tossed onto the step next to me.

"Try not to spend that money all at once," she says, already climbing the steps again.

I stare at her, stunned, unable to make any reaction. She wriggles her hips, moving away from me.

"Madame," I splutter at last, "this is a mistake, madame..."

She turns briefly and gives me a smile, convinced that my astonishment is caused by the amount of the gift. I stand up and look as she walks away. In a second, I dismiss the idea of running after her and explaining the confusion. I would only frighten her. I continue looking at her until she disappears from my sight.

I pick up the coins from my hat. Fifty-five koruna. Fifty-five Czech crowns. Two pounds sterling. I'd signed a contract for hundreds of thousands of euros a few hours ago and now I was getting a pittance of fifty-five crowns... I have to laugh.

I walk back down, and the coins jingle in my pocket. I think that the incident was fatefully extraordinary. The woman seemed special to me. Even if I had met her under different circumstances, on the street, in a restaurant, in a shopping centre... she would have caught my attention. I would have looked at her and hoped, believing in fate. I'd believe that somehow, we're all destined to meet someone on our path of life with whom we'll unwittingly fall in step. Someone we shouldn't just let go.

I get the nagging feeling that somewhere out there, beyond our comprehension, the foundation for one of a thousand stories may have been laid. My story. I want to believe it. No, I believe that her footsteps and mine fatefully led to the castle steps...

* * *

That evening, I'm sitting in the hotel bar with my Staropramen lager, and I close my eyes. I have an early flight back to Birmingham the next morning so I will have an early night. I warm the few coins in my palm. I imagine I'm home and looking out into the darkening garden and think of her. The dancer. Rusty lies at my feet, and somewhere in the back garden a mole is burrowing... and the sound of silence is the sound of my night fairy's dancing footsteps pressing into the lushness of the soft lawn. I give vent to my dreams. There are tiny steps and then a leap… She stops. A dancer.

The moment is silent with tension, only the branches of the trees rustling against the night sky. Softly now, footprints imprint in my direction before turning and slowly walking away. One step, two, three… they turn in a second, and in that second, my dancer's face is gone.

I'm kidding myself, I think.

I open my eyes.

The episode stirred the surface of my life. It was the kind of tingle you get when you managed to skim a pebble over the surface of the water. Wheels on the water they formed by that action, racing along the surface until they gradually disappeared, I thought. My mind, momentarily agitated, also quietens. It's calm again, as if nothing had ever happened. Only the image of this beautiful woman, like the motionless pebble on the water's bottom, lies in my memory.

Chapter 4

"May I speak to you?" Aisling asked Eddy quietly, and went on at once, without waiting for an answer, perhaps fearing that the old man would forbid her. "You have a magnificent house; I confess, I didn't expect that—"

"Did it not occur to you that the man who made you such an indecent proposal might have a decent home?" Eddy interrupted, with a smile.

"No," she hissed guiltily. "Sorry, I was afraid it would be more like a dump, and you'd be a fat…" She searched for a word that wouldn't offend. "Gentleman."

"Yet you came."

She remained silent.

Silence fell over the room. Only the ticking of the antique grandfather clock that stood in the corner of the room suddenly broke the silence. But only to enhance it and create the tension she had been dreading.

"I need the money…" She kneaded her sweaty palms and was about to add something else to drown out the sound of the clock, but the old man raised his hand and held up his index finger, a clear gesture that all had already been said.

"Good. Okay then..." she repeated nervously. "Are we going to do it here?"

He didn't answer. He just waved his hand, like a conductor making a grand gesture to encourage the musicians to come forward.

"All right. Very well then."

She remained seated in the deep leather chair, avoiding his gaze with anxiety in her eyes. She didn't want to see the old man with the old face and shrivelled up skin she suddenly feared.

"But only for me to take my clothes off. Nothing more. That's what we agreed, isn't it...?"

Eddy remained silent.

This isn't going to end well, she thought. *He'll want more,* she realised now. *Why did I just come here? Why! Why did you come here? Because I desperately need the money. I desperately need money!*

She unconsciously licked her lips, but immediately realised it might have looked alluring. *Oh, no!* She took a deep breath. She mustn't show him she was afraid. Maybe that's what he was waiting for. Maybe that's what turns him on.

It was silence in the darkness of the room, punctuated by the ticking of the old clock. Only the light flickering through the drawn blinds portrayed two figures sitting in leather armchairs, facing each other. If you were to frame this scene, the painting would be titled *The Old Man and the Girl*.

In the silence of the room, an unbuttoned shirt rustled. Clearly one button... and a pause, and a glance into his eyes; hers are wide open and his are calm.

A second button, a third…

"I wear a padded bra, and I'm not wearing a thong, but another time I will—"

A raised hand and forefinger: all has been said.

She stood up and pulled the shirt off her shoulders. The straps of her bra slipped from her shoulders. She smiled as she undid the clasp behind her back in that uniquely feminine way, and the bra fell onto the floor. Standing upright, she took off her jeans and underwear, standing before him naked. She watched his face and… smiled at him.

The clock was ticking, but the ticking suddenly didn't seem ominous.

The seconds ticked by. She counted them; twenty more to the minute, ten more…

She remained standing upright. The dim light multiplied her beauty. She knew it.

The seconds ticked by. She wasn't counting them anymore. A minute? Two? Three?

She could hear his heavy breathing in the silence of the room, punctuated by the ticking of the clock.

"You're letting me have more than we agreed. I don't deserve that," Eddy said.

"What makes you think that?" She smiled at him. "You had your eyes closed all the time I had my clothes off. You weren't looking."

Chapter 5

Today, Aisling walked up the castle steps slower than usual. She was on an extended lunch break but couldn't make herself go back to her company's office just yet. She needed to somehow resolve the nagging sense of self-loathing she had. *How far have I fallen? What am I doing selling myself, and my body, for money?*

Back home in the UK, a couple of nights ago, I went to this old man's house where I obligingly took all my clothes off. To pleasure him, and only for money, of course. Just for money, I risked being beaten and violently raped by him, being killed. But it turned out well, nothing bad happened to me… but it could have! He could have come at me with a knife to my throat and forced himself onto me. He could have rolled his ugly body all over me and his breath would've stank…

She shuddered in disgust.

What am I doing? How far have I sunk? Am I going to feel this way each and every time after prostituting my body to oblige a different client? But what can I do? I know that I have no other choice. How else, other than as being an up-market escort, am I going to get this kind of money quickly? No one will lend me a large amount of money because I'm already mortgaged to the hilt on my apartment. Each and every time I see a new client, I risk being violently raped by these old, and some not so old, men in their hotel rooms, or in their homes while their wives are out. Because if I don't, my life is over. I'll lose my job and end up in jail because I embezzled thousands of pounds from my employer. Forty-five thousand, to be exact, which I had taken out in cash from the fund account safe, and I have to pay back before they find out.

It turned out well a couple of nights ago, I got lucky…

With a fleeting sense of satisfaction, she carried on climbing the castle steps. She passed a sitting beggar, cap on the step next to him, begging for beer money. It wasn't until she passed him that she realised he wasn't quite so lucky today. His cap was empty. She walked back down those two steps and tossed him all the small coins she had in her purse. Not pushing her luck, she praised herself mentally. *I'm going to need it.*

* * *

Only the image of the pretty woman, like the motionless pebble beneath the water's surface, lies in my memory. Yes, I think of her often, no longer with a troubled mind. I've let go of the sense of fatality of that encounter. Of course, no foundation for our story was laid, and our steps were certainly not fatally led to the castle steps. I only wished it at that moment. I wished it so much, for it was she. She with a capital 'D'. The Dancer. The dancer of my dreams. Slender body and legs, flat-chested, and narrow, swaying hips… *clack, clack, clack*… hair falling into her eyes. Come on, fate!

Actually, it did. I was blessed to meet the woman of my dreams. How many men can say that? I was treated to twenty seconds I'll never forget for the rest of my life. That's it.

And my life goes on. I carry on making hundreds of thousands of pounds more each and every month. And yet I kneel in the flowering rockery, weeding the soil and stroking the flowers with my dirty fingers, and in the evening… In the evening I sit on my expensive patio chair, and I warm the few coins in my palm. I look over the darkening garden and think of her. Rusty lies at my feet, and somewhere out there, a mole burrows… and to the sound of silence, the footsteps of my night fairy are pressed into the soft density of the lawn. As I give vent to my dreams, there are tiny steps and then a leap… She stops.

My night fairy, the dancer.

Chapter 6

I've been making improvements to my house. For almost a month, workmen were here. They were replacing the standard-sized patio door, leading from the living room out onto the patio, with a large, panoramic seven section door. It involved installing a large, long RSJ beam to span the new opening and support the existing brickwork. I was worried about kitsch, as was the case with the pool, but I don't think it happened.

So the garden of green tussocks, trees and shrubs, and the still blooming rock garden entered through the patio, full of flowerpots, through that huge glass patio door and into the house. During the day, the room is flooded with sunlight, unless I draw the blinds. But later, if the patio door and the blinds are opened, side and long shadows and damp scents enter the abode in the evening. A magical atmosphere is created so conducive to unusual thoughts. Then I perceive the splendour and wonder of how it could have come into being.

I see the sky full of stars and think of the universe. Distant worlds. The universe. *On which of those worlds is there a garden like this?* I wonder. There, on that little star, just one among thousands I see, maybe there is one, fragrant and just as blooming. Who knows.

From the armchair in the living room, I watch the world through my large patio doors. I can see the blanket of flowers on the terrace and the still coloured rockery and a bit of green lawn beyond. Just a bit, because the rest is lost in the dark shadows of the lawns. And beyond that I can just make out the trees and bushes, and above them the dark sky full of stars. I can see the whole world.

Even as a schoolboy, and later as a college student, I used to paint, and I was quite good at it. I went and bought paints and a selection of brushes, and I'm trying to get back into it. I'm trying to capture that magical atmosphere, the coming dusk. But I can't do it, I remind myself slowly, throwing away one sheet of paper after another, hoping that after a while, perhaps I will. I repeat the same motif over and over again: the flood of flowers in the foreground and the darkening green of the grass, bushes and trees, and above that the dark sky dotted with stars. It's not easy at all to paint flowers to be flowers, trees to be trees, but the hardest part is capturing the mood of the scene. To capture the fading light that no longer has the power to reach the corners of the garden, to capture the waning of the day and the triumph of the night, and also the sadness that spreads. Twilight.

But I enjoy it, I've completely fallen for it, and I paint in every spare moment. And what really pleases me, when I look at my latest attempts, is that I'm getting better. I take a step back from the drawing board and... there it is. The flowers are flowers, and the trees are trees, and even

– and this is what I'm most happy about – there's at least a hint of the mood I was trying to capture. The painting is brooding, quiet and somehow smells of a garden.

I'm trying to paint on canvas and I'm actually starting again. Only slowly is my hand remembering my earlier skill. I also bought a few books on drawing to educate myself. It's fun. Painting brings me satisfaction. The paintings I create I would be reluctant to show anyone. They are probably naive in content and execution, but I enjoy them. I paint mainly the garden. Not just the magical view from the living room anymore, but also the view from the other side, from the lawn towards the house, where the rock garden is the dominant feature, and the blossoming terrace is in the background. Even behind it there is the house with a large patio door that reflects the whole garden, and that patio door actually becomes the painting I have been trying so hard to achieve.

I try to remember the dancer's face. Short hair, a fringe falling into her eyes that are not dark, perhaps light grey, or blue… and a smile. I want to capture on canvas her expression when she turned to me in that second: the hair that swung into her eyes, the smile that so charmed me, and the figure, erect and slender and lithe as a cat's body. Feeling a slight shiver, I try to find the curves of her body and the shape of her face.

I'm not satisfied. No, it's not her. I throw away one attempt after another. A figure? It's not easy to capture her at all, but the face is even harder. There was no mercy in that face, there was not a prior kindness that is evident in my last sketch. I'm on the wrong track, I realise. I let the circumstances of our encounter get the better of me. I have forgotten that the smile was preceded by an expression of defiance. When our eyes first met, she frowned. Yes, she frowned, and I looked away. But before I looked away, in that last split second... no, it wasn't defiance, it wasn't anger, it was sadness.

I carry on painting, and I paint, and paint. More attempts. It's exciting. It's like we're walking towards each other, and the meeting is within reach.

I step back from my last painting. I think I'm close. It emerges from the fog of my memories.

Chapter 7

The fund was set up by Mr Wang. Perhaps he originates from the large and densely populated Xinjiang region in China, or from Hong Kong – no one knows. No one knows his full name properly, either. He has lived in Leicester for many years, running a thriving business, and to everyone, including all his employees, he is Mr Wang. He owns several companies. It's said that he made an absolute fortune from North Sea gas supplies and North Sea oil supply fraud. He also lent money on a mammoth scale and charged a huge amount of interest, which he then collected in harsh ways. When he accumulated those millions, and he laundered all that money in his companies, something stirred in him, and he started a fund to help cancer patients called the CRO Foundation. Why CRO? Does it stand for Cancer Research Organisation, or Clinical Research Organisation? Who knows. He never explained it to anyone. So it remains plain CRO Foundation.

Mr Wang remains such a mysterious character.

Well, at the time the fund was founded, Aisling was applying for a job in one of his companies, and she was given a really unusual opportunity when Mr Wang personally offered her the position of manager of the fund. A really top-notch job. Head office located in Leicester, not far from the cathedral, with its remains of King Richard III, and with another, smaller office in Prague, at the top end of St Wenceslas Square. She has her own well-appointed, modern offices at both locations where she is her own boss. She's the only one who pays Mr Wang's bills; no one else does that.

When she first sat down in the leather chair behind the massive desk and read on the computer the directive with her job description, she alternated between feeling ecstatic and apprehensive.

What had she done to deserve it? She had left Oxford University with a first class honours degree in economics and management, but no experience, and suddenly she was going to be managing a multi million pound fund. She was going to find sponsors, convince them and negotiate the amount of sponsorship. She was going to persuade hospital managers and also Foreign Office buyers – the government – to purchase from them various equipment and supplies for different hospitals and Foreign Office oversees departments. She was to negotiate with various suppliers to give her discounts and concessions. A top-notch luxury job for such a young woman.

Aisling realises that her looks played a big part in landing the job. She knows full well that she's attractive. She always has been. She's flattered by the looks men give her and the words of beauty, elegance and grace they utter in real amazement at her looks.

But sometimes her beauty bothers her. Like now. She knows she didn't get this job because she was qualified for it, but because of her cute little face and her perfect figure. Should she despair? *What would another person give to get it?* she thinks to herself. *It's a dream job, and any one of the applicants would be ecstatic and jumping with joy to land it.*

Yes, sometimes her beauty bothers her. Maybe that's part of the reason she's always alone. Men are attracted by her, but they are also afraid of her. They don't dare to have a long relationship with her. So far, they've all run away. Each one left something behind. The scars on her body and soul, a few books on the bedside table and dirty socks in the bathroom... after the last one, hell, gambling and debt.

It was he, Nigel, her great love, who first introduced her to the gambling circuit and showed her the tantalising flashing machines.

"In this magical darkness, just in the light of those machines, you are by far the most beautiful woman here," he told her. And when they were alone in the darkened far corner of the gambling room, he would approach her from behind, put his arms around her and whisper the same words in her ear as he lifted up her skirt and stroked her inner thighs. His hands would stray up to her lap, and Aisling, sitting on a stool in front of the gambling machine, would succumb to the gentle touches and spread those thighs as wide as she could, for his pleasure and her own, and in the knowledge that they were also being watched on a security camera.

They gambled together. It lasted quite a long time. Six months. A record.

Then, all of a sudden, he packed his bags and left.

She never got used to the pain of break-ups. On the contrary, each one hurt more and this last one hurt the most.

Only the gambling machines always made her feel a little better. Here, in the captivating darkness of the casino, the memories came, here were the smells and the clinking and the clanking sounds. No, at first, she hadn't cared about money at all. Perhaps she didn't even want to win. She inserted tokens, coins and notes, indifferent about losing them. She just wanted that moment of happiness back, just wanted to light up and make the machine hum with colours and tones that evoked memories of Nigel. It was working. The machine blazed and sounded cosmic, and Aisling, upright on the stool in front of the machine, sucked in the resulting fluid and only moaned softly when she dreamily felt warm palms on her legs…

Only later did the awakening come. Later, when it was too late. In the epiphany and panic that had taken hold of her, she played on. She needed to erase the debt she had incurred when she had recklessly 'borrowed' money from the fund's coffers. What a vanity. Deeper and deeper she sank into trouble.

Often her dreams came back to her at night.

The lion is chasing the doe. They both run and run, zigzag, jump over bushes, stones. For a while, it seems that the doe will save herself, the distance from the pursuer lengthens… but then she stumbles unhappily, and the hunt is over. The lion catches up with its victim but doesn't pounce on it, doesn't immediately crush the neck of the poor animal with its powerful jaws. The unexpected happens. The lion lies down a short distance away from the trapped doe and they both exhale sharply. They look at each other and rest after the chase. It's as if it's not a race of life and death, but just a friendly rivalry between two animals.

Death will come, but it will wait a little longer…

I'm going to run away too; I'm going to run with all my strength, zigzagging and jumping over obstacles, Aisling thinks, when the terrifying dream wakes her up. *I must not stumble! Or has it already happened? Have I fallen? Am I lying down, and Mr Wang is standing over me? Does he know? Does he know I'm stealing from him? Has the beast caught up with me and is resting before he clenches his fangs? Will he kill me? Yes, he'll kill me!*

She wants to scream, but she just sighs softly, her eyes fixed on the flames shining through the blinds, like the eyes of a beast.

Chapter 8

I flew to Prague to be present at the delivery. I don't usually do this, leaving this job to my staff, but in this case, I'd felt obliged to be there. Perhaps I was a little remorseful, and with hindsight I'd found my behaviour towards these Czech associates stupid and disrespectful. So, I'd put on a dark suit and shaved, and I'd tied my long hair into a ponytail as I was loathe to cut it. This, combined with wearing the suit, gave me the appearance of an extravagant conductor.

The two male buyers were waiting for me at the airport. They offered to meet me there, and with that Czech calmness, dressed casually in jeans and a smart jacket, without the need for any words, it was a moment of silent reflection. It let the sympathetic contrast of the confusion of our styles shine through.

In good humour they drove me to the hotel. There, once more, they indulged me in more proverbial Czech humour. In answer to their question 'who's Rusty?', which they asked me in response to my telephone call to my Market Harborough neighbours. When I replied that it was an old dog, they accepted the information with the laconic remark that 'there weren't many dogs in the Czech Republic who were able to make a telephone call'.

Later that day, I handed over six large lorries with trailer load consignments of cardboard packaging, which were already waiting at their premises. We signed the handover protocols. As I expected, they were satisfied.

We had dinner together, and it was initially an evening of casual conversation, the kind of terse humour I like so much, where a joke is often 'finished' with a glance, a raised eyebrow or a gesture. Only a slight shadow flickered when I was caught off guard by Pavel's equally brusque question, "Wife or girlfriend?"

I responded with a look so unhappily accompanied by a stiff smile that it immediately revealed to those perceptive boys just how vulnerable a subject this was for me. Not even my wannabe witty reply of, "No, thanks, I'm still happy single..." could save it and we never went back to it.

But then we got drunk. We downed many pints of Staropramen, followed also by more pints of Pilsner Urquell, and ending up finishing off a bottle of Becherovka between the three of us. Simply put, gentle humour was replaced by stupid humour. No, we weren't vulgar, nor did we insult anyone, we just neighed like horses at every stupid thing and were loud enough to shout over a nearby table of Russians – but it must be said that we were a few lagers up on them.

* * *

The Castle Steps

In the hotel room the witches seemed to be dancing around my bed and in my head. Yes, I was in a drunken stupor. I ripped the elastic band off my ponytail and shook my hair out straight, so that I must have looked like one of the witches. They tempted me to dance wildly. But I fell into bed fully clothed, closed my eyes to escape the witches' rants, and before I passed out – no, it definitely wasn't sleep – it occurred to me that these thoughts were creating electromagnetic waves that propagate in spheres through the infinite universe. Now, if it's 'her', the dancer, we're on the same frequency and our waves are coherent. It could be that somewhere in the depths of the universe, the spheres of our thoughts touch, interfere… and our minds connect. I haven't figured out the rest of that stupid thing.

I dreamt about Rusty all night.

Chapter 9

The Vltava is the river flowing through Prague. Even here, the masses of water roll in silent amazement because they were in these places for the first time. Few of the waters have been here before; they have evaporated here and fallen again in the form of raindrops in an endless cycle.

But I am here for the umpteenth time. I just love being here.

I walk along the waterfront and stare into the water. The river flows through the city, passing through time as it remembers many events in a long history…

Just like Tower Bridge over the Thames, Charles Bridge over the Vltava allows the water to flow underneath it, exactly the same as it's been already doing for many centuries.

I'll be returning back here again, and again…

* * *

On my return from Prague, I rush to my painting. Like a smoker craving a cigarette, like an alcoholic in urgent need of his drink, I have an urge and a physical need to paint. I'm fascinated by the white surface of the canvas. I don't even know exactly what I'm going to create on it yet. I'm just looking, not thinking, waiting to see what my heart tells me. Today, it won't be a landscape, or a garden, or a terrace with pots of flowers…

I set up my easel in the living room, right next to the panoramic patio doors, to take advantage of the light of the already fading day, at least for a while longer. With my eyes darting from the canvas to the living room chairs, I make my first brush-strokes.

I know now. I can see it now, feel it. It's going to be a dancer.

No, I will not paint her as I did before, as an ethereal being in an indeterminate space, I will paint her as a real, beautiful woman who is with me in this room.

Tonight I won't be alone, she'll be here with me. We'll talk, we'll laugh…

This evening will be happy.

I'm painting quickly but surely. I paint with my heart, not with my head. All that which is fermented in me, all that which is tormenting me, all that in me which is filled with longing in Prague, all this I transform into a feeling that guides my hand.

Yes, that's it. Go on.

My hand doesn't falter. It's steady, as steady as it was almost forty years ago when I started painting. I don't fail a single stroke.

Time is running out. I don't pay much attention to it. It's dark outside and I've moved the easel from the patio doors to the lamp in the corner of the living room. I've slowed my pace, but I keep going. Tonight I'll just finish the painting, my idea. I have to. I won't be alone today.

I couldn't accomplish that; it was well past midnight when I finished. But it was done. I painted the picture. I painted my dream, my desire; everything I wished for was expressed in that painting. Although, looking back, there is not much in it: two figures sitting in chairs facing each other, one of them an extraordinarily beautiful woman, the other figure being me, and in the background of the scene a large grandfather clock, which I had imagined was to create an atmosphere of peace, tranquillity and silence.

I'm standing back a little, looking at my work. It's not bad. It's a good one. The dancer sits upright, one hand resting on the back of her chair, the other, just the backs of her fingers, supporting her chin. Is she thinking? Listening? I've portrayed myself quite faithfully. I recognise myself. Grey hair pulled back in a ponytail and wrinkles on my face. I'd be lying to myself if I didn't make my figure hunch up slightly…

I'm looking at my work. I'm waiting for the reward for the effort. I expect a feeling of satisfaction, a warmth…

It doesn't come.

Nothing.

On the contrary, I'm a middle-aged man. I shouldn't be, but I'm a bitter, middle-aged man. I can see it in the painting. I portrayed myself in the presence of a very beautiful young woman, creating a contrast that stung.

The grandfather clock, it's supposed to convey peace, quiet and serenity, but so far… time.

Disappointed, I take the painting off the pedestal. Rusty watches me silently.

Before I put it away in the utility room where I store my creations, I write in pencil on the back of it: *Middle aged man and a girl.*

Chapter 10

Aisling watches Eddy's face. It's calm and composed; not a muscle moves in that face, not even the closed eyelids flutter. The deep wrinkles on the forehead, around the eyes and mouth do not disfigure that face. Together with the thinning grey hair – which is carefully cut and combed, and only in a little disobedience has become loose in a few strands over the forehead – they give the face an expression of dignity and self-discipline. Eddy, an old man, sitting in the chair opposite, wearing grey trousers and a light-coloured shirt with the sleeves rolled up above the wrists, seems to Aisling at once quite sympathetic.

She hadn't noticed that when she was first here. Her eyes, dilated with fear, saw him differently. His calmness seemed ominous to her. Not now. She may be sitting naked from her waist up and defenceless in front of him again, but she's not afraid. On the contrary. She watches his still face, and suddenly she feels rather sorry for him. She knows now that she has before her a man who has understood that he has put all this beauty of the world behind him. She just wants to smell him, just to touch him with her thoughts... Aisling knows that he feels and senses her warmth, and behind his closed eyelids, a film of the most beautiful moments of his life is running.

She leans in, reaches out and touches his knee.

"Open your eyes, I'm here for you."

Slowly, he lifted his hand from the back of the chair, propped his chin up with his fingers, and looked. He looked directly into her eyes, not for a second slipping his gaze to the breasts that Aisling, still bent over, offered him in the most beautiful image. He smiled kindly.

Aisling smiled too. She remained in that position for a few seconds, in a kind of emotional determination to please the old man. She wasn't sure of the result. He didn't move his eyes.

She straightened up in her chair.

"I am here for you," she repeated kindly.

"I know, I'm paying you for it."

They were both silent for a moment.

"What do you need the money for?"

"I'm in some trouble, but I'd rather not talk about it." Aisling sighed, disappointed that the subject had come up.

"You don't have to explain, of course. I can imagine how worried you must be…"

"That I'm experiencing all this?"

"Yes, that you are experiencing all this."

Feeling suddenly ashamed, Aisling unconsciously put her hand across her breasts and reached for her bra with her other hand.

"Are you mocking me?"

"I don't know which one of us is more laughable."

That put her at ease.

"Can I get dressed?" she asked softly.

He didn't answer right away, and for perhaps the first time, his gaze lingered on her breasts.

"I could lend you money. How much do you need?"

The bra hand paused.

"And you'll then expect more of me?" she whispered after a moment. "More than just to get naked?"

"Yes, I will," he replied dryly.

"Going all the way?"

"Going all the way."

"Without a condom?"

"Without a condom."

"I owe forty-five thousand pounds…"

He looked her calmly in the eye, unmoved by the information.

"I can't let you have that much, but I can lend you ten thousand right now." And then he added, to make it perfectly clear to her, "You can pay me back later, when you have money to spare."

She returned his direct gaze long and wordlessly. Then she stood up, unzipped her skirt, slowly wriggled it over her narrow hips, and let it slide to the floor. She stepped forward and pushed the skirt aside with the tip of her high heel shoes. Then she slipped down her legs the thong, standing before him completely naked.

I will do it, her mind went. She'd known from the first moments of tonight that she was going to do it. She had already made up her mind that she was going to let Eddy go all the way even if she wasn't going to be lent the money.

Chapter 11

I'm an old man's comforter, Aisling told herself as she drove home from Eddy's house in the up-market village of Church Brampton near Northampton. It was way past midnight. A short while ago she had toyed with the idea of staying with Eddy overnight, but then decided she'd better leave. Strangely enough, she didn't have such a low esteem of herself as she had the first time she had visited him. This time there was no longer the feeling of disgust, or the need for a long soak in the bath afterwards…

Eddy. The old man was Eddy. He was over forty-five years older than she was. One more record. She felt like laughing.

She had ten thousand five hundred pounds in cash in her handbag laying on the passenger seat of her car. Five hundred pounds were for services rendered. It would have been five hundred more had she spent the night with him. Being a high class escort paid really well…

Eddy had kept his promise and lent her the money. She didn't have to sign anything, she didn't have to swear an oath, she didn't have to do anything more than what they'd already done. She'll pay him back. She'll pay him back someday, but she'll not go to visit him again as an escort. He didn't want her to visit him as an escort again, either, as she could tell when they parted. He was too wise to ruin the good times of last night by trying to make any sort of sequel.

In her bedroom, which was also her dressing room, she undressed and entered the bathroom in only a light robe. When she'd furnished this apartment, she hadn't given any of the rooms as much care as she had the bathroom. Her pride and jewel. She had spared no expense here. Not a lot of floor space, perhaps some forty square feet, but the Italian marble cost an arm and a leg. A standard-sized bath – there was no room for any other – and a folding shower screen to one side of the bath taps. A large frameless mirror above the sink with gold-plated taps, hangers of the same material, all perfectly coordinated, not by an architect's hand, but by her heart guiding the hands of the craftsmen.

She remained standing in front of the large mirror, the light above it tinting her hair the colour of those golden rosettes of the basin faucet. She thought of Eddy… of Eddy? Nigel? Suddenly she wasn't sure. Her memories swirled shut, and out of the swirl came the face of an old man who intrigued her. Was it Eddy? Was it Eddy after all? Her memory lapse made her feel ill.

She looked at her own face, and after a while she was satisfied with it again. Still, she reached for the dimmer switch and flipped it, which allowed her to dim the light, until even the little wrinkles by her eyes had all disappeared. Then she untied the belt of her robe, pulled it off her shoulders, and her naked body lit up with that dim light above the mirror, exposing itself to the reflection in the mirror like an angelic apparition…

It didn't matter, she thought. It was lovely, strangely exciting, but fleeting. It was kind of satisfying, like skimming a pebble on the surface of the water. Wheels are formed by this. They run over the surface of the water until they gradually disappear…

She thought of this with a strange smile.

* * *

Mr Wang carefully placed the cash-book and the cash box, containing large used notes in sterling, back into the safe. This was built into the wall of the office at floor level. Then, just as carefully, he slid the leather chair to the desk exactly where it had been before he sat down in it. When he reached the door of the office, he turned around and checked to make sure there were no traces of his late night visit to Aisling's office.

There are some 'sharp guys' who have it written all over their faces, and it's a small advantage that when you meet them, you know immediately who you're dealing with. Mr Wang's past certainly allowed him to be considered one of the sharp guys, but anyone who didn't know it would never guess that this fit, mild-mannered, good-looking man with smiling eyes could be considered in any way dangerous. But he is very dangerous. It's this combination of good looks and cold, ruthless thinking that has enabled him to acquire a vast fortune.

He's known for a little while that Aisling is helping herself to cash from the safe. He could have put a stop to it long ago and use tried and tested methods to get his money back, but he's waiting. He knows her assets; he knows where he can let her go. He's also intrigued that she returned ten grand to the cash box a few days ago. Where did she get it? He'd made it a priority to find out that she frequented casinos and gambling parlours; he also knows she doesn't win that much. He needs to find out. His predatory instinct tells him that this clue promises fatter prey.

Chapter 12

I sold my customised Maybach because I felt it wasn't me. Not, perhaps, because of people who can't buy such an expensive, luxury car, or because of the envious looks some of them give me. I didn't want to stand out in this way. I sold it for feeling guilty about myself, as I was betraying the beliefs I had which came with that car. I've come to realise that nature is my only and true value, and that it was the plants and flowers in my prized rockery and the butterflies that flitted over them that really mattered. The buzzing of insects and the birds chirping in the tree branches were the only things that made sense. I got rid of the car because I also felt guilty about its high emissions and what it's doing to the environment. I felt guilty about the dead animals and birds that are crushed by the wheels of cars every day. I also felt guilty for us, as a race, for building all the motorways, roads, bypasses, and car parks that deal mortal blows to the landscape. They are built only to make cars like my Maybach go faster, faster, and faster still… but to where? Where am I going in such a hurry? To work? Shopping? Somewhere in the countryside? To the seaside? It's so laughable that I could cry.

I ride my bicycle from Market Harborough to my factory in Corby on most days, otherwise I work from home, and I continue looking for answers to all these questions. I don't want the money I made selling the car. I don't need it. I know that it won't save the world, that nothing will change. I also know that new roads will continue to be built, and more and more hedgehogs, rabbits, foxes and badgers will perish under the wheels of the cars and lorries. I also know that the world will continue to go down these ecologically slippery slopes, but I have decided to donate the money from the sale of the car to some victims of 'progress' and try to make my small contribution for a better world. I donated lots of money to cat and dog charities and animal protection groups that I found on the internet and offered to help financially. I donated a relatively large chunk of money to the RSPCA as they are the largest animal welfare trust in the UK, also to the PDSA and the National Animal Welfare Trust. But, in spite of my eccentric and critical views, I've never stopped loving people. That's why I also donated a large amount to a charity to help cancer research – the CRO Foundation.

Chapter 13

It's a beautiful Indian summer and perhaps the string of sunny days is the reason I am thinking of her again. Thoughts of the dancer come in waves, when a period of oblivion caused by a lot of work and all kinds of responsibilities is replaced by feelings of emptiness, loneliness and sadness. It's this vacant space she enters. I let her enter. I call her in. I call her in to comfort me.

I take out the painting of the middle-aged man and the girl, which I store in the utility room, and I look at it. A straight back and leg over leg. High-heeled shoes form her feet and calves into a graceful curve, and this flows into the tantalising line of her thighs… I confront the curves of her body captured by the drawing with the image stored in my memory.

Such beauty.

These images have awakened the man in me. The movement of her legs and the undulations of her narrow hips as she ascended the castle steps flash torturously and insistently before my eyes. I don't restrain my imagination, and in my mind, I transform the drawing into a kind of comic strip. It's there that the dancer's fingers – a moment ago lightly supporting her chin – undo the buttons of her blouse, one by one, until the last one is undone... and the blouse slides off her shoulders.

I close my eyes to escape the tantalising scene, but I can't help but feel the warmth of the bared flesh as even the bra falls into her lap... I shake my head to banish the vision until my long strands of grey hair have become the mane of an old, solitary lion.

"Oh my God," escapes my lips.

Only after a moment do I reflect on my sigh.

Yes, I'm an atheist, but sometimes it's hard to be one.

* * *

The lion has caught the doe was the first thing that ran through Aisling's mind as she stared, deathly silent, at the door of the floor-level office wall safe. The thin, almost invisible slither of Sellotape she had stuck across one corner of the door to the frame had become unstuck. Also, the objects she had strategically scattered on the floor in front of the safe had been moved to enable the door to open.

She had set this trap because she had an uncomfortable feeling about the safe... and now, there is a clear indication that someone had opened it late last night, or perhaps the night before. She looked around the empty and eerily silent office apprehensively. Was she really alone in here? What would happen now? What was next? She started to despair.

It couldn't be anyone but Mr Wang. He must have checked the cash in the safe against the cash ledger and couldn't help but notice that there was a shortfall of forty-five thousand pounds. *He'll have me about that, that's for sure. But what next? Will he hit me? Beat me up? Kill me? What can I expect from this mobster?*

She put the cash box back into the safe, locked it and set the trap again.

The late summer sunlight streaming in through the office window couldn't help her forget the anxiety that gripped her heart. Not even the butterfly that had wandered into the office and was perched on the window frame, displaying itself in colourful splendour, could dispel her gloom.

Eddy, flashed through her mind. *Eddy, help me... I'm a trapped doe.* She picked up her mobile phone and pondered if she should call him. *What would it achieve? Ask him for more money? Offer myself to him again?* She watched the butterfly that seemed to breathe with its wings, opening them in full glory and closing them again, opening and closing, slowly, repeatedly, in time with her breathing. *No;* she put the phone down. *I can't do that. It's a lot of money. He certainly doesn't have that much in cash, and even if he did, he won't lend it, and even if he wanted to lend it... I can't accept it because I'd be paying it back for years. I'm like a trapped doe... but I'd like to be that butterfly and fly away from the claws and fangs of the beast.*

* * *

The ping of an incoming email message snapped her out of her heavy thoughts.

She clicked it open.

I would like to make a significant contribution to your fund. Please send me a donation agreement, together with a Gift Aid declaration form for a single donation to a UK charity.
  Sincerely – Russell Steel.

A significant contribution. How much did Mr Steel have in mind? She mused unperturbed as she promptly sent the donation form with the charity Gift Aid declaration and thanked him in advance. Five thousand? Ten thousand? She knew from experience that it would probably be that much. As a rule, it was the parents of sick children, who had witnessed the hell of treatment, who donated contributions like this. Perhaps they want to atone for a cruel fate, but their outgoings are already so decimated by expensive private treatment that they can't afford to send more. High profit companies and wealthy businessmen have to be persuaded; they will usually contribute, and not just a little, but they have to be enticed by various events and also a promise of wide publicity for their charitable action. A voluntarily and unselfishly given 'significant amount'… it was never going to be a large amount.

Those few minutes of work distraction did put her mind at ease, after all. *Wouldn't it be better if I called Mr Wang, asked for a meeting, and tried to explain everything to him? He won't call the police as this is laundered money, and I probably won't escape the sack either, but maybe he'll understand and give me a chance to pay the money back. No*; she dismissed it out of hand.

The rumours surrounding Mr Wang gave no hope. She'd be enslaved. She'd be his slave for years, and his plaything. He'll suck her dry, wring her dry, and kill her in a slow death, but not before she satisfies his sexual fantasies. Or, in the spirit of underworld morality, he'll kill her now. After all, she stole from her master, and that's unforgivable.

Eddy. Eddy! she screams in her inner voice, outwardly silent and helpless. *You are my only hope.* She thinks again about the choice she has made. *Or shall I try to recover this shortfall in the casino?* The devil suddenly awakens, embedded in the furthest recesses of her mind. Bet it all? On the red, or on the black?

She puts the phone away. *Bet it all*, whispers the devil, who took the tiny opportunity to take over the whole brain. Yes, it was him and not Aisling who put the phone down. And now, in her eyes, he spins the roulette wheel and puts the ball on the lucky number or colour… how irresistibly beautiful the solution is. You see?

Aisling's eyes remained glued to the computer monitor. But then she held her breath as it was Aisling again who clicked on the incoming message. Mr Steel. She was surprised at how quickly the man handled his business. A completed gift aid declaration form and a terse cover letter: …*You may scan the signed agreement and send it to me for signature. You will receive it signed and I will pay the donation by bank transfer.* He's fiddling with it; he could have sent the money straight into the account. What's the point of a donation agreement? She glanced at the amount, and it took her breath away. She stared in disbelief at the amount. Fifty thousand pounds. A huge donation!

Chapter 14

The long-tailed black and white sprightly bird, a pied wagtail, was perched on the bird feeder, his tail wagging absent-mindedly. Suddenly, and to my surprise, he fluttered down to the patio table where I was sitting, just inches from the coffee mug. Without stopping wagging his tail, he cocked his head to the side and looked into my eyes with the bead of his eye. I didn't breathe, I didn't blink, just so I wouldn't alarm him.

The movement of his tail is in time with the seconds. I counted them in my head: twenty more to the minute, ten more… and I don't really know why. A strange silence has fallen. Only the ticking of the long tail emerged from the silence, but only to amplify it and create the tension I was afraid of… I exhaled, scaring away the wagtail and the shadow in my mind.

What was it that disturbed me? I wonder. *What did I see in the dark bead of my eye?* I don't know. Perhaps the singularity of the moment, the confrontation with uncommon perfection, the unexpected reminder of nature in all its simple complexity. And also, like a glimpse of eternity.

Or perhaps I saw myself in that beaded mirror? The image of a lonely, middle-aged man.

A middle-aged man and a girl... I was reminded.

It's strange how strongly this tiny incident affected me. This is what happens to solitary men. They sit in silence, undisturbed by anything or anyone, and in their overwhelming loneliness they are open to unusual thoughts and unusual incidents. Then they are rewarded with the company of a small bird or butterfly, and they hear silence and see darkness and reach infinity and glimpse eternity.

I have a new painting. I painted it on the evening when the wild horses of my imagination ran wild inside me, when the dancer undressed... just a horny man pouring out his desire on the canvas. No, not an orgy. I didn't abuse my ability to almost perfectly portray the dancer, the beautiful woman I met for the first time on the castle steps, to create the image of my erotic dreams. Of course, I didn't rape her. I tamed myself and painted a picture – a beautiful picture. Yes, I painted her nakedness and her beautiful face and her hair, with a fringe which falls into her eyes... but I didn't humiliate her. I didn't draw her as if she were a model in a kind of submissive position. No, on the contrary. I was the one who, in shame, in the role of the peeping Tom, painted this beautiful woman. I drew her image in the mirror! She stands there, unaware of me. A colourful robe full of flowers lies at her feet, her hands are pulled back as the robe trails down them, and her naked body shines in the dim light above the mirror, exposing itself to the reflection in the mirror like an angelic apparition...

Chapter 15

What kind of a person can give away fifty thousand pounds, just like that? What made him donate such a sum? Illness? His, or someone else's close to him? Conscience? Or is he just a generous man who can afford it? Russell Steel. *Russell Steel of Carton Fabrications*, Aisling read in the gift agreement she printed out. Fifty thousand pounds. The amount resonated in her mind. *That's enough to buy back my life and still have some left over.*

She closed her eyes; *my life, and there will be more...* The lion lay there but trembled with excitement to attack. She saw him, she felt him. Another second and he would attack. One more second. *The last second of my life.* The attack... She opened her eyes. *Let me become a butterfly;* she gasped. *May I be a butterfly and fly out of the beast's reach.*

But she sat at her desk, oblivious to the text of the contract she was wandering through in slow speed. She couldn't concentrate. She just sat staring at the sheet of paper and suddenly... she heard music. A song emerged from the silence. It grew louder, louder. At first, she didn't recognise it, but after a while – *yes, Janis Joplin is singing* Piece of my Heart. *Is this real? Is the song really coming from somewhere? No, it's just a hallucination, but still, it's as if that wounded animal, Janis, has crept in through the open window. Where was the last time I listened to Piece of my Heart? Where was it?* she wonders. *I'm freaking out. Oh, God, I'm freaking out. Yeah, in the casino. It was in the casino,* she recalled without enthusiasm.

The devil nudged up the volume a little.

So shall I give it a go and play? A thought crept into her mind. *Bet it all and spin the roulette wheel? Should I also take more money off Eddy and play?* She thought of a lesser risk. The whirlwind in her brain was a centrifugal force, sweeping away the last vestiges of sound judgment. *I must, I must do something. But what?*

Unconsciously, she typed the name of Carton Fabrications into the business registry search engine. Carton Fabrications, production and sale of packaging, owner and CEO Russell Steel, based in Corby, Northamptonshire. She went to the company's website: *About Us, Products, Contact, References* – Austria, Belgium, Bulgaria, Czech Republic, Finland, France, Germany, Hungary, Italy, Netherlands, Norway, Poland, Portugal, Romania, Slovakia, Spain, Sweden... They manufacture and ship packaging all over Europe. Successful company, a wealthy man – *that's why he can donate fifty thousand pounds.* The devil even got into the website. She reverted to thinking. She sat and thought for a long time. The whirlwind had died down, and the thoughts Aisling had been trying to catch were still flying around in the wilderness it had caused. She caught them and weaved them into strange shapes, and her bond was not rationality, but emotion, as a mixture of longing, fear, hope, and apprehension.

For perhaps an hour, maybe two, she sat like this at her desk. The computer monitor had long since gone dark in sleep mode, and when Aisling finally moved and tapped the keyboard, the monitor lit up with the Carton Fabrications website. And all that was missing was something like a fanfare to complete the picture of the revealed solution. This, Aisling perceived as the illuminated image of 'hope', but it was, in reality, a blur of dark 'fears' that was more deserving of the drumbeat.

As if in a daze, she bent over the page of the donation agreement and typed in her own address and bank account number, together with her bank's sort code, in the recipient's account box. She filled in the other missing details of the contract and scanned it. She wrote a short letter, enclosed the contract as an attachment, then took a deep breath and clicked *Send*. The email went out immediately. She then deleted her correspondence with Russell Steel and placed the printed contract in her handbag. Mr Steel had never written, and no contract had ever existed.

She sat at her computer for a moment longer, feeling that the wilderness in her mind, a moment ago seemingly illuminated by the sun's rays with that brilliant idea, was suddenly darkening again. She closed her eyes to escape that impression. Silence. Just music from somewhere in the distance…

Cry Baby.

* * *

It had been a terrible night, perhaps the longest of her life. She couldn't sleep, and when she did fall asleep for a while, that horrible dream of the course of life and death came back to her. Dawn was breaking and Aisling could no longer stay in bed. She got up and walked around the apartment in an attempt to turn her brain off. In vain.

I shouldn't have done it. No, you shouldn't have. Russell Steel, before he sends that much money, is most definitely going to check all the details: address, bank, sort code, account number... He'll work it out. He'll find me...

Tired, her head full of tormenting thoughts, she sat down on a chair in the kitchen and put her feet up on the table. Her long, slender, naked legs glowed white in the gloom of the waking day as her nightgown slid down them to her lap. This contrasted inappropriately with the dark shadows of the apartment and Aisling's mind. And then she wondered further if perhaps Mr Steel had sent the money to her account; after all, he had the gift agreement on his computer. Maybe he'd even printed it out and had it filed somewhere. That would convict her someday. Her correspondence with Mr Steel, which he certainly wouldn't want to delete, and the contract, will one day land her in jail. Or send her to the grave, depending on who discovers the fraud first, HM Revenue and Customs, or Mr Wang.

Why didn't I think of that yesterday? she reproached herself. *Why, oh why? Because it doesn't really matter*, she answered herself. *There's still that enormous wad of cash missing somewhere. Either in mafioso Wang's cash box, or in some of Mr Steel's account.* She resigned herself to making a gross error of judgement; it didn't bring her relief. She sat down on a chair, drew her knees up to her chin, rested her head on her knees, and in this huddled position let the tears trickle down her face.

* * *

The money arrived in her account that same day. The honest man, Mr Steel, had fortunately not allowed for the possibility of fraud. But perhaps he had seen through CRO Foundation after all. *I'm sure he did. He checked the foundation records, checked the website… no account number. How?* she wondered. *Is that even possible? I think so, but he just believed it.*

But Mr Wang doesn't trust me anymore. He's checking up on me. What does he know? He knows there's forty-five thousand pounds missing. She looked at the balance in her bank account and found it unbelievable. *Why hasn't he done anything yet? What's he up to? What's he waiting for? I'll withdraw the money from my bank account and return it to the foundation's coffers. I'm sorry, Mr Wang, it was just a loan… don't kill me,* she consoled herself.

Chapter 16

I've travelled to London. Not on business, but on a short break. I like London, and I like to wander around its interesting places. To get on the train in Market Harborough and escape to London from the mundane, even if it's only for a short time. Escape all the worries of my company, escape the loneliness of the long evenings.

It has also got to be said that I don't mind flying. Yes, I'm a little scared, probably like everyone else, but up above the clouds a calmness enters me. I have this pleasant feeling or knowledge that I have not only physically detached myself from the world below, but that I have also broken the invisible bonds that were keeping my mind grounded. I see things differently, more clearly. And I'm enjoying it. I'm really enjoying it. So why a trip by train to London and not a flight to another European city? I don't really know. I suppose it's whatever takes my fancy.

In a strange way, my love of nature and the seductive lure of cities compete. I love forests and meadows, and lakes, and rivers and mountains, and all that is untouched by human hands… but even a big city, come to think of it, I'm able to see that way. I can see then that this age-long human footprint, where man builds houses and streets and whole blocks and interconnects them and interweaves them and spreads them out, leads to his work being outgrown. It's so cluttered that if it weren't for the motor car it would become an insurmountable jungle. What a pity that man invented the motor car.

In London, my first steps lead to Abbey Road. It's raining and the weather is inclement, but I want to see the sacred place that every Beatles fan must visit at least once in their lifetime. And I do. I'm standing at the pedestrian crossing where John, Ringo, Paul and George are in the photo that was used for the cover of their *Abbey Road* album. I'm standing there soaking wet, looking at the pedestrian crossing, and I see all four of them marching towards me. The ghost of John Lennon all in white, followed by Ringo in a long jacket, barefoot Paul and skinny George... I see them all. And I hear their songs. They were all born here, in this place. All those familiar melodies still ring through this space, seeping through the studio walls, rustling in the branches of the trees that shade the walls, carrying over the passage... I listen and I get wet. *I'm Eleanor Rigby*, I thought.

Yes, I'm alone. I feel alone, and in that state, I always think of *Lady Madonna*. Hush.

* * *

The next morning I have a full English breakfast in the hotel restaurant. Cereals, followed by full English breakfast of bacon and eggs, sausages, black pudding, hash brown and baked beans. To finish off with, toast, butter and jam. Ugh, I couldn't eat that every day. Then over a pot of tea, I relax and watch the people around me. I enjoy it. I'm in a good mood and looking forward to a day of wandering through the city, which is all ahead of me.

Adding to my good mood is the woman who, neatly groomed, in a decent business suit, with her flowing hair combed back, trotted demurely, in her high heels, to the buffet, picked up a tray and a large plate, and immediately loaded a huge portion onto her plate. A heap of fried eggs and bacon, several sausages, also a bowl of beans, followed by several rounds of toast, butter and jam, a bowl of yoghurt and cornflakes, a banana, pastry… I look around to see where the Rambo was to whom she was serving this portion, but she's on her own. She sits down at the table, spreads a napkin on her knees, and eats this incredible mountain of food with an endearing demeanour that is the most striking feature of her personality. She dabs her lips with the napkin, folds it, and weighs it down on her plate with her knife and fork. She stands up and, with her expensive designer handbag hanging from her forearm, walks off. I smile after her. Good morning.

Good morning. What a pity that man invented the motor car. When I take away the thousands of cars that block my way, a wonderful new world opens up. I don't have to wait for the right moment to cross the road to the other side. I don't dread the unpleasant noises, the honking, screeching and rumbling. I walk calmly through the valley of high-rise buildings. I descend down to the Thames and enjoy the blossoming of the bushes and the shade of the trees that decorate the space between the blocks of houses.

In this dream world, I meet smiling people in no hurry. They don't know what a rush is, perhaps because there is nothing that unnaturally speeds up their lives. A garden in the town and the town in the garden. I walk along the waterfront and continue to dream my crazy dreams. I wander through the jungle. I don't hear the cars. No noise, just The Beatles' *Lady Madonna* humming in my head as I was reminded of it yesterday. I have no destination. I'm not planning anything. I'm just walking and walking and looking around. Wandering through the jungle. Walking the streets and exploring. I even cross the river by that strange natural formation called Tower Bridge. Yes, it was the power of nature that gave birth to this bridge. It wasn't all Horace Jones.

I'm watching the river. It's the artery of this jungle. *It ought to be*, I admit to myself. She gave it life and is its mother, but looking into her waves, which roll grey as they mirror the similarly coloured sky and the cliffs of the coast, I fear for her. The river gave birth to a town. Yes, it's a town, not a jungle. The river gave birth to the town and I'm wandering through the town. I'm walking through the streets, and I can't keep my eyes off the thousands of cars. As aphids attack and choke a flowering bush, so the cars choke the town; a smile comes to mind.

I resign myself to my dreams and make my way not through the thicket of flowering bushes, but through the crowds of people on the pavements. Still, I'm not uncomfortable; I love forests and meadows and lakes and rivers and mountains and all that is untouched by human hands, but even a big city, come to think of it, I'm capable of seeing that way.

At the bus stop, I board the first double-decker that comes along and stay for a few stops, then get off and continue on aimlessly. I arrive, I don't know how, in Trafalgar Square. The weather has improved a little. At times, the sun even peeks out of the clouds and brightens the square and people's faces. I wander through the square and stop and turn my face to the sun as it offers rays to bask in. I'm enjoying it. The crowd of visitors paddle all around and vary in the twinkling sun, giving rise to a sense of belonging and the shared joy of the moment.

After a while, I leave Trafalgar Square and I make my way to the National Gallery where I admire the works of true masters. Such extraordinarily beautiful paintings…

Chapter 17

In the silence of the gallery, my mobile phone buzzed in my pocket. My kind neighbour informed me, in a pained voice, that my dog Rusty had died. Silently and with the phone to my ear, I walked out of the gallery building. I couldn't manage a single word.

"Mr Steel, Mr Steel, can you hear me?"

After a while, outside, I answered. We talked quietly. I told him that I was going to cut my trip short, and I would return back home as quickly as I could. I also told him that I would bury Rusty in my back garden under the large spruce tree.

Then I sat down on the low wall that formed the bank of the clipped lawn, clasping my hands back and exposing my face to the cold sun. Tears streamed down my face. My loyal dog Rusty had died… I sat there for a long time, oblivious to what was going on around me. Until an old lady came up to me, put her hand on my knee and raised the other to the sun.

"Look, the sun is shining, don't cry," she consoled me.

My sun was extinguished. The good old companion that always crouched painfully to welcome me home, had died. I tried to smile, and the old lady smiled back.

Thanks. I could only manage an embarrassed one.

I phoned my PA, Olivia. I asked her to buy me some white linen so I could bury Rusty in it. She promised to make the arrangements and was genuinely sorry.

"Oh," she rushed in just as I was about to end the call, "there was a young lady looking for you."

"Who was it? Did she say who she was?" I asked unenthusiastically.

"Well, not exactly. She wouldn't give her name and insisted on talking only to you. But I have to tell you, she was a very attractive, elegant lady."

I wondered who that might be. But I couldn't think of anyone.

"Was she a customer?" I tried.

"I don't think so. I had a feeling she wanted to deal with you in person – perhaps on some private matter…" Olivia chuckled, but immediately became serious again. "She was just wondering if you were in and if she could talk to you. Nothing more. But something didn't seem right about her behaviour, Russell… I told her you were on holiday and wouldn't be back until Monday."

I was intrigued. A very attractive, elegant lady who only wanted to talk to me, apparently on some private matter… I sensed a contradiction there.

"What did she look like?" I blurted out as Olivia was saying goodbye.

"A cat. In a single word – a cat."

"Cat, cat…" I growled. "Describe her to me. Small? Big?"

"Model, a dancer – slim, tallish, but not too much. A beautiful face, perhaps blue eyes… what do I know how to describe her to you. Just a pretty woman at first sight. What am I saying – a really very beautiful woman."

My heart skipped a beat at the word dancer.

"Hair? What kind of hair did she have?" I blurted out.

"Do you know her?" Olivia asked, taken aback by my insistent tone. "Hair? Dark. A short style of dark hair… and a fringe that fell into her eyes," she continued when I didn't answer.

* * *

Mr Wang didn't get it. The money that went missing just a few days ago was back in the safe. How did this woman do it? Did she have a win in the casino? No way. He knows she's gambling and has lost this amount. He also made it his business finding out that she hasn't set foot in the casino lately. Then where did she get forty-five thousand pounds from? First, she returned ten thousand pounds, and now she's returned a further thirty-five thousand. Has she savings? No way: he dismissed this immediately. If she did, why would she then take money out of the safe? It made him angry and amused at the same time.

He leant back in Aisling's chair, propped his chin in his hand, and thought. He didn't have to think long: he realised that he had an answer. *I wonder how such an exceptionally elegant and attractive woman would come by that kind of money so quickly?* he asked himself. He smiled. Only one way. Of course, why hadn't he thought of that before? That beautiful lady manager of his, she's on the game. She's got clients, but not just any clients, it seems. She's selective and it's the wealthy men who pay her handsomely for being their companion.

Now he was just enjoying it. Thrilled by the epiphany, he sat back in the plush chair and leant his elbows on the desk. *So Miss Aisling is a luxurious companion and escort to wealthy men. Well, that's wonderful. I wonder...* He rejoiced in his mind. Watch, he decided immediately. Follow and find out the names of the patrons. After all, that's what he'd always wanted to do, that's why he'd set up CRO Foundation in the first place. Besides improving his reputation, he could gain direct contact with some rich, but adulterous, people. It's not just a question of the possibility of more money, though he'll never get enough of that. It's a passion. It's the hunt that makes him run in the footsteps of these money men, his next victims.

Chapter 18

Aisling withdrew forty-five thousand pounds in cash from her bank account, but it didn't happen straight away. The bank clerk insisted that she had to give the bank at least twenty-four hours' notice to withdraw an amount over five thousand pounds in cash.

She immediately returned the thirty-five thousand to the foundation's coffers, and ten thousand she would return to Eddy. He'll probably find it very strange that she's returning it so soon. She wondered if she should pay him back in instalments. No, she'll repay him in one go. She'll pay him back all the money now. Who knows what the next few days will hold for her. Revelations? Arrest? She'll make sure she pays at least one debt.

What about the other fifty grand? She'll pay it back to Russell Steel, she's decided. She must find some way to pay him back.

She called Eddy and asked to meet him. He was surprised, but eventually agreed. She could tell he was hesitant about the meeting place. He finally gave in to her unspoken wish when she merely made a significant pause at his question, 'where?', and told her to come to his house.

Yes, she wished to return to that beautiful house for a while. Not, perhaps, in an attempt to revive memories or provoke further adult activity. No. Eddy was more like a father to her now, and his house was her temporary refuge. She felt that way. In these days of tension, fatigue and fear, she needed a haven. She needed to hide from the world, at least for a while. She was a butterfly here. A beautiful, admired butterfly that has escaped the claws and fangs of the beast.

* * *

Eddy silently and without question accepted the money Aisling handed him. Then they sat together in the luxury leather armchairs and talked. The precious antique grandfather clock struck silently both on the half hour and the hour in an effort not to remind of passing time. It bore witness to Aisling's youth and Eddy's old age.

All evening they talked in this way, and it was deep into the night when they parted.

Chapter 19

Aisling couldn't sleep. The events of the last few days were stopping her from sleeping. She didn't even switch on the lamp beside the sofa on which she laid. She just curled up in her short dressing gown and engaged in deep thought.

She was trying to be positive. After all, she had returned all the money to the safe and paid Eddy's debt, so she was in no immediate danger from Mr Wang. Perhaps. She hesitated, then continued her internal monologue. *After all, I could always tell him that I took a liberty and borrowed the money... I needed it badly and I borrowed it for a short while. I knew I'd pay it back quickly, so I didn't say anything to him...* stupid, but she could get away with it.

Perhaps he hadn't even found out. *Maybe I'm panicking for nothing.* She kidded herself further that perhaps the slither of Sellotape along the corner of the safe door could have just peeled off on its own, and that she might have forgotten how she set out the scattered items on the floor in front of the safe.

But what about Russell Steel? What about this complete stranger, Mr Steel? Somehow, I'm going to have to pay back that fifty grand. But how am I going to pay him back? How? And over what period – ten, twenty years? She couldn't answer the questions she was asking herself in her mind.

For the start, he's got my correspondence and that damning contract stored on his computer. That incriminates me for cheating them both. Russell Steel and Mr Wang. I stole Steel's money that he wanted to donate to Mr Wang's fund. Steel's going to have me, and Mr Wang's going to kill me.

You can't remain positive with a weight that size hanging over your head. You can't. *I should pay back the fifty thousand, not to Mr Steel, but back into the fund… put the money back, fast, where it belongs. But I won't have time for that.*

She pulled her exposed legs to her body, suddenly tired to death. *I won't have time for that… time… t-i-m-e.* She stretched that word into a dream.

T-i-m-e.

With that strangely twisted word, she woke up. *What time is it?* She realised she'd fallen asleep, but she just couldn't make herself get up in a hurry. She was remembering. Even in the early morning, in the throes of waking, she knew what she was going to do today. She will go to see Russell Steel. She'll meet the man in person and tell him absolutely everything. She'll tell him how she stupidly fell into debt. She'll tell him how scared she is. She'll tell him how she succumbed to temptation when, as if by magic, she was exposed to it. She'll tell him that his financial donation came at the very moment she was praying for a solution. She'll tell him that she can't go on like this. She'll ask him to give her a chance, that she'll pay the money back. She'll ask him for compassion, and to give her time.

Chapter 20

The forest of violins. The sound of a thousand violins carried through the garden as I stood over Rusty's grave. Then, though it wasn't necessary, I raked the ground of the place. In the spring, I'll lay new turf here to fill in the resulting bald patch, and then perhaps mark the grave with a headstone inscribed with Rusty's name. But there again, I may not put a headstone here, and only my memory will hold that my dog was buried here. My loyal dog Rusty, who kept me company during the loneliness I endured so hard, who was my friend and companion during the long evenings.

But who was that woman that Olivia's description fitted so well? The question kept creeping into my mind as I stood in the farthest corner of the garden under the tall spruce tree. Is there something between heaven and earth? Is that fate that made the dancer from the castle steps, from a long distance away in Prague, find me in Corby? Why? Why would she come to me all this way? What reason would she have? Did I, by any chance, woo her? To want to see me on the same day Rusty left me…? I stood in the darkening garden and smiled indulgently at my silly questions. I stood there for a long time, until the chill came over me and that indulgent smile froze, fossilised and lost its condescension.

Who was that woman?

A forest of violins. I hear again the beautiful sound of a thousand violins. *Who was the woman who came to me?* I repeat to myself. *Who was that woman, Rusty?* I just can't let it go.

It's getting dark fast, but I'm still walking in the garden. I don't want to go into the house yet. The moon is so close to full that it illuminates the house from the side. It appears to me, from the shaded garden, like a mysterious castle with dark windows. I look at it and it seems sad and deserted, with the partly empty rockery in the foreground and the patio ceramic pots in need of fresh flowers. It's sad and lonely and I don't want to enter it. I remembered reading somewhere a question without an answer: what would the world look like if man had the nature or heart of a dog? In this world of mine, in the world of my garden and my house, it's now as desolate as desolate can be after the passing of an infinitely good and faithful friend. And that is my answer.

I don't want to go into the house. I stand in the middle of the garden and look at the large folding patio doors that darkly reflect the space in front of it. Somewhere in the darkest shadow of that mirrored glass that is the patio doors, is me. I must be there. I raise my hand and wave it against the distant patio doors. I squint and focus my gaze... nothing. I try again, but I drown in the deep shadow of my image in the mirror-like glass wall which didn't return my greeting. *I'm alone*, and it came upon me with great force. *I'm desperately alone.*

I don't even turn on the lamp in the living room. I just pull back the patio doors, sit in the armchair, and through the chill that crept into the room, I let the whole world in too. Just to forget the awful feeling of loneliness that literally paralysed me. But it didn't.

Was it her? I couldn't help but ask the question again. It surfaced in my mind again and again, competing with the memories of Rusty. And along with those memories, at least easing little the agonising feeling of loneliness. A dancer? Not as an ethereal being imprinting dance steps into the lush grass of my garden lawn, not as my dream, but as the real woman from those castle steps – who came all this way to see me for some reason? For a reason... but what reason? I wonder. It doesn't make sense. There's no explanation. What else could we have in common besides that little incident on the castle steps? Nothing. That's all there is. Or did she want me to give her back the money, the fifty-five crowns she gave me? I smile at last. Or is she a potential customer?

I again reject the idea that it was her. But why such reluctance? She could have told my PA she wanted to order something, she could have left a request, a business card... I just don't understand. I think, I remember, I look for the context... and nothing. I can't think of anything that could have brought that beautiful woman to my company.

The sky darkens and the darkness spreads through the garden and into the living room. It gets quite chilly, but I still don't shut the patio doors. I am uncomfortable with the idea of enclosing myself within the four walls of this deserted room. Rusty's departure has really got to me, and the question marks surrounding the mysterious woman don't help either. I slouch in my chair and stare into the black shadows of the garden.

I don't last long. I realise that I have succumbed too much to the sadness and strange tension of the last few days. *I must do something*, I tell myself. Something to occupy myself and dispel the gloom. As I have done countless times in my life, I must pick myself up, shake myself down and move on. I pull the patio doors shut and turn on the light. I think for a moment about whether I should get on with business, or watch television, or read something, or perhaps paint something… I haven't really decided yet, but somehow, unconsciously, I move the painting board closer to the light and stick a sheet of white paper onto its surface.

Yes, I'm going to paint. Painting brings me satisfaction and calms me down, and everything else can wait. I pick the charcoal up into my hand. No canvas today, no paint. Only charcoal, in shades of black. Will I create something? But what? I can't think for a moment, but, as usual, I listen to what my heart tells me. What's bugging me? What wants to come out? I miss the light, I miss the colours, I miss the joy, I miss the beauty… I calculate. But how do I express all that I miss in charcoal? Black charcoal. First stroke and with my middle finger I blur a thin line. Then another. I blow away the tiny grains of charcoal dust and move on. I lean as close as I can to the surface of the paper and hold my breath to hit the intended curve. There you go. I step back and check the accuracy of the lines. I bend down again and with quick, short strokes, I blacken the surface, which I then smear with my middle finger until the resulting shades of grey give the image depth, soften the contours and make the image light and translucent… I like it. Yes, that's it. *That's the real thing.* I stay with it for a long time.

It's after midnight when I finish the picture. I step back and assess my work. I think I've succeeded. Does it have everything I'm missing…? Yes, I am enjoying the scene: a sun-warmed stone drowned in the silence of flowers and on that stone a colourful butterfly. It's there.

I'm looking at the picture and it comes to me. It's just a flicker of a thought, an instant idea, an epiphany, like when you pull the last screw of a complex mechanism and all the cogs in the gears slowly turn. That could be an explanation. That could be a clue; my mind is spinning faster.

I switch on the computer and continue to chew on the idea during its start-up. Then, when I click on the CRO Foundation website, I am firmly convinced that the young lady, or perhaps Ms, originated from here. After all, I had gifted them a lot of money and a personal thank you would be the logical explanation for the visit. And then, we have a donation agreement: they know me, they know my address, they know about me…

The pages load: *About Us, Who We Help, Photo Gallery, Contact…* I click on *Contact*; the board members are all men. There's a little photo next to each name. The manager of the foundation is – I know her from the donation agreement – Aisling Hunter. *Aisling is a beautiful name*, I think. Aisling. She's got a little photo here, too, but even with glasses, I can't see much. I click on *enlarge image*... it takes a moment... I'm breathless with excitement...

The incident has stirred the surface of my life. It was a kind of gurgle, like skimming a pebble onto the surface of the water, I remembered... wheels were formed by the commotion, it ran through the surface until it gradually disappeared and my mind, momentarily agitated, also became quiet. It's calm again, as if nothing had ever happened. Only the image of the pretty woman, like the motionless pebble beneath the surface of the water, lies in my memory.

At last. It hasn't enlarged much, so I hold my glasses to focus perfectly and... the image of the pretty woman, until now motionless like a pebble under the water surface, shudders with an eruption. It rises from its quiet place and with that unforgettable smile, watches the tsunami that pours from the banks of the river of my life. It is she! The beautiful woman of the castle steps, the dancer of my dreams, the mysterious woman who visited me... Aisling Hunter, of the CRO Foundation.

Chapter 21

Aisling examined her face in the mirror, flicking the dimmer light switch until the shadows around her eyes, caused by sleep deprivation, disappeared. Mr Steel wouldn't understand. He wouldn't understand anyway. He wouldn't understand and he wouldn't forgive her. No one could understand, she was suddenly certain. She looked at her face. No, it hadn't been a good idea to go to Carton Fabrications, and perhaps by the grace of fate she hadn't been allowed to meet Mr Steel. He would have exposed her, turned her in. *But how do I get out of this mess? How? How? What do I do?*

The rain pattered outside the living room window, which she could see through the open bathroom door. At first it just rustled, tiny drops tapping on the windowsill, but then it grew stronger and after a while it drummed violently. Intrigued by the sound, she stepped out of the bathroom. Her bare feet left footprints in the thick pile of the carpet, as if in the sand at the beach. She stopped at the window and opened it.

Through the delicate pattern of the curtains, she watched the rain fall. The darkness of the room and the curtains, like a thick veil, didn't allow even the nearest windows of the opposite house to see her nakedness. She became aware of it, however. And it was the nakedness of her body against the backdrop of the roaring elements that multiplied her vulnerability. Fear. The heaviness weighed heavily on her. *My life is ending*: the blackest thought occurred to her. *By my own stupidity, I have ruined it and...* She crossed her arms over her chest to ward off the encroaching sense of threat. But after a moment, with her hands first on her shoulders, she slid down to her naked breasts... finding no way to make things right, she finished the thought.

With her palms on her chest, she stood by the window, and then in the fading sound of the rain, her mind also calmed. The rain reverberated like a receding train, and so did Aisling's distress. No, it wasn't a liberating sense of peace. Apathy, perhaps, or resignation. Like the diagnosis of a serious illness, when initial dismay is replaced by regret, then belligerence, and finally a soothing awareness of the inevitability of fate. *It has happened and it can't be undone. Calm down. Calm yourself. After all, life ends and there are things I no longer need to do; it's suddenly a comfort.*

I don't have to worry about what's going to happen, because nothing will happen. That's the result of even a faint relief – I don't have to worry any more. The bad has already come and so I don't have to worry about it coming. The anticipation of pain and suffering is often more painful and distressing than the pain and suffering itself.

Such thoughts ran through Aisling's mind. But were they running? No. Flowing is more accurate, though it's not said of thoughts. Water flows and time...

Aisling stands at the window, with only a little rain outside, and her thoughts are... flowing. *Eddy*, she suddenly remembers. *Eddy, how alike we are now. All the beautiful things are behind us, and we are just waiting for...* she didn't even finish it in her mind. *And we're just waiting. Period. That's better. Eddy, like you, I close my eyes now, and behind my eyelids runs a film of the most beautiful moments of my life.*

Nigel. The love of my life. Nigel's hands and the colourful music flicker through the darkness. Darkness. Turning off the mind's alluring play of coloured lights. She'd rather see the darkness, because in the flashes she saw the face of the devil. The devil? No, it was Nigel's face, but in the stroboscopy of the flashes, she wasn't sure anymore. Eddy and Nigel. *What's next? What more beautiful things can I remember? What about all those lovers before, and after them? These two men trumped everything that came before.* She didn't open her eyes, but the film wasn't running. It stopped, or looped back to Nigel and Eddy. *That's it? That's all?*

Out of nowhere – she didn't understand why – she remembered the bald violinist with the overgrown remnants of grey hair just in the back. An ugly, fat man – but he played beautifully. He played for the guests of the very expensive hotel where Nigel had once taken her. He played, and as he played, he rolled his eyes angrily at a group of guests who, unimpressed by his playing, were talking noisily among themselves.

"You rude imbeciles," came from his whispering lips. "You morons," he hissed in the shadow of his violin. "Even the money doesn't entitle you... you pathetic specimens!"

But he didn't drown out the glorious sound of his violin. He carried on playing. He played exquisitely.

"That was just for you, princess," he said when he finished playing, smiling sadly at the little girl sitting at the nearest table. He put down his violin.

"I'll take a short break. Will you let me?" He stroked the little girl's head and left with dignity. He stood it all, humbled.

I must keep playing too. Aisling breathed. *I must go on living, because… because life is as beautiful as the sound of a violin.*

She sat down on the thick pile of the carpet. In the tilted window, the mirror reminded her of her nakedness. She propped herself up on her elbows and covered her lap with her bent leg. After all, life is a beautiful sound of violins, a thousand violins… She watched her image in the reflection of the window. Then she tilted her head. *A forest of violins*: a strange thought occurred to her. She remained in that position. Like a model posing for a nude painter, she remained motionless, only sensing the sensuality of her body projected on the glass. She sensed the breasts that glowed from the shadows, and the paleness of the bent leg covering the lap that dominated the image. A forest of violins.

A slight shiver ran through her body. A shiver.

"I must live. I must," she whispered.

She rolled onto her side and slipped her relaxed palm between her thighs, into a fist, squeezing with all her strength. She closed her eyes. *I must live.* She didn't loosen her grip on her thighs. She could feel the hand clenched into a fist. It wasn't her hand. It was Nigel's. No, Eddy's… She squeezed it and heard his breathing quicken. Without moving, just with the cosmic energy concentrated between her thighs, she gripped the man's hand. For a long, long time, until his gasp became a muffled cry that echoed through the room through her mouth.

Chapter 22

I'd gladly give one hundred thousand pounds not to have to buy love, I remembered saying some while back. Was my exclamation, so absurd, heard? Fate? I have given fifty thousand pounds and am I halfway there? I believe I am. I'm not stumbling in the mud of my loneliness, but I'm on my way and I'll see my destination.

But my brain, trained to rationality, is fighting a battle with something that creeps in, something between heaven and earth... whose only proof of existence is the fact that it is...

* * *

The seventies song *Aqualung* is playing in the luxurious hair salon near the Clock Tower in Leicester. I'm sitting here, waiting for the hairdresser, who's gone off somewhere for a while. I've been listening. Jethro Tull. The song tells the story of a character also named Aqualung, a homeless person, who spends a cold day in a park in London. I get feelings of guilt about the homeless, as well as fear and insecurity with people who seem a little scary. But I like that wild man with the flowing hair, hobbling on one leg with a flute at his mouth. I see myself in the mirror in front of me. I look like him. I look like him with that long flowing hair…

What am I doing here? I think to myself. *Do I want a change? Do I want to be different? If I do meet Aisling, do I want to impress her? Charm her? Fools. Crazy*, I answer in my head, my eyes fixed on the mirror. I can't expect a miracle even at the price they charge at this hair salon. They'll cut my greying mane, somehow comb what's left, but they won't get rid of the worried look on my face and the wrinkles at my eyes. I shouldn't be, but I'm a middle-aged man. An uninteresting man who… who lately, vainly, needlessly, agonisingly, accidentally, has met the woman of his dreams and in a foolish belief in fate is arming himself to attack her in a battle for her favour. Ridiculous. Vain. I rise, ashamed, catching myself in foolish naivety. The song of Aqualung reverberates as I leave. The amazing guitar riff at the end of the song. I am Jethro Tull and I'll remain Jethro Tull.

"Sorry to keep you waiting, sir. I'll be with you right away," the young hairdresser blurts out as I collide with her in the doorway. "Would you like a wash and a haircut… or a colour?" She sizes me up as she deftly adjusts my chair. The song has died down.

"Just a wash and haircut." I sigh.

The comb has sharp points and slides painfully over my skin as it straightens my cropped hair into a style, but after each painful stroke, a sensation of pleasant warmth remains under my hair. Done. Checking the result… Am I different? Better? I'm different: my hair is washed and carefully cut, and styled; only a few strands have come loose in a minor disobedience to my forehead...

* * *

I'm travelling to Market Harborough from Leicester on the X7 bus. Outside, the landscape is passing by. I watch the trees by the roadside and my gaze wanders to the fields that have already been harvested. I see a hare, uncomfortable with the crop of barley around it as far as the eye can see. It's scurrying about in an attempt to escape from the monsters that scare and chase him with their noise. The world goes on down those roads. The modern world. It's never been sadder.

How could it be that the dancer I dreamt of actually came into my life? I changed the subject of my thoughts. *What a coincidence. Is there really something between heaven and earth that caused this? Did the spheres of our thoughts intersect somewhere deep in the universe?*

I remember the babble of the drunken night. I laugh involuntarily and the lady sitting in the seat next to me looks up in alarm. *Yes, I am crazy, madam.* I nod to her. I keep my eyes on the landscape outside the window. *I'm a nutcase who wished for something so much, it came true. That doesn't normally happen, ma'am.*

What next? What am I going to do about it? Should I look for her? Approach her? I've been thinking seriously.

I know where to find her. I have the address of the foundation she works for. I'll find her. It won't be a problem. But what else? What do I tell her? You know, I've known you for a long time, you've been dancing in my garden for months. First as an ethereal being, invisible, just your bare feet in the lush grass in dance steps... then, one day, I saw you on the castle steps in Prague. Do you remember? No, you don't. You gave me a pittance – fifty-five crowns. No? I still have the coins. Look, I didn't spend them as you feared. And I painted you too, Aisling.

You have a beautiful name. Aisling. I painted a picture of you reflected in the mirror - where your naked body shines a dim light over the mirror, exposing your reflection like an angel's apparition...

I was struck by the inner dialogue, where silence was always the answer. *Is that what I'm going to tell her? The truth that I dreamt of her? That the spheres of our thoughts intersected in the depths of the universe, and our minds connected?*

"You are a fool, sir," she will answer me. "You are a middle-aged fool."

Outside the bus window, the landscape passes by. *No, I won't look for her. She wouldn't understand me.* No one could understand, I was suddenly certain.

Chapter 23

"Police? Why are you calling me?" Aisling stiffened in surprise.

"Is your name Aisling Hunter?" The policeman ignored her question.

"Yes," she whispered after a moment of silence and slowly resumed walking. But then she was oblivious to his next words. They blended into an unintelligible murmur that couldn't cover the storm of her animal thoughts. *Has it burst? Had they discovered my deception? Who? Russell Steel? Mr Wang?* She walked down the street where the call had caught her by surprise, her mobile phone still held to her ear. But the panic that had taken suddenly hold of her made it impossible to control where she was walking next or to understand the meaning of the words the policeman was saying. It all finally surfaced…

"Hello, Miss Hunter? Can you hear me? Hello?" His urgent words, which he was literally shouting into the phone, did wake her up.

"Sorry, it's a bad line," she spluttered. "I couldn't hear you properly. Why are you calling me?"

"We need to talk to you in relation to a case we're investigating jointly with Northamptonshire Police, and which involves you. But I can't explain it over the phone. Give me your address and we'll come and pick you up and continue this conversation at the police station."

A short statement. She didn't repeat her question again, but within a second, she also cast doubt on whether the man on the phone was really a police officer. But no doubt he was. *The doe is caught...* She gave him her address.

"Will you be at this address in about twenty minutes?"

"I will," she replied resignedly. "I'm only a short way from my apartment."

The balding man, about forty-five years old, who rang her apartment bell exactly twenty minutes later was in civilian clothes. He showed his warrant card – a Detective Constable... she couldn't read the name and didn't really care.

"I'm DC Peters. Can we...?"

She didn't answer. She merely slammed the front door behind her and locked it. She was calm, ready and resigned, and even descended the stairs with a sort of relief. She mentally appreciated the officer's gallantry as he walked two steps ahead of her and held the door open for her on the ground floor. His much younger colleague was waiting for them in the car. He sat behind the wheel, clumsily hiding his astonishment at Aisling's attractive looks. He just smiled and nodded his head in greeting and the unmarked car sped off.

After a moment, DC Peters broke the oppressive silence.

"Miss Hunter, what is your relationship to Mr Eddy Foreman?"

"To Mr Foreman?" Aisling breathed a sigh of relief to the question, startled, for it was only after a moment that she understood who he was speaking of. Of course, she knew Eddy's surname, but she had never actually used it. He was never Eddy Foreman to her, but always just Eddy.

"Yes, to Mr Eddy Foreman," the police officer repeated patiently.

"Why? Why do you ask?" Aisling didn't understand.

"Can you answer me, please? What is your relation, Miss Hunter, to Mr Eddy Foreman?"

"In what relation? Acquaintance, friend? Friend. Why do you ask?"

The car sped down the street, only to come to a stop at a red light and then rush off and stop again. It turned left and then right and travelled through the heart of Leicester.

"We're here," said the young policeman at last when they arrived at Euston Street Police Station.

"We'll continue our conversation inside, Miss Hunter," said DC Peters, Aisling's intent gaze no longer held.

They climbed stairs. The detective constable walked beside Aisling, the young policeman two steps behind her. She knew that more than gallantry, the reason for the young man's distance was his desire to look at her behind. The bars that separated the floor from the stairwell clanged metallically as the police officer unlocked them and yanked them open, and even his polite holding of the bars did nothing to ease the heaviness that fell on Aisling. The bars. Her chest ached. The keys rattled again as he unlocked the door to the interrogation room. She closed her eyes briefly.

DC Peters shivered with excitement. "Please." The officer motioned with his hand.

Eddy. But why was he asking about Eddy? How had the police located her through Eddy? She didn't understand.

"Please go in," the policeman repeated when Aisling didn't respond.

She opened her eyes. She hesitated a second longer, but then stepped inside.

"Why am I asking you about Mr Foreman?" The policeman began with a rhetorical question. He offered Aisling a chair and sat at the one opposite her. The young policeman sat at the desk too. He opened his laptop and tapped something on the keyboard.

"I always find it difficult to inform family members or acquaintances about death…"

Aisling's hands tingled and the tingling ran through her entire body and exploded in her brain in a second, like a bolt of lightning that struck and knocked out all of Aisling's senses so that she couldn't see or hear for a moment. Then she put her trembling hands to her face, only her astonished eyes uncovered.

Eddy was dead? Dead? Do you mean to say that Eddy died? she asked with those eyes.

"By misfortune. I am sorry to inform you that Mr Foreman is dead."

"Dead…?" she whispered into those hands. Then she placed her hands in her lap.

"Miss Hunter, it appears that your friend has apparently died of a heart attack. That's the up-to-date information we have from the duty doctor so far. But the reason we're involved with this is something else. For Mr Foreman called our colleagues at Northamptonshire Police shortly before they found him dead in his house, saying that he was…" The policeman paused for a while. "Being blackmailed."

"Blackmailed?! Blackmailed by whom?" Aisling was startled, but like another flash of lightning in close succession, the answer flashed through her brain. Wang! It was certainly Mr Wang!

"Mr Foreman called to report that he had an unexpected visit at home from two rather unsavoury characters. The two men are already known to us as coming from the Leicester area, thanks to the pictures captured of them on security camera. They threatened Mr Foreman and demanded some favour or perhaps commitments – in return for not disclosing compromising information."

Aisling struggled to understand the meaning of these sentences. Thoughts whirled through her head. *I put Eddy in danger. I brought Mr Wang to him*, she reproached herself. *His people followed me, found out everything… but why? What does Mr Wang know? Why is he doing this? Does he know everything about me? Does he know about the money? Will he kill me? Will he kill me too?* A barrage of questions.

"Why? Why are you interrogating me?" she finally responded.

"You're the last, and, in fact, the only person he's spoken to on the phone recently. We found this out from his mobile phone."

He paused for a moment, watching the impact of his words in Aisling's eyes. Then he continued: "Didn't he talk to you about his troubles? Do you have any idea who might have blackmailed him and what compromising information it might have been? For Mr Foreman refused to tell us anything more about it." He looked her in the eyes.

"Am I a suspect? Do you think I'm somehow involved?" Aisling couldn't stand the look. "Shouldn't I have my solicitor present?"

"No, we don't suspect you, and you are free to go after we ascertain some facts," he answered unconvincingly, but then continued in a more conciliatory approach. "We need to get to the bottom of this. Please understand, our colleagues in Northampton got a call from a man saying he was being threatened, blackmailed, and they found him dead shortly afterwards. He didn't appear to die a suspicious death, but someone helped him along in some way. Scared the living daylights out of him. That's why I'm asking you. He didn't tell you about his troubles? Do you know who could have frightened him so?"

"I have no idea," Aisling replied blankly. "I really don't know."

"How did you know Mr Foreman?" DC Peters abandoned his conciliatory tone with the question Aisling had been dreading for minutes.

She hesitated, realising at once that the hesitation was a mistake. He didn't believe her. He suspected her, and she had only confirmed his suspicion with that small hesitation.

You are his bad conscience, she read in his eyes now. *You are the weak spot, the compromising information…*

"How did I know him?" she repeated, only to have the next seconds of silence say no more. "I don't even know anymore. Maybe we met at some charity event… I really can't remember."

"You've spoken on the phone a few times recently. What did you two talk about? Why did you call each other?"

Aisling stumbled into that self-preservation mode… there's no escape. So she stared silently into the eyes of her conqueror.

"Have you visited Mr Foreman at his house in the last few days? Have you met up?" The lion struck the fatal blow.

"Yes," she sputtered. "I was at his house a few days ago."

"The reason?"

"Do I need to talk about it? Is it important?"

"It's very important, Miss Hunter. You have to tell us everything."

Chapter 24

No, I won't look for her. She wouldn't understand me... Or is it fear of failure? Of rejection? Yes, I'm within reach of what I've wanted so much, dreamt of, and now that fate has contributed so much, I'm afraid to do my best not to spoil everything. I dreamt of her – the dancer who danced through my night garden. Then I met her – no, I was privileged to meet her by that strange chance. I painted her, dreamt of her – and dreamt her. She came to me when we signed the Gift Aid declaration forms. Thank you? To look at the fool who gave so much away? Or is fate still playing tricks? I sit in my chair in my office, holding the contract we signed, and smile at my thoughts. I look at our signatures. Is that even possible? Is it true?

* * *

It's evening outside my office window. All my employees have long since left; I'm left alone. I don't know why, but I don't feel like going home tonight. I don't want to go to that empty and sad house. *Tonight I'll stay in the lonely and sad office*, I think bitterly.

I get up from my chair and turn off the light. I stand for a moment to get used to the complete darkness, and then sit down in the chair again. That's what I like: darkness and complete silence which calms my mind.

Yes, my decision was definitely the right one; my thoughts return to Aisling. I can't, at my age and with my nature, approach that beautiful young woman with any suggestions. I would feel like a fool. I'd be a fool... I'll go back to my dreams. With my sense of beauty, I'll only dream of beauty. I'll dream dreams that I won't fulfil, and they'll stay dreams, they'll stay that gentle tingle at the thought, they'll stay a scent, they'll stay a sweetly pretty sadness I remember.

I draw my chair close to the window so that the window frame doesn't obstruct the view. I look up at the night sky and admit to myself the thoughts of the solitary man that I am. Strange thoughts, the kind that only come from solitude. I look up at the dark sky, to those distant worlds, and my mind wonders: *why, from where and to where? Space, time, life... death. Why? Why is it so? Where's the answer? Is it far out there in the universe? Or somewhere close? In the human mind? Can the human brain comprehend all this? Can it find the answer?*

I think it can. It's part of the universe; it came from the universe. Human consciousness is expanding in the same way, and one day it will reach its limits. The universe and human consciousness will become one. Maybe the answer we get will be simple, obvious; how is it possible that we had to wait so long for it...? It also occurs to me that the depth of emotion is comparable to the magnitude of the universe. Like the universe, emotion is an infinite space where a force called desire sets in motion the mechanism of being…

Clack, clack, clack; it's ringing in my ears. Our story has shifted only slightly. Actually, it hasn't even begun. Can I really call it a story? It was only a brief encounter. Hardly anything. It was just a flicker, like skimming a pebble on the water. It formed wheels with the commotion, carried on following the surface of the water until it gradually disappeared…

I fall asleep and dream – of Rusty. He has somehow got caught up in my dream, and as if I am only half asleep, I dream that he is here in the office with me, lying at my feet, asleep, dreaming his dreams…

But suddenly, in the dream, Rusty raises his head and listens.

"What's up, doggo?" I say to him.

He just groans weakly and stares at the door. I listen too. Nothing. All my staff and workforce have long since left, and surely no one would be wandering in at this hour. They shouldn't. I soothe myself in my reverie.

Chapter 25

The dream continues and Rusty never takes his eyes off the office door. It makes me feel uneasy, but I remain seated and listen. And suddenly – footsteps. *Isn't it just me?* I wonder in my dream. Quiet, careful footsteps. I hold my breath, that's all I can do, as the footsteps reach my office door. Rusty doesn't even manage more, standing on his unsteady feet, but by then the door handle has moved and the door slowly opens. I stare in surprise at the bright cone of torchlight that bounces across the walls and furniture, until it catches my eye. Then I wake up.

"What's wrong?" I shout against the real, blinding light. "Turn it off!"

For a second, the scene is silent, but then the light disappears, and the dark figure staggers in the doorway. Perfectly awake, I run out into the corridor and immediately turn on the light.

Leaning against the wall, face pale with terror, there stands a young woman. Her pale face contrasts with her black sweatshirt and leggings. She holds a torch in her right hand and extends the left towards me, perhaps to stop me hitting her.

"What are you doing here? Who are you?" I stammer.

She remains propped up against the wall, only her arms lowered along her body. We look at each other… and then I recognise her: Aisling. Aisling Hunter. Oh my God.

"What are you doing here?" I whisper. She leans down until her hair bunches up in her eyes, but she doesn't answer.

"I said, what are you doing here, Aisling?"

She slowly lifts her head and there is wonder in her eyes. Immense wonder.

"Eddy…" she breathes.

"Eddy?" I blink in surprise as well. "I'm not Eddy. Who are you confusing me with?"

She looks at me and seems to understand.

"No." She sighs resignedly after only a moment.

Then there is silence. Am I still dreaming? My mind is going. This can't be real.

"Rusty!" I call to the open office door.

Nothing, of course. Just another question mark in Aisling's eyes: *who is he calling? How does he know my name? Who is this man?*

No, it's not a dream anymore. Aisling Hunter is real and she's standing next to me.

"What are you doing here? Do you even know where you are? Do you know it's night?" I was questioning her sanity.

"Are you Mr Steel?" she asks, not answering my question. Her look is suddenly so disarming that I nod.

"Yes, I am Mr Steel. The owner of this factory you just broke into."

She looks away. She remains silent.

"Can you explain?" I ask. After a moment, I motion with my hand towards my office door.

She raises her head to me. She is breathing through her open mouth, and there is a sudden strange calm in her eyes. That's my answer.

"I'll explain," she says, though no words were needed, and enters the office.

I turn on the lamp on my desk and offer her the chair at the coffee table. I take the other chair myself. The light is dim, warm, and once again gives me the impression that I am dreaming.

In this strange, dreamlike atmosphere, I watch Aisling. The dancer. She sits upright, one hand resting on the back of the chair, the other, with just the backs of her fingers, supporting her chin… A middle aged-man and a girl, I suddenly realise, involuntarily straightening my hunched back. This is the scene from my painting. Only the grandfather clock is missing. Time… the time has come. *Have you come, fate?* My head is spinning.

"I'm not here to rob you," Aisling begins, not noticing my confusion. "I came…" She hesitates a moment. "I came to cover my tracks because…" She takes a determined breath. "Because I've stolen from you."

I don't understand. "What tracks? When did you steal from me? What did you rob me of?"

"Can you show me the donation agreement you signed with the CRO Foundation?" she says quietly.

I stand up and, with surprise still undisguised in my eyes, I pick up the donation agreement that has lain on my desk since the early evening. I hand it to Aisling. Aisling, too, is astonished that the contract is immediately to hand. Her trembling voice betrays how much this instant upsets her.

"You see, here's my signature. Yes, I'm Aisling Hunter..." She paused for a moment, as if waiting for an explanation of where she knew me from. "And here's your signature," she continues when she didn't get one from me. "And here is the donation... and here..." She takes a deep breath. "Here's my personal bank account number and sort code..." She looks at me, her eyes glistening with tears. "Those are my own bank details," she repeats, her eyelids closed and squeezing the tears from her eyes as they trickle down her cheeks.

I understand now. I lean back in my chair and gasp at the shock her confession has caused me. Her eyes are still closed, and I realise that, despite all the words that have hurt me so much, I am noticing her beauty above all else. My mind is in perfect turmoil: I marvel at the beauty of the woman who just told me she robbed me.

"Why?" I ask after a moment. "Why did you do it?"

Aisling hasn't held back the tears and remains in her position, like a pianist, with her back straight, one hand resting on the back of her chair and the other, just the backs of her fingers, supporting her chin. She isn't looking at me, but somewhere into the space behind me, and in a slow, quiet voice, she begins to tell her story. She speaks of Nigel, of Mr Wang, of Eddy, of love, of being a high-class call girl, of debt, of temptation, of fear, of hope...

"Mr Wang will kill me, as he killed Eddy, when he finds out that I stole from him…"

I listen, and the sound of footsteps from the castle steps is the background of her story: *clack, clack, clack…*

That's how fate strikes.

Dream

Dreams have only one owner at a time.
That's why dreamers are lonely.
(William Faulkner)

Chapter 1

Is there some connection between heaven and earth? Some people think there is. Things occur that we can't explain, or perhaps we don't want to believe. That's because we are pleasantly stirred by a sense of mystery, of something that transcends us, that tantalises us with the scent of the unknown and hope, that makes us forget the mundane. Particularly where life goes on, day in and day out, while being stuck in a rut.

And yet when it does go off those tracks, it's still only the work of the explicable, the predictable. It's the work of us, humans, who do both good and evil to each other. The evil in particular can be unimaginable, but it's earthly and doesn't come from the space between heaven and earth.

So is there something between heaven and earth? I remember a verse I came across a while ago:

Somewhere between heaven and earth
Where you think there's nothing except space
Just alternating darkness and daylight
Your dream is somewhere born there…

Something happened to me recently... Was it a dream or a distorted reality? Actually, I don't know. Dreams come while we're asleep, when thoughts, which are otherwise tightly bound if we're awake, break free of those bonds and wander through our minds. They project themselves in images so unreal that when we wake up – and, of course, if we remember it – we just shake our head in disbelief. I certainly wasn't asleep when it happened to me, so it couldn't have been a dream. It shouldn't have been. Looking back on those few days, I'm certain it really happened to me. I saw photos as proof; they were real. I'm not blind, nor I am senile. But there was a dream visible in those photos... so was it real or just a dream? I really don't know.

Before I start telling my story, I'll try to complete the verse with a few lines of my own:

It lives there and it observes, I know
My dream that I dream
It hesitantly approaches, perhaps ashamed
But what pleases me...
It's how beautiful it sees me.

Chapter 2

It's raining, and I don't understand why my trainers, which were the only footwear that matched the skirt I chose for today, are called trainers. They're actually the least appropriate footwear for the heavy downpour that's bouncing off the pavement. They're now full of water, but fortunately the water doesn't feel cold. The few sunny days in May that preceded today's downpour have warmed the air, so the wet doesn't become intrusive.

I hurry, but the car park where I left my car is still a long way away. My umbrella, which is more designer-orientated than practical, is a flimsy shield against the worsening downpour. I begin my retreat from the deluge and slip into a café I know well, as I often come here with a friend. Fortunately, it's not crowded and even the table by the window, where we usually sit, is vacant. My designer coat is soaked through and not really suitable for this kind of weather. I take it off and hang it on the coat rack in the hope it will dry a bit before I leave.

I order a mug of Americano – black, no milk, no sugar, just as it comes; good, hot coffee. Crossing my legs, leaning back in the chair, I shake out my hair. I'm always at ease here. I sip the delicious beverage and I think of my best friend, Kym. Hopefully it was just a slight smile that flitted across my face when I thought of her and not a goofy grin, because the man sitting at the opposite table would have thought I was otherwise nuts.

He's peeking, I notice. Not a looker, I could tell. Forty-something, like me... Kym and I call our age group 'recycled teenagers' – and I want to smile again but stop myself. I look out the window at the people hurrying down the street, huddled under umbrellas or with the hoods up on their raincoats. The rain hasn't let up. On the contrary, it seems to get worse as it hits the window. As it runs down the pane of glass and harmonises with the café, it murmurs with people's voices.

I wonder if perhaps it's still leaking through the roof of my old static caravan, pitched close to the woodland just outside town. I proudly call it a retreat: a two-bedroom static caravan with a minute garden, which, at this time of year, is also a place to get away from it all. I like it there. In fact, I love it. When I'm fed up with the hustle and bustle of the town, its where I like to escape to. The silence, the tranquillity, the night sky full of stars, the smell of the pine trees...

I must go there soon. Tomorrow, I decide.

I sip my coffee and with the mug tilted to my mouth, I check out the man at the opposite table with my eyes. His table is not exactly opposite, but a little to one side, so I have to turn my head slightly. But when I do, I almost sputter because at the same moment that I am hiding behind the mug, he is checking me out with his mug lifted to his mouth, and then our gazes meet: my hazel eyes over the rim of my mug, and his brown eyes over the rim of his mug. It was only a fleeting glance, lasting a second, maybe not even that, but…

I look out the window again, but I don't see the street, and I don't see the hurrying people I'm so interested in at other times. But I still see those eyes of his over the mug of coffee. No, he's not handsome, I realise that, but those eyes – how can I put it? They're nice, kind, welcoming, as I realise in that fleeting second. If I were to determine the personality of a man with such a look, I can only think of one thing: he must be a good, decent man.

If my sixth sense isn't deceiving me, I'd say he's watching me. I can feel him looking at me and I'm convinced that he's no longer hiding behind his mug, but cheekily eyeing me up. His look is certainly defiantly long, unbearably long, but I hold out and don't look in that direction again because I'd lose the advantage I hope I still have in this exchange. I fumble for my mug and don't take my eyes from the window as I finish the rest of the coffee. It's only after a moment that I realise the rain has stopped.

"Can I have the bill?" I nod to the waitress.

I don't turn directly to the opposite table, but I can still peripherally see that no one is sitting at it anymore. He's gone. Discreetly I look around. No, he's not here.

I pay and find myself feeling disappointed. I remain seated, still thinking of that second when our gazes met. I find it strange how his gaze captured me, and I mentally rage at myself for dwelling on it too much. At my age I should be above it, at ease, and not see something in such a familiar and fleeting moment that might cause me a kind of mind quiver. Well, it did. I smile.

I'm snapped out of my thoughts by my phone. I fumble in my handbag. It's Kym.

"Hi. Well, where would I be right now? I'm sitting in our favourite café because it's been chucking it down. Yeah, right. Don't worry, I didn't forget. I'll be over tonight... I was sure you'd send me a reminder..."

With my mobile phone in my hand, my thoughts return to the man's eyes, but I am interrupted by a beep. I get a WhatsApp message from Freya, my sister-in-law, sending me a new photo of her children. They are lovely. I save them and then, I don't know why, I click on *Photos* to make sure they got transferred. Yeah, all right. I am about to put my phone away into my handbag when the last photo, that precedes the ones I have just saved, catches my eye. What's that? I don't understand. I tap on it to enlarge it. That's just not possible...

I stare at the photo: me sitting at this very table, legs crossed, leaning back, chest out, shaking out my hair...

"That's me," I mutter to myself. The photo must have been taken just a couple of moments ago...

Someone took a picture of me?! Here and right now, and from across the other table! Then somehow, mysteriously, saved it in my photo file without my knowledge, or me saving it first? I look around the café once more. Mr Mysterious? No, he's not here so it couldn't have been him.

"Can I get you anything else?" the waitress asks me, apparently surprised that I'm not about to leave after paying.

"No, thank you."

I get up. My coat is still damp, of course, but I put it on.

It's now pleasant outside. The rain has definitely stopped. Even the sun is peeking through the broken clouds.

I can't get the incident with the photo out of my head. I don't get it. There's just no way that someone could have taken a picture of me, with their mobile phone, and then saved it to my phone without me knowing. They would have had to send it to me somehow – by text, by WhatsApp – and I would have had to click onto it first before transporting it to my photo file. I don't understand.

Distracted, I walk down the street to the car park where I left my car. I look around, unconsciously searching the faces of the men I pass. I would recognise those eyes.

No, he just disappeared into thin air. Mr Mysterious.

Even at home, it still bothers me. I look at the photo again. It's strange, though, that I'm the only object in focus and the entire background is a blur. Did he have time to edit it? Crossed legs, chest out, head tilted back, and fingers entwined in a strand of hair. But in the photo, I am looking extraordinarily beautiful. I am aware that I'm not too bad-looking for my age, but in this photo, I look like a model – and a young one at that... really strange.

Chapter 3

I've known Kym since my school days. We've remained friends ever since and our friendship has survived the long years that have passed. It has survived our weddings and our divorces, and I dare say that the similar life stories of both of us have made our friendship even stronger. We often get together – just for catch up, to exercise in the gym, to go to the theatre, the cinema, on trips… but today I realised for the first time that I desperately needed her.

I arrived at her place earlier than agreed. I couldn't stand it any longer. I let myself in the back way and Kym was in the shower when I arrived. She came out a few moments later covered in a large bath towel.

"Sorry to come so early, but I have something I need to tell you," I started immediately. I sank into the chair and took a moment to gather my thoughts.

Kym was drying her long, wet hair with the towel, standing right in front of me. The towel was swaying with her movements, alternately covering and revealing her naked body. Looking at her firm body, I could see the hard work we're putting in at the gym was paying off because she's in pretty good shape.

"What? Some kind of trouble? Ex?" she asked, unperturbed.

"No, nothing like that. My ex doesn't give me any grief, thankfully, but let me show you." I fish my phone out of my handbag and hurriedly recount what I encountered. "Like I told you, I was in our café because it was chucking it down outside. I'm sitting at a table, sipping my coffee, minding my own business, and I notice a man, forty-five ish, eyeing me up. Such…" I searched for the right words to describe him. "That you wouldn't look at him twice. An unremarkable man, a bit overweight, going bald on top, not a looker, but with very nice, kind eyes."

I took a deep breath and continued, "We are both sitting there, and we drink our coffee. I could tell that he's eyeing me up. I don't give him any eye contact, of course – actually, I kind of do – well… and then suddenly he's gone. He kind of disappeared rather quickly."

"So what?" questions Kym. "That's it?"

"Wait, the main thing is yet to come." I tap my phone screen with a finger that is trembling with excitement. "Let me show you something." I tap on the photos. "Here are Freya's children and here…" I scroll through dozens of photos several times, up and down, and… nothing. I scroll through all the photos again. "Holy shit." I'm relieved. "The photo isn't here."

"What photo? What are you looking for? Don't tell me you took a picture of him?"

"Shit," I whisper, scrolling through the photos again.

The photo isn't there anymore. It's gone!

"I don't get it," I stammer. "I had a photo here, of me, taken in the café, and somehow it got saved in my photo file. Someone – probably the man sitting at the other table – took a picture of me and then sent it to me, and then, wait for it, somehow managed to save it into my photo file."

"He sent you a picture?"

"No, he didn't actually send it to me. I really don't understand. I just discovered it in my photo file when I was saving the photos of the children. I don't know how he did it, but the photo of me, which was definitely taken today, in the café, and which then mysteriously appeared in my photos album… is not there anymore."

Kym looked at me suspiciously. "That sounds strange. If I hadn't known you better, I'd say you made it up. I reckon he took a picture of you and then he sent it to you – via Bluetooth, I don't know. I don't understand that much, but surely you would have had to open it first and then save it into photos yourself."

I couldn't do more than shrug.

"What I can't understand," Kym continued, "is that he'd then somehow deleted that photo from your mobile. Sorry, but that's if there was a photo of you in the first instance. You would have had to click onto it before deleting it."

"I realise it sounds strange. But trust me, the photo was there earlier on, and now it's gone."

"Okay." Kym sighed. "So what was actually on the photo?"

"Well, it was rather nice and most complimentary." I smiled awkwardly. "I'm sitting at the table in the café, both hands in my hair, chest out – I look pretty and sexy – and the background of the photo is sort of in a haze." I try to explain but feel stupid as the story becomes harder to believe.

I talk, trying to convince Kym and myself that it wasn't a mirage, that the photo really existed and that it had been stored on my phone. When I had said what I had to say and I realised that I was only repeating the words and sentences I had already spoken, I finally paused. The silence that fell, which Kym should have broken as I hoped she would, but didn't, was annoying. It only reinforced how futile my efforts to explain the unexplainable had been.

"Say something," I urged her.

Kym hesitated for a moment before answering. The hesitation actually said more than words could as then any spoken words became futile. For the words spoken, carefully chosen so as not to hopefully hurt, were only meant to stop the pause.

"Strange. I never would have thought it was possible… but after all, what do we know about what is possible and what isn't?" Kym said unconvincingly.

"Kym, I'm sorry that I brought it up in the first place and I really regret bringing it up now."

It hadn't given me an explanation as I had hoped, but instead I felt an oppressive sense of being left all alone to figure out the mystery.

We talked for the rest of the evening as friends do, but although we didn't bring the subject up again, there remained on both our tongues an aftertaste that even good wine couldn't wash away. It was the aftertaste rather than the wine that weighed heavy on our tongues, and our conversation, at other times so lively and refreshing, was ragged and only multiplied the aftertaste. And so, going round and round in a circle that had changed our mood, my leaving became my rescue.

It was only at home, as I was going to bed, that my thoughts returned to the café and I looked at the photos stored on my phone again. But the photo of me had simply disappeared.

So was it really there in the first place? I suddenly had my doubts. Was I seeing things? Is Kym right when she thinks that I must have gone off my rocker?

I sat up in bed. The doubts that crept in my mind had made me nervous. No, I'm not stupid and I'm not blind; I refused to accept it. But who is this man who's playing tricks on me like this? It had to be him, there was no one else sitting in that direction. Anyhow, how did he do it, this Mr Mysterious?

I put my phone down on the bedside table and I remained sitting in bed for a while longer, my legs bent at the knees, my arms wrapped around them and pulled close to my body, with my head resting on my knees. I asked myself yet again: *who is this man?*

I closed my eyes. I should be scared, I should be terrified of this, but I'm not. I'm calm now. I remember his look. Nothing more, just his kind and friendly gaze.

* * *

Dream

In my sleep the previous night I had a dream. A crazy dream that I tried removing from my memory immediately upon waking. But I'm not sure that I'd managed to remove it all. Was it really that which was bothering my sleeping mind? Or was it perhaps just a feeling I had that something had clicked in the back of my mind? I don't know.

In my dream: *I saw Kym drying her wet hair with a beach towel before using a hairdryer. The towel was swaying with the movements of her hands, alternately covering and revealing her naked body. I looked at her and dreamt of touching her, which she didn't resist. I dreamt of the smell of her skin as I touched her breasts, hips and thighs...*

I just sat and watched as the towel carried on swaying and I saw her spread her legs for a second... And then I heard the rain and the distant thunder as I was transported to the sea. I waded into the water and the sea reached my calves and as I spread my legs, it reached my lap... I felt the heat and then the cold, and then the seawater wet my hair and made my thin shirt translucent. I covered my breasts with my hands as I looked into the stranger's dark eyes while I drank my coffee...

But I realised that it was all just a dream.

* * *

I stay in bed because it's Saturday, and I don't have to get up too early. I can lie there and close my eyes and let the dream fade away. It reverberates like a receding song until it fades into silence and its shards slowly crumble into dust. When I open my eyes, the sunny breeze that blows through the window blows the dust away and only a kind of sweetness remains in my soul…

I touch the screen of my mobile phone. It's eight-thirty. A time when, even on Saturdays, I have to get up, and especially today as I can't indulge in any more lazing around. This is because I want to check on the caravan to see if it's still leaking and how much water had collected in the bucket. I also need to get out of town for a rest and clear my head. I need to get away from people, and not bump into Kym, who somewhat disappointed me yesterday.

Actually, it wasn't disappointment. I'll have to apologise to her when I see her next, as, after all, yesterday's incident in the café was hard to comprehend. I can't blame her for it as my thoughts go back to the dream I had last night. I realise that it wasn't just a coincidence, as during yesterday's visit to see Kym, when she stood partially naked in front of me, I felt arousal. My desire to touch her body surprised me and I thought then whether she was perhaps thinking the same thing. I don't recall her ever standing so invitingly for me before. I also realise that last night, the second I woke up in the middle of that dream, I was full of determination to confide my feelings to her. But now, in the morning, I find the idea absurd and ridiculous, and I know I could never confront her with it.

I sit up in the bed determined to get up and put an end to these thoughts. I grab my mobile phone and look at the time and then, sort of automatically, I tap on my photos because, somewhere in my subconscious, yesterday's episode still nestles and teases me with its inexplicability.

I scroll through all the photos up to the ones with Freya's children, which should have been the last ones, but aren't. I am startled to find another photo. This I click on to enlarge, and a chill runs down my arms and all over my body, for it is a photo of me again. Not the one from the café, but one from last night… when I was sitting in bed, legs bent and pulled up to my body, my head resting on my knees, my eyes closed, dreaming…

I don't know how long I stare at the photo in a kind of a daze. I don't know, either, how long it takes me to realise the horror that someone must have been in my flat and that someone had taken a picture of me. Only then do I jump up and run to the front door to find, with relief, that the door is locked and secured with a chain. No one could have entered the apartment unless they had somehow managed to get in before I arrived home. Terrified, I look into the kitchen, the living room, the bedroom, and open all the cupboards. I look under the bed, into the bathroom, and check the windows to make sure they are shut… and nothing. I am alone in my flat.

I look at the photo again, but I am unable to concentrate and somehow logically explain what had happened to me. I walk around the bedroom with my mobile phone in my hand, trying to find the spot from where the picture was taken. I am certain that I found the actual place, and it is clear to me that I couldn't have taken a selfie in some kind of a frenzy. It would be impossible to take a picture of myself sitting on the bed, hugging my bent legs and with my head on my knees and my eyes closed as if I were asleep… impossible.

I stare at the photo for a long time, taking in every detail, and find no clue. There's nothing that would give me a clue, only the fact that I am in the photo, just as was the case with the first photo, and I was made to look incredibly beautiful.

In a hurry and skipping breakfast, I put the things I would need to spend the night in my static caravan into an overnight bag. I leave the flat with the oppressive feeling that I couldn't escape from someone who had invaded my privacy, my life, in such an agonising way.

This person is torturing me and making me feel defenceless. I get into my car and I leave the town at great speed, still with that oppressive feeling, that even at the speed I'm going, I can't escape my pursuer, and panic takes over.

The fear is too much to handle, and I slow down until I'm driving very slowly down the road. Other cars are overtaking me, and drivers are sounding their horns and gesticulating furiously. Those who can't pass me are right on my tail in an attempt to force me to speed up. But I don't speed up and I carry on driving slowly down the road until I finally come to the allotments with the track leading to the caravan. The slow drive slows my mind and the panic and heaviness turn almost to apathy. But I still find the strength to think about the photo and I tell myself, finally, that there must be some plausible explanation, that it must be somehow logically possible to take a photo like this.

I park my car and step inside the caravan, which appears to be in order with no water collected in the bucket. I take a look at the photo again; I am sitting curled up and dreaming, and made to look unusually attractive. And it's then that I start casting doubt that there is a reasonable explanation, contradicting my thoughts from earlier on. I realise that I'm all on my own. I can't confide in anyone: no one would believe me. I can't even tell Kym, because the photo would disappear, and she would look at me again like if I had gone mad. I could read in her eyes how weird she thought I became. She would doubt if there ever was a photo, that I must have taken it somehow myself, and that I was just making up a stupid story because I was getting old and senile…

I open all the windows in the caravan to air out the mustiness of the few weeks I haven't been here. I clean the place top to bottom to forget for a while, to distract myself, and I spread my bedding over the railing of the small patio to air it out. Here in the caravan is where I'll sleep tonight, but I'm afraid of the night to come. I'm afraid that I'll be afraid forever, because I've lost my sense of security, my security of being alone, though it was loneliness that I feared most after my divorce.

When I finish cleaning, I boil the kettle and make myself a cup of tea. I then sit on the patio where the May sun is beginning to warm the air. I turn my face to the sun and its rays caress me soothingly, but there is a cool air blowing in from the woodland, reminding me gently that summer is still a few weeks away. I clasp my hands together to keep my chest warm, and with only my fingers to support my chin, it is like praying.

The sunny weather lasts all day, but by midday the sun has moved over the roof of the caravan, and it shades the patio. I move into the small garden behind the caravan, which gets the sun at this time of day, sitting on my folding chair. My small garden is just a patch of lawn with a couple of rose bushes and a small rockery to decorate it. But it doesn't really decorate it at the moment because it's overgrown and I haven't had time to tidy it up in the autumn. Now the weeds are growing all over and I'm glad of it, in a way, because it's going to keep me busy. The effort will make me feel good and it will calm me down. By evening I feel tired and am grateful for that, because maybe it will allow me to fall asleep easier.

I wonder if I should take a look at the photos again. Should I clear my mind, or should I just give up and try to go to sleep? But when I lie in my bed, the bedding smelling fresh after airing it on the patio all day, I am slowly relaxing. I touch my phone screen because I know that if I don't do it now, I'll think about it and do it in an hour or two. I scroll through the photos, and I know that the one I'm looking for follows the ones of the children. But then I'm not surprised to find that the photo is gone. It's not there. It's disappeared! It's as if it's only set to stay for a certain amount of time, or maybe it always disappears when daylight fades to dusk… what do I know. It was definitely there earlier and now it's not.

I put my phone down and I turn off the bedside lamp to try to get some sleep.

Chapter 4

Earlier on I was afraid I'd remain scared forever, but now I'm not. I don't know why, but I'm suddenly positive that somehow this will all get logically explained, that I'll get through this. Perhaps it's so set in the human brain that it's impossible to be permanently afraid, just as it's impossible to be permanently happy. It works like the Stockholm syndrome, where fear of the captor is replaced by some positive emotion we feel towards them. Or perhaps, in my case, it's due to the fact that I was captured so beautifully in those photos that they couldn't have been taken with malicious intent. Who knows?

Sleep doesn't come as I hoped. I lie with my eyes closed to be closer to Mr Mysterious and I want to think of nothing else. But the darkness behind my closed eyelids is the blackest it's ever been, so I prefer to keep them open. But I see the same darkness all the time, for the blackout blind is pulled down and it blots out the light of the moon and the stars and doesn't allow any light to enter the bedroom. So I alternately close and open my eyes, and it's still darkness. Like a dark canvas, I project into the darkness the images that come in my mind. I want to see the garden and the rockery that has become beautiful to me, and the green lawn, and the woodland behind the caravan that smells of pine trees and rustles in the wind… and I want to see Kym drying her hair with a towel, and I want to see those brown eyes looking at me over the top of the mug with coffee… and I want to see the sea and the mountains…

At that, I fell asleep.

I wandered through a woodland. I followed a narrow path that only wild animals used. The sun shone through the treetops, and I kept on walking, but when the path suddenly disappeared, I carried on to where even animals didn't go. The woodland thinned and I hoped I would soon reach its edge.

When the sun was setting and only a faint glimmer of light shone through the tree trunks, I came out of the woodland. But there was nothing before me but an unseen landscape… and the dream, which had no story and was just this endless journey, unfolded like a boring movie. I carried on, hoping for an ending, and I climbed up the hill that stretched out in front of me. When I got to the top, I looked around and the sun was shining over the horizon, and everything was dreamily transported into a magical picture.

I stood and looked, and suddenly I heard a voice from somewhere. "I'm an uninvited guest – you know – and the photo you see is for fun, when you sleep and dream. Just say 'that's enough!' and you won't see it again."

I heard the words and then the sun went down, and everything went dark and silent. The darkness was the blackest I've ever seen and as I closed and opened my eyes in the dream, there was no difference, just the same darkness...

And then I woke up.

When I looked around, I was relieved to see that dawn was breaking outside the window. A new day was beginning, and a new day was coming through the window. I won't get up. I want to lie here dreaming, because it's Sunday and I have plenty of time. I love these sleepy mornings when I wake up and the sun is shining outside.

What was I dreaming about? I'm trying to remember. I'm slowly recalling the strange dream and remembering the uncomfortable feeling of darkness as I opened and closed my eyes. I saw nothing but the blackest darkness all the time and the uncomfortable feeling overshadowed my sleepy morning.

I remembered the photo and that upset me even more. But I also remembered the eyes of Mr Mysterious looking at me over his mug of coffee, and then the words I heard in my dream pushed to the forefront of my mind. I remained lying there, remembering more, and then I was convinced they were the words that sounded like a verse.

I am an uninvited guest, you know.
And the photo you see is for fun,
When you sleep and dream.
Just say 'that's enough!'
And you won't see it again.

And suddenly I realised that I knew, that I had it all worked out. I reached for my phone, and I tapped on photos. I was certain that I knew what I'd find... and I scrolled through the pictures and... I'm holding my breath with excitement. I find a photo of me after the one with the children – that should be the last one, again, but isn't. And when I click on it, I see myself... facing the sun, my hands clasped together to keep my chest warm, and my fingers propping my chin up as if I'm praying... and I look a million dollars.

I made myself a mug of coffee and I sat down at the caravan table. I looked at the photo that Mr Mysterious, Mr Dream, Mr Uninvited Guest sent me, and I kept looking at it for some considerable length of time. Then I raised the mug to my mouth until my hazel eyes covered the top of the mug, and I visualised his brown eyes covering his mug... and I smiled until tears flowed down my cheeks.

It's when the photo on my phone fades and disintegrates into raindrops, which run all the way down my legs and into my trainers, that I command in a loud voice: "*That's enough!*"

Abrielle

Chapter 1

The strange incident could have happened to me on my way home from work, or on my way from shopping... anywhere. But it happened in a place and time so unexpected that perhaps the resulting contrast amplified my dismay.

I'm a mean, lying piece of shit, I thought as I covered up my wife lying in bed. I told her that I was going for a pint and I'd be back soon. What a lying toad, because I'm not going to the pub, and I won't be back soon. I'm off to have fun. I'll get into my car and drive to Aviemore, ten minutes away and, in a place that plays music all night, I'm going to enjoy myself. I'm going to dance, and I'm going to sing and freak out in the arms of other women. And if I'm lucky, I'll have sex.

Lying toad. But who doesn't lie nowadays? Because everyone lies at times. Husband to wife, wife to husband, boss to employees, employees to boss, politicians to the electorate... They all lie, and they're not always kind lies. Some are evil lies meant to hurt, to insult, to humiliate...

One more look as I turn round from the door. "Bye, love, I'll see you soon."

Then I quietly close the door and stand still for a while listening intently, even though I know I won't hear a sound. Ella is lying in bed with the covers pulled up to her chin, staring motionless into the darkness, just as she would be staring into the light if it was left on. I'll find her in this same, motionless position when I return in a few hours. She'll still be lying on her back with the duvet pulled up to her chin, and maybe just those eyes will be closed, and she'll be asleep. But will she be asleep? Does she sleep at all? I don't know. She utters the occasional muffled word, but mostly an incoherent sound as if she wants to tell me something, but she's not able to get the words out.

Chapter 2

Ella's forty, two years younger than me, and she's turned from a bubbly, happy-go-lucky person into a cabbage. She's suffering from the effects of acute decompression sickness. It's been almost two years since she became ill. We were on holiday in Egypt, scuba diving in the Red Sea, because diving was our great passion. Together with a few friends, we were returning to the coast on a chartered yacht from one such trip. We were laughing and the sun-drenched world seemed amazing. Behind us, the vast sea, and ahead of us, the distant foggy coastline.

"Here's to those deep sea experiences." Ella laughed, toasting the others with a can of lager. "One hundred and fifty-five feet down. Our record!" she managed to say.

And then she slumped into her canvas chair and the lager spilled onto the deck. Ella didn't continue with her scene, which we thought to be a theatrical performance. She silenced us all with her stillness. We remained silent for a few long moments. We stared at her in confusion, suddenly realising that this was no longer a play and that something serious had happened, which took us by surprise and shocked us. When we recovered from shock, we whispered her name softly at first.

"Ella, Ella, what's wrong?"

But it was me who finally yelled at the top of my voice, "Ella!"

All the way to shore I massaged her heart, and we gave her mouth-to-mouth resuscitation and I kept shouting, "Stay with us, Ella, stay with us. You mustn't go to sleep."

She didn't come to until she was in hospital. She moved her arms, left and right, and her legs moved a little.

And so it remained.

With help, she could sit and stand, shuffling her feet on the floor in a kind of parody of walking. She has aphasia: a brain disorder which impacts her speech, hearing and coordination. She occasionally mumbles something unintelligible but doesn't speak and is unable to communicate her feelings. But it seems that the sea remained in her eyes – wide, unseeing – and also in her ears, where it thunders and roars, drowning out any spoken words.

I am her carer, and I will never leave her. She had endless hospital stays and procedures, all kind of tests. Now has palliative care at home, in the house I bought with Ella's insurance payout, and which was specially adapted to suit her needs. I pay for a home help and a nurse, but I still do most of it myself: serving meals, toileting, bathing... I now only work part-time and I'm with her most of the time. I give her prescribed medication, exercise with her, cook her meals and feed her like a baby. She's a baby. She's not a grown woman anymore... and I can't treat her like one. She's distant, and her mind is probably as dark as the sea depths of the one hundred and fifty-five feet she had dived to.

Abrielle

But here at home is where the shyster in me woke up. A shyster? A piece of shit? Am I really a piece of shit if I put Ella to bed night after night, whisper soft words into her ear and then sneak off to a nightclub where I fool around, where I forget, where I live for a while…? Yes, I suppose that does make me a piece of shit. But it doesn't stop me from going anyway.

Chapter 3

It's snowing heavily. I carefully manoeuvre past parked cars and join the main road which, after a while, continues through a dark forest. It doesn't take me long to shake off the weariness that always falls on me in the dark.

In sight is Aviemore, which shines with a hundred lights and also with the sweet promise of the adventure of this evening. With a kind of trepidation, I approach the town, and then at last I am in its streets. Then, via a shortcut I use often, I reach my destination. An inconspicuous large building at first glance, where only a small neon sign above the entrance somehow casually and unobtrusively invites me in. Not many people know that inside, beyond the staircase that takes guests down to the basement, a new world opens up. There, each step brings you closer to a massive wooden door.

I ring the bell and the door opens. I am greeted by a bouncer who checks my booking before letting me in. The heavy wooden door then closes behind me, and after going through another door, the noise hits me full on. The loud music with the magical light suddenly surrounds me. The spotlight of coloured lights cuts through the darkness of the space and catches my eyes.

But neither the noise nor the lights are unpleasant. I hear a lot of laughter and see curves of beautiful women. That very second when I step through the door is a high for me. It's a sweet experience preceded by eager anticipation of the night's adventure – all the touches, the looks, the fragrance worn by women. How different this world is, and how little does it take to change that grey, troubled outside world, now covered in snow, for pure enjoyment.

I head to my reserved table. I pass the dance floor and take in the glances of the women as well as the heady scent of their perfumes, and I feel like a king. I am the king, and I am on the threshold of a night that will be mine. I'm forty-two and suddenly I'm a young man again. Gone is my aridity and weariness from the burden of fate that has been weighing on my shoulders for the past months. Here I always manage to unwind. I rejuvenate here as I'm like a plant left to fend for itself to survive in a dessert, and suddenly watered with lifesaving rain.

I settle into a comfortable chair so that I have a view of the dance floor and order a large glass of white wine from the waiter, who helpfully heads to my table. The three hours I have ahead of me are long enough to get rid of some of the alcohol in my system. I lean back comfortably and look around. There is carefree exuberance everywhere. Men and women chatter and laugh, and the warm lighting on each table makes everyone, regardless of age, look carefree and happy. If there was nothing more, and if I just sat there and sipped wine all evening and watched this little island of happiness and well-being, it would be three hours of sheer, warm satisfaction.

A DJ plays dance music. Gloria Gaynor sings *I Will Survive* and the petite lady on the dance floor undulates her hips seductively and flicks her long dark hair. Her short dress shows off her shapely legs, teasingly highlighted by the dim light of the dance floor. Yet it draws out the arched buttocks that hug tightly until the image sends a wave of excitement through my stomach and reminds me of how long it's been since I've enjoyed this with my wife...

But there will be more. I'm certain of that... I hope.

I sit and watch. I can put up with this for a long time, but at the next ballad I get up and ask the petite lady to dance. She doesn't refuse me. It's all so simple and natural here.

We dance and I see her face close up. She's not quite as young as she seemed earlier when I looked at her from my table, but she's attractive. How old could she be? Thirty? Thirty-five? I can smell the scent of her hair and feel those legs brushing against mine, and her breasts pressing against me.

I keep reminding myself that I'm the piece of shit who left his sick wife alone in the bedroom. But I love it when a woman looks up and searches my face for the reason I'm here. I quickly smile into those eyes because this isn't where gloom belongs, as this is paradise. *This is heaven*, I repeat to myself, *this is absolute heaven*... but somehow, I can't let my hair down today. Yesterday and the day before, I was out here chasing women and scoring, but today... I can't seem to do it.

We're dancing and I'm taking in the scent that's supposed to make me forget my troubles. I put my arm around her waist and squeeze her tighter. She responds and puts both arms around my neck so I can put my other arm around her waist. I squeeze her lightly and again the wave of excitement…

"Are you here alone?" I lean towards her.

She looks up until our lips are almost touching.

"No, I'm here with a friend…" And she looks around the dance floor and then nods towards a blonde young woman dancing with an older, bald-headed guy.

We dance for a while and then we go to the bar. There she has a few glasses of champagne which I'd put on my tab. Then we continue chatting at my table. Sophie is her name. But she doesn't believe me when I tell her that my name is Owen. I didn't lie to her. I didn't feel like lying to her, and if she'd been interested in knowing my surname, I'd have told her it was Robertson. But she didn't want to know that.

"Did you come by car?"

She surprises me with the question. I nod and we look long into each other's eyes. The look is long and eloquent and says it all. It is almost unnecessary to add anything else.

"Will you give me a lift home?" She smiles ambiguously.

I understand but don't answer at once. A piece of shit? Am I really such a piece of shit? Again the remorse that haunts me today.

It is only now that I noticed her long fingernails. Each nail is painted a different colour, and I realise that those nails bother me…

"I'm sorry, but I can't."

She isn't upset. Her eyes, which dart around the place, search for her friend.

"Too bad," she just says with a smile and then we veer away.

Chapter 4

I climbed back inside the freezing car with an equally chilling feeling of doom. This evening had everything I wanted, but still the overriding feeling with me was that it hadn't worked out.

Was I supposed to have sex with her at her place?

The wipers didn't have the power to clear the snow off the windscreen, so I got out and cleared it with a scraper. I then drove slowly through the snow-covered streets. It was still snowing and every now and then the rain sensor turned on the wipers, which can just about handle the snowflakes already sticking to them. *This is how it should have been three weeks ago at Christmas*, I thought.

Aviemore is blanketed in snow and it's as if the town had been freshly cleaned up. Everywhere looks white and clean. The streetlamps betray the next batch of settling snow as they give off a shimmer of light. This is reflected off the snowflakes, which fall thickly from the sky. Everywhere is deathly quiet. The ghostly calm around me and the romantic backdrop outside the car improve my mood and make up, somewhat, for the disappointing evening.

Suddenly I'm glad I resisted the temptation and didn't go back to her place. Those long, multicoloured nails –

which she probably painted a different colour each time – would have dug into my back like some kind of claw. I didn't care much for the idea. No, she wasn't a woman I'd have enjoyed having sex with. Young, beautiful, yes… but those nails and the ease with which she would let me have my wicked way with her… I'm glad I resisted.

I carried on driving out of town. Snowflakes danced wildly in my headlights, hitting the windscreen and keeping the wipers busy. This seems to always be accompanied by an annoying squeal as the rubber scraped across the wet glass. I turned on the radio, which I hardly listen to normally, but immediately turned it off again when I heard the strains of a hundred times overplayed hit.

I carried on driving slowly along the road, which started to climb towards the woods, and at times I had to be careful that I didn't end up in the ditch. I looked at the temperature gauge: it's minus two degrees outside. Not unduly cold, but the snow keeps falling and falling.

Then I suddenly couldn't believe my eyes. I saw a figure walking in the road, just a few yards in front of the car. It looked like a woman. She wasn't in my way, and she kept to the side of the road, but I still slowed down. I got close to her. She had her hood up and she stood upright, her hand shielding her eyes as the headlights and the snow blinded her. She carried on walking, but when I got alongside her, we both stopped.

"Are you okay?" I addressed her through my half-lowered window. She didn't answer my question and leant towards the car.

"Would you give me a lift?"

"Oh, yeah, of course. Jump in."

I raised the window with one button and unlocked the doors with another.

She opened the passenger door, climbed inside, and slammed it as fast as she could to escape the swirl of snowflakes chasing after her. She pulled her hood down. A young woman with short blonde hair.

Twenty? Twenty-five? I'd be guessing.

"Where are you heading? I'm going as far as the old barrack's estate."

"That will be far enough," she replied. "I'll tell you where to drop me off."

I drove slowly. We followed the road through the forest, with snowflakes dancing in the cones of light. They were silent, and I felt the need to break the silence somehow.

"All that's missing here are wolves," I tried to joke.

She didn't respond.

Out of the corner of my eye, I checked her out. She was pretty. I discreetly moved my gaze to her hands. She had manicured, pink nails that are just long enough... I mentally scalded myself for comparing her to Sophie.

"Excuse my curiosity," I said. "But can you tell me what a young, attractive woman is doing in this weather and in such flimsy clothes and shoes walking along the road in the middle of nowhere?"

She was silent. She didn't answer and that made me feel nervous. We drove through the forest and the stifling silence, enhanced by the gloomy scenery outside the car windows, was annoying me.

"Did someone hurt you?"

No reply.

"You don't have to worry about me. If it makes you feel any better. I'm Owen," I introduced myself, not sure why.

"Abrielle," she finally replied. "Please stop here."

"Here?" I wondered. "Right here in the forest?"

"Yes. Here, please." That made her sound strange.

I slowed down and came to a stop.

"Do you live around here?" I wanted to understand.

Again it passed in silence. She opened the door, got out, and before slamming it, she just said, "Thank you."

I looked at her. She walked away, shuffling her feet through the snow, perhaps fearful of slipping, and with that walk she reminded me of my wife, Ella. *Strange*, I thought.

I put the car into gear and slowly drove off. I glanced in the rear-view mirror, but I couldn't see her. I was shocked. What the hell was that all about?

Chapter 5

The road left the forest and in the distance, I could see the lights of my estate. I couldn't get the young woman out of my head. *What could she be doing out in this weather in the middle of nowhere? I don't recall seeing a house here, and I don't even recall there being a track that would perhaps lead to a dwelling. Did I scare her? Did I say something stupid and frighten her? I don't understand.*

I can't leave her there; they'll find her frozen to death at the side of the road in the morning if I don't do something. The thought scared me. I knew that I'd always regret leaving her there. I slammed on the brakes and skidded to a halt.

Oh, shit! I was relieved as I carefully did a three-point turn in a lay-by and managed to turn the car round. I headed back in the direction I just came from. I was no longer concerned about the snowflakes hitting the windscreen and I was ploughing through them at a higher speed. I just wanted to get back to the spot where I'd dropped her off a few minutes ago.

As I got to the forest, I slowed down. I was almost lying on the steering wheel just so I wouldn't miss anything a few yards in front of the car. The wiper blades were wiping away a steady stream of snowflakes with a whine.

Here, at this very spot, I had dropped her off. I pulled over, switched off the engine and got out of the car. I left the lights on. The tracks were probably covered with snow by now, but this was it. I looked around. No one was there.

"Abrielle," I hollered into the darkness, but I scared myself by that strangled-sounding voice of mine.

"Abrielle," I yelled, trying to sound normal.

"Abrielle, show yourself to me... you can't stay here. You'll freeze to death."

Nothing but silence.

I walked a short distance from my car and looked down the gentle slope at the end of which the forest began. The snow crunched under my feet.

Nothing, just nothing. I walked a little farther, into the shadows where the car headlights didn't reach... and then I saw it. There was a car overturned and lying on its roof like a big dead beast. My heart stopped. *For God's sake...* I subconsciously took a few steps back. My eyes never left the silent, dark object that looked monstrous and menacing with its wheels up and belly exposed.

"Shit, shit, shit." That was all I could muster at that moment.

I stood still, gasping in shock. It was only after a few minutes that I managed to put my thoughts together. I felt for my mobile phone in my pocket. *Do I call the police... or do I call for an ambulance? But they'll ask me immediately if there's anybody hurt so I'll have to go and take a look...*

I took a deep breath and with my heart in my throat, I slid slowly towards the scene of the accident. The snow was almost up to my knees. The accident must have happened a while ago, because everything around was covered in fresh snow. It was impossible to see any tyre marks or the direction the car had come from.

I took three steps forward to the wreck. I crouched down and peered inside. There was no one in the passenger seat as far as I could see. No one in the back seat either.

I calmed down a little.

I made my way to the other side of the car to check the driver's seat as well.

Hopefully everyone who was in the car escaped, I prayed.

I had to lean forward to see better. The driver's window was smashed. I pushed the airbag away... and flinched with fright. A strangely twisted figure, head facing down and thrown back as the deformed roof of the car pinned it down...

A woman.

I felt sick and gasped violently.

Oh, my God! Is she alive? Can she still be alive? With her head twisted like that, no way.

I got my phone out of my pocket. *I have to dial 999*, I thought frantically, *but they're going to question me.*

Then I decided to turn on the light on my phone. I shined the light inside the car... I saw a young woman with short blonde hair, with the hood over her head... On seeing that, I collapsed and slumped down in the snow.

I shined the light once more. The fingernails of her hand seemed to be manicured, and were painted pink and of normal length... Abrielle? I stared in disbelief. Abrielle!

Chapter 6

The police, ambulance and fire brigade arrived almost simultaneously.

"I was driving out of town and saw the car," I explained to the policeman. "I immediately ran down to see if everyone was okay," I stammered breathlessly, "and then I called you."

"You were driving out of town, but you've stopped your car in the opposite direction," the policeman observed.

"Well, I drove past moments earlier. I realised what I actually saw and then I turned around and drove back," I lied, not sure why.

After that, I was just a spectator to this. No one paid any more attention to me. I stayed on the side of the road and watched the goings on below.

"There's nothing for us to do here," I heard the paramedic say. "She's dead and has been for a good few hours," he continued.

I didn't understand. Then it couldn't be Abrielle. I had given her a lift half an hour earlier... Is the dead woman her twin sister and Abrielle is wandering around in the forest somewhere? I was looking for an explanation, clutching at straws.

I saw the firemen cut open the car roof. It took a while, but they finally got her out and put her in a body bag, then zipped it up.

"Call the undertakers," one of them said, which I thought was a bit heartless.

"No, she's coming with us," the paramedic interjected.

I looked out for the policeman I'd spoken to, to explain that there was another person wandering around – the twin of the one who'd been killed, and her name was Abrielle… I was determined to confess everything, how it actually happened. That I'd given her a lift, and she'd apparently wandered off in shock. That she'd been confused, and I'd dropped her off here and then I returned…

I caught sight of him rummaging through the stuff in the glove compartment and I made my way down to him carefully. By the time I got there, he was leaning against the car, talking on the phone. He was supporting his mobile phone to his ear with his shoulder and had some papers in one hand and a torch in the other hand, shining it onto the papers.

"One adult female in the crashed car, the only victim of the accident," he reported to someone. "Name Abrielle Hargreaves, born…"

I couldn't listen to him anymore. My eyes narrowed and I felt a chill run down my back, down my arms and all over my body.

In a daze, I turned and scrambled back up to the road with an indescribable feeling of terror. Something had just happened that was beyond my comprehension, which I didn't understand. And that scared me.

Chapter 7

I don't remember anything of the journey back. I don't remember where I turned the car around. I don't remember if the policeman called out to me, I don't remember anything. It wasn't until I closed the front door of my house behind me and leant against it, perhaps to prevent the terror from penetrating the area, that I took a deep breath and tried to comprehend what had happened. *What on earth was all that? Was I dreaming? Am I asleep?*

No, I couldn't find an answer.

I stood leaning on the door for some time, and in the whirlwind of my thoughts, I found none that would bring me an explanation, a bit of respite.

I walked over to Ella's bed without putting the light on and I bent down to her. She was asleep. Well, she looked as if she was asleep. I sat down in the chair. I realised that I wouldn't be able to sleep tonight. I stared into the dark shadows of the room and the swirl of thoughts slowly turned; they were no longer thoughts, just images... a snowy landscape, snowflakes seen in the car headlights, ng nails, each one painted a different colour...

* * *

Abrielle

The silence in the room became eerie. But all of the sudden it was broken by the deafening sound of thunder as lightning struck and passed through the chair, sending an electric charge through my body. I stopped breathing as my body convulsed and tensed like a coil spring. For above the din, I could clearly hear Ella's harrowing scream of '*w-w-w-h-y*' as the ear-deafening echo of thunder resonated in my ears…

Acknowledgements

With special thanks to Fran Pollak, Robert Pollak and Rod Barr for the seemingly endless task of proofreading and editing the manuscript.

Thanks too to Sue Beardmore for additional editing, and Grahame Chalk for keeping this book on track.